ASYLUM ROAD

ASYLUM ROAD

Olivia Sudjic

BLOOMSBURY PUBLISHING
LONDON · OXFORD · NEW YORK · NEW DELHI · SYDNEY

BLOOMSBURY PUBLISHING
Bloomsbury Publishing Plc
50 Bedford Square, London, WC1B 3DP, UK
29 Earlsfort Terrace, Dublin 2, Ireland

BLOOMSBURY, BLOOMSBURY PUBLISHING and the Diana logo
are trademarks of Bloomsbury Publishing Plc

First published in Great Britain 2021
Copyright © Olivia Sudjic, 2021

Olivia Sudjic has asserted her right under the Copyright,
Designs and Patents Act, 1988, to be identified as Author of this work

'Between the fear that something ...' from *Signs by the Roadside* ©
Ivo Andrić (Sezam, 2015)
'A specter is haunting ...' from *Imagining the Balkans* ©
Maria Todorova (Oxford University Press, 1997)
'What one wonders about ...' and 'nothing ever, perhaps, quite safe ...' from
Pleasures and Landscapes © Sybille Bedford (Daunt Books, 2014)

A catalogue record for this book is available from the British Library

ISBN: HB: 978-1-5266-1738-5; TPB: 978-1-5266-1739-2;
EBOOK: 978-1-5266-1741-5

2 4 6 8 10 9 7 5 3

Typeset by Integra Software Services Pvt. Ltd
Printed and bound in Great Britain by CPI Group (UK) Ltd, Croydon CR0 4YY

To find out more about our authors and books visit www.bloomsbury.com

For Miša and Seja

Between the fear that something would happen and the hope that still it wouldn't, there is much more space than one thinks.

Ivo Andrić

A specter is haunting Western culture – the specter of the Balkans.

Maria Todorova

MOUSEHOLE

I

Sometimes it felt like the murders kept us together.

I'd suggested taking a break, which turned into the holiday, to remedy our real problems – but I knew we'd need one more for the road. They distracted me from my thoughts, from his silences. Murders and holidays were a quick fix that worked.

We drove through London as another body disintegrated, reaching the tunnel at dawn.

Maybe it was ghoulish, my fixation with true crime, but I hate tunnels, and being underground, and the channel one is fifty kilometres.

He knew that about me almost from the start. On our first proper date I went to meet him at the Olympic Stadium. It was 2012. He had tickets for the opening ceremony. Since moving to London I'd avoided the tube and it was July then so I walked, following my phone north across the river, a route which turned out not to be a bridge. That tunnel was designed to curve so you can't see light at the end – so horses wouldn't bolt. As the ceremony began he asked if I wanted his sweater, he could see how badly I was shivering.

Inside the tunnel, the episode ended. We got out, ignoring signs to remain in our vehicle, into the throat that had swallowed us beneath the waves. There was a loud rumbling, but it didn't feel as if we were moving in any particular direction.

Luke hunched over, then pushed his chest out several times. Something cracked. He was stiff already and we hadn't reached France. The complaint was directed at me because I couldn't share the task of driving. I said nothing, showing him alleviating stretches, manipulating him with my hands. The people in the car behind seemed to be staring at us. I felt Luke constrict as he became aware. Maybe they were listening to something as well, I reasoned, their intense concentration focused elsewhere. But I felt paranoid, post-homicide, and we shut ourselves back in the car.

When're you going to learn again? I mean actually take the test.

I sighed and shut my eyes.

I'll pay for it this time. Start when you've got the thesis done.

It was him behind the wheel and I did not have a licence, true, but it was really me who was actually driving. I remember being set on happy-ever-after. It amuses me now, how I thought about it as a physical place at the end of a long road. A place where I could unpack, lie down and never have to move again, and the future became an ending.

Eventually everything stopped, quietened, the car rolled forward a little. We drove out into pale sunshine, a sparse landscape, exposed. He grimaced and tapped the visor down but the brightness came from the road. A shining white fence rose on one side of us and, along it, dust from the ground, or mist. A delicate velvet sheen hovered just above the muddy fields as the sun spread out and silhouetted grey factories. It was peaceful after the tunnel, quiet but for the gentle drone of articulated lorries far-off. Little lakes flashing with white birds. Allotments. A few glinting skylights in the attics of strange homes.

The holiday had begun. I would be on my best behaviour from now on.

I looked over to see what kind of mood he was in.

Luke avoided short-haul flights for environmental reasons. He said he preferred scenic drives. So far, the view was emptiness. The occasional wind turbine standing still, little metal boxes moving up and down the belts of asphalt.

We stopped for coffee at a service station. I waited in the car, staring at a lay-by for HGVs, watching their drivers get out to piss or smoke, remembering the man who'd abandoned a truck crammed with people and left them trapped in there to decompose by the road. A pink rosette of what looked like ham printed on the side, a mysterious beige sauce, a grey lock on the outside of the doors.

Moving again, I opened the window, let the headwinds pummel my cheek. In front of us a truck swerved across the road. Luke shook his head, then slowly, deliberately, switched lanes.

Without knowing the rules of the road, his driving always struck me as exemplary. With other drivers I felt nervous as a passenger, a hand on the door keeping me in but also so I could be ready to jump out. With him I did that very rarely, and then only when another car came too close. He was confident but never reckless. Driving, at least, he never gave me any reason to doubt his ability to read the intentions of others or communicate his own.

Now I concentrated on the gentle incline on one side. When it thinned, or the road rose, I concentrated on the endless brown fields beyond, the outlines of slender trees in rows.

OK Loris? You're very quiet.

I nodded.

Carsick?

Loris was one in a series of names. The cute primate, which at one time colonised parts of the internet, clutching a tiny umbrella or stretching their arms into the air. The people who buy these creatures illegally don't realise the saliva is poisonous. Even with their tiny teeth removed, the venom can be deadly.

We passed names on the map that made me think back to school exams. The mist disappeared. I could make out steeply pitched roofs – pitched, he said, for snow.

They'll get flatter as we go south. South of Lyon the climate changes.

I admired how he knew these things. These invisible rules of the land, like the road. Or not quite like the road because they were innate.

My skin felt greasy and I closed the window. The silence between us grew. I resisted the impulse to play another true crime episode and rubbed my hand beneath my chin. We passed memorials and where Charles de Gaulle had lived, my fingernail grazing back and forth along my jaw.

Luke rarely commented on this now, but initially he'd compared the habit to stereotypic behaviour. I'd thought this meant stereotypical but in fact it's a kind of death drive:

The mysterious, repetitive range of actions displayed by captive animals such as pacing, picking without

purpose, and even self-harm, indicative of psychological distress in artificial environments since it is not
observed in animals in the wild.

I never said what I was actually doing, which was feeling
for the sharp hairs that surfaced there. An insurrection-
ary beard I was always monitoring. I forced myself to
stop now and examined my hands. My knuckles would
need shaving.

I knew other women who'd given up that unwinnable
war with their bodies, even the jawline razor wire, but
I'd now concealed my natural state so long, why spoil
things when I'd succeeded?

Of the things I cared too much about then, one was
appearing civilised. In ethical terms but also in aesthetic
ones. I had read the right books, bought thrifted designer
clothes, gained several degrees at elite institutions and,
in Luke's flat, arranged an elegant mise-en-scène that
in fact held no emotional resonance. They were props,
these objects I combed from life, smooth pebbles that
had once been cliffs.

I love that first bit out of a toll station, unmarked, where
you can move away on clean road. Those were the times
it seemed to me I might like to drive myself.

*

We reached our stopover in the afternoon and eventually found the hotel. The small dining room was all couples, none of whom spoke much. Cutlery on china, teeth on glass – I saw Luke going inward to escape it. He said he was too tired for more than one course, leaving before I'd finished.

When I came back to the room, minutes after, it was pitch-black and I could hear him breathing. I moved toward the bed, tapping the mattress in the dark, and climbed, in facing away. A few minutes passed before he turned, curled round, and, after momentary resistance, I hooked my foot behind his knee.

I waited for his hands to find me, but gradually his body lost tension until he jerked. I turned over – his dark shape like a hill faraway.

My phone said it was midnight, which meant it was our anniversary. On the first one I remembered feeling warm, insulated from the outside world. The second, I kept sensing what I thought was a phantom draught. The third I saw a detailed map of hairline cracks spreading out across the table between us. I did not mark our fourth but waited to see if he would. He did not. Today was our fifth. I'd reminded him when we booked the holiday.

Christopher said it was a natural response to capitalism, these tensions in what he disparagingly called monogamous, cishet relationships – particularly my sense that sex was a job, and not doing it the one way I could hold power.

He often referred to a friend who lived in a commune. They seemed to have a lot of sex. Feeling square, anxious just thinking about it, I reminded him my parents were communists. But it was true that nostalgia had replaced hope. When we did have sex now it was usually followed by a feeling of dissolution that seemed more intense than normal post-sex loneliness, at least for me. Solving a murder was a better way for us to feel connected.

I woke up and knew he was gone before I saw it. I listened for sounds in the bathroom and tried to remember whether we'd had an argument at some point in the night.

Our arguments were mostly silent, or silent on his side. Often in the dark, lying in bed so neither face could see the other. Not an argument then, but a pressure. A malignant quiet that sank into the mattress until I couldn't bear to lie there. I would get up in a dramatic fashion, go down to the sofa, then crawl back in a few hours later when he was sound asleep. Once he'd left for work in the morning, an email would usually arrive with a link he knew I'd like, and it was as if the night's events had been the product of my imagination.

He would have gone running, I told myself as I lay in the hotel bed. There was a path along the perimeter of the hotel grounds that cut through woods. Someone had tied colour-coded ribbons onto branches to mark two routes. Blue led you in a circle round the property, green took you on another path out of the grounds. We'd walked the blue route together soon after arriving the previous evening, ending where we began after half an hour or so. He'd said then he might wake early to do it.

I told myself I had no reason to feel rejected, dressed, then went back to the same table we'd eaten at.

I put my book down, split open, and watched as the other guests began to notice me. Last night's wine had sedimented in my lower lip and without thinking I peeled away a strip. I could taste the sourness of my own blood, pulsing.

After a while I realised breakfast was self-service. Standing by the buffet table, I held a napkin to my lip and made a show of examining the pastries wrapped in heavy cloth. I cut a slice of breakfast cake with slow precision. The other tables emptied and I became more self-conscious. The blood was still blooming into the napkin. I could not touch my food, except to cut it into smaller and smaller pieces, as if I were the kind of lonely, greedy woman liable to choke while eating. When I couldn't cut anything in two again, I left the knife at an inconclusive angle, as if to say I was still considering what I might do with it.

Two maids began clearing. I finished my glass of cold green tea and got up with what I hoped looked like nonchalance, as if Luke was never supposed to join me. I held the book to my chest, feeling my heart begin to thud against it, and went back to our room.

Not there.

I opened the shutters, looking around as if I'd lost an inanimate object that could not reveal itself. The sun was high, bars of it crossed the floor. The bedcovers were still thrown back on his side, his boxers and shirt on the floor where he'd shed them.

It was habit to think of crime scenes. I told myself to concentrate, looking around slowly and noting his phone, dead on the bedside table. The table was actually a bookcase of warped paperbacks and crisp hardbacks never read. My eyes rested on a title about survival. I drew it out. On closer inspection, a survival A–Z. The novelty kind with illustrations. I'd owned something like it as a child, or perhaps even the same one. Dangers were illustrated in a way that felt calming, like the sedate line drawings of airline safety manuals. I'd remembered one instruction, in particular, that if you fell down a waterfall you were supposed to close your legs to prevent internal rupturing.

I looked at the dust jacket with the uncanny sense it was my own copy transplanted here. The spine cracked as I opened it. Quicksand. The trick with that I knew already. Lie very still and flat.

On no account struggle or attempt to pull yourself out.

I plugged his phone in, switched to my canvas shoes, then went to find the pool, hoping I would see him swimming or reading. The sun was hot as I marched along the passage that led away from the main building, shielding my phone to check the time.

At the pool I swore under my breath and circled the loungers. No sign. I stood over my reflection at the deep end. A dead scorpion swayed on the bottom. I told myself this was not a sign of anything. I was reading into things again. This was simply absence. Absence with an absence of meaning.

I went back to reception. The same woman who'd cleared the breakfast and observed my solitude. I asked her in French for a bottle of water and she extracted one, unsmiling. I bared my teeth gratefully as she handed it over. She checked my room number, wrote it down, then went back to a game she had been playing on her phone.

*

I stood in the shade of the front gates and watched time creep closer to something categorically wrong. He knew how I hated to be left, with or without warning, but would've decided to forget how this went. He liked to assert his freedom by doing it I guessed. While he was gone I'd go through all the best-case scenarios, pacing like someone under house arrest. The narrative becoming ever more complicated. By the time he returned I'd be hysterical, then livid, then contrite. I would find myself apologising to him, neck bent, applying pressure to some part of him, begging forgiveness for my offence.

Our walk the previous evening had taken maximum forty minutes at a slow pace. I hesitated at the other external gate that marked the start of both routes – the simple choice now fraught – before embarking on the blue. I would retrace my steps. I would find him reclining somewhere along the path in the shade. And if not, he would have taken the green route into town and settled somewhere picturesque. I imagined a large white umbrella in a concrete stand and a glass ashtray into which he would have deposited wet olive stones. The same light that had suffused my vision of this trip. He would greet me with a bemused expression, to remind me I did not own him.

The wood was dense and the way obscured by branches. Alone, I had to focus harder on following the route. The path was sandy and my calves began to burn. I could feel blisters rising behind my heels and sweat prickling beneath the hair against my neck. Occasionally something Luke-sized would appear – the reptilian markings of a shoe – but these would slip away into sandy crests which went off in all directions.

It seemed safe to assume no other guests would be walking in the heat and that it would be possible now to shout his name. It was an ostentatious thing to do. If he was nearby and could hear me, I would feel humiliated. The silence, on the other hand, felt oppressive. I tried it out but couldn't raise my voice above a whisper. I stood still, panting, trying to summon something louder. Sweat crept into my eyes. The heavy glass bottle was now empty, sliding in my hands. No sound.

In the distance then, a bell. I strained, trying to decide if it was coming from ahead or behind, moving back and then forward again, then running, steps erratic on the sand. The bell grew louder and at the next turn, the trees thinned. I stopped, my throat thick with dust and saliva I couldn't swallow. A dozen horses stood in front of me in a clearing, tossing their heads in the shade. The bell hung from the neck of the most magnificent. It rang each time the horse moved its head or passed the heavy air through its nose.

I sank to my knees, heart at my temples. I knelt in that pose as a child, waiting for absent people.

From kneeling I soon lay down, thinking not of happy endings to this situation, but what it would be like to hear the worst. The horses snorted and kicked the air, perturbed. My nose stung, as if I was about to start crying, but then, as the minutes passed, the pain faded. It began to seem like another thing I might survive and my breathing slowed again.

I grew quiet, save the occasional gasp, and eventually very still, feeling the heat of the earth against my back, staring at the branches swaying. From survivable it became tolerable. And from tolerable, gradually, something else. My heart soothed inside my ribs. I felt a kind of unity with my surroundings. The old trees, the rocks that had endured. The horses grew accustomed to my presence, and I with them, until I realised the worst now felt desirable, like release.

2

After my brother died, my father said a suicide could be hard to detect because the person, having decided on death, has accepted the worst and may feel more at peace. They might seem happy even, the struggle and indecision lifted, an end to the tunnel near.

But when Luke returned from his solo excursion he was agitated, packing without meeting my eyes, paying the bill in a hurry, then driving us further south for hours in almost total silence. I decided he was not suicidal, he had simply wanted a morning alone to see the town, but I felt my body brace, like the drawing of the woman before the waterfall, everything sealed to protect against the rupture.

When I told the story of what happened after, I described the golden-hour heat and the view. Us seated on a balcony overlooking a small fishing port. A still pool shaded by umbrella pines. I didn't say I thought he was about to break up with me.

Anya, he said.

The cicadas seemed to intensify. All at once their separate mating calls surged as one siren song. A rasping sound that rose from everything on earth. He took my phone from my hand and set it aside, began to speak of a fork in the road. Something rose in my throat, hard and tight, I put my hand to it and hid by pressing into him, feeling our separate heartbeats hammer away in mutual dread. He released himself, got up. I thought he was leaving me but then he knelt. He lifted his hands, offering me a box.

The yellow diamond flared green and white. On my finger, I could see it even out of the corner of my eye – an aurora that followed me everywhere.

It had been his grandmother's. Now, he said, sounding unconvinced, it would be mine.

We stayed to watch the light bleed out. Somewhere an insect beat relentlessly against a screen and the sky turned a pink so saccharine my teeth began to ache.

I stopped sleeping. Luke's sleep changed too, which I knew because I only slept intermittently by day beside the pool. At night I watched him. I told myself the cause of my insomnia was the heat and mosquito hordes. The mattress was too hard. I watched the retreating tail of the green repellent coil, the hours burning off.

He'd look angry in his dreams. He'd twitch then make a startled noise and lurch upright, hot and damp

– What? he'd shout, like I'd shoved him. What're you doing to me?

In the mornings he'd rise stealthily and go running. I'd pretend to be asleep.

When he came back I'd be waiting. I'd watch him through one eye as he undressed. Waiting again while he took a shower, watching again while he dried off. His penis pale beside his darkening legs. It started to look sickly. If he caught me with my eyes open, I turned my gaze to the yellow diamond, turning it slowly and deliberately so that it would catch the light.

I'd taken several books by Sybille Bedford with me on that holiday. Every place, person and meal she described sounded like a secret language of sophistication. I read them in the sun by the pool while Luke read his apocalypse books in the shade, their titles all in sans serif. I found myself wishing to be like her. Bedford. Hedonistic. Denying my own hunger for security.

One of the books Luke read revived his idea of getting a communal smallholding and living off the land. I wondered why he'd suggested getting married if society would soon collapse but I didn't ask out loud. Not just because Luke talked about environmental issues in increasingly technical terms, as if irritated his pet cause had grown popular, but because the subject of our engagement quickly felt too awkward to return to.

When I thought about it I felt a peculiar foreboding. It was not the feeling I'd expected when I imagined this initiation into married life. Though we inhabited the same villa and had nothing else to talk about, we barely spoke of it again. Without the ring, I'd have convinced myself I'd imagined it.

I reasoned that this was probably for the best. I did not want a white wedding or the associated rituals. Weddings seem like hubris and perhaps they invite disaster. But I wanted the institution of marriage. To change my surname to Luke's and be shielded by it. Bedford had become Bedford by one of those strategic marriages that happened between Jews and gays in the 1930s.

Most people we knew were married by then. Christopher said it was reactionary. Luke and I owed our first meeting to the wedding of our only mutual friends, and since then I'd paid attention to ring-fingers, to the self-confidence of these women, like expensive cats that had all been microchipped. My ringless finger marked me as a stray among them. Something pitiable and out of place, which made me want it more, not just for protection but as validation. By that summer, listening to tales of yet another engagement could produce strange reactions in me. I'd ask the newly affianced if she'd been uneasy, following her suspicious-acting partner out onto some remote cliff face like that. A rock to the head instead of the hand! Only I would laugh at this.

I laughed louder just to cover Luke's unnerving silence, but there was resentment I could barely hide. A cold part at the very centre of me, painful, as if my underwire had pierced my flesh. My smile would droop on one side. What's wrong? he sometimes asked as we left the creamy folds of another marquee. You look like you've got Bell's palsy. My feet would hurt from being bound in foolish shoes. I'd run a bath in yet another B&B, soap my arms and slide the razor, going carefully round each wrist.

Now I had a ring of my own. This was what I'd wanted. This was where everything in my life had led. This rented villa in the South of France. This man beside this pool. Occasionally dozing or plunging into the freezing water. But the longing was still there. I stared at the ring to remind myself of my new status, and, fresh from a dive, the breeze cold on my skin, the sun warming it, the view beyond the trees could then suggest something infinite, some new place I now had access to.

The last Bedford book I read was her travel essays. One describes her drive across the Italian border and then through Yugoslavia. She is driving slowly, in a sturdier car than her own, rented so as to be expendable, apprehensive not only regarding the roads but of entering a socialist federalist republic where *their* idea of freedom is not the same as *ours*. Where 'communism is the price for peace'. She describes the road to Split along the Dalmatian coast – the mountains, the green of the sea, the mist like a bloom on a peach – as the most wonderful drive she had ever experienced.

When we returned to London, Big Ben had been stopped, and scaffolding now obscured the clock tower alongside parts of the Houses of Parliament. When I pointed this out as we drove past, Luke said that given the current situation the symbolism was too crude to mention, as if this was what I'd said.

We dropped the car at home then went straight out again to an Italian restaurant where his friends congratulated us. We had them back to the flat and the toasts continued with wine Luke had brought from France. The women inspected the diamond as if for flaws. My drooping smile returned. Now it was my turn for Mason jars. For personalised vows like annual reviews – helping someone live their values.

I went to bed long after him, having cleaned the kitchen. He had put a crime podcast on and fallen asleep but I lay there listening to it.

The following morning, the sticky remains of a bird could be seen when I stood at the kitchen sink washing the wine glasses that were too large to go in the machine. I'd bought them for his birthday. A stupid purchase I could not afford. It seemed too high for a cat to reach the slate roof which jutted out from the back wall, so how, I wondered, had it got there?

He came in as I was drying them and told me his parents had invited us to Cornwall. He'd go that afternoon and make the most of the holiday he still had left to take, I could join them on the weekend.

They had known what Luke was planning to do in France. His mother had provided the ring. It was unclear what remained to be discussed privately between them, but I agreed to stay behind.

September was ending but the temperature reached a sinister twenty-nine degrees. Every day was meant to cede to storms. I waited for rain to wash the tiles of the bird remains. The city heat made my insomnia worse. Finally I gave in and bought an expensive fan. Once I'd carried it home the heatwave ended – and it rained non-stop for days.

The noise of the downpour helped me sleep, and in sleep it also entered my dreams. The sea levels had risen so that half of the British Isles were flooded. Luke directed me by text to meet him at a safe place but I had to sort out something first with my family. Once this was done, I could no longer find the message with Luke's instructions, and the water meant I could no longer find my way back to the flat as all landmarks had been submerged.

When I woke I texted Luke to tell him, even though he has no interest in these things. His reply came slowly but was comforting:

I'm sorry. It's hard to get back to places in dreams.

On Friday I walked most of the way in the rain to the station, relishing the new smell of the earth.

I meant to work on the train but spent the hours watching the landscape change. I'd requested forward-facing with a table but was given a rearward seat. This happened every time I took the train to Penzance. I suppose they rarely know which way carriages will be facing when they allocate seats, but somehow it felt personal.

I could have switched – there were empty forward-facing seats – but I hated doing this. I couldn't stand the tension when the train arrived at each station and new passengers got on, their eyes boring into me as they moved along the aisle. And I couldn't bear the shame of being told to move if I'd taken a place that did not belong to me.

This paranoia was most acute on the way to see his parents, perhaps because of everything I knew from Luke about the native Cornish view of outsiders, or 'emmets' as he called them. His own mother had moved there as a child but made up for it with Cornish nationalism and loud suspicion of second-homers, which her own parents had once been.

The journey to Mousehole was by then familiar. There were stretches of scenery I knew to look out for. I liked the thunk thunk of the doors and the whistle each time we pulled away, ever closer until I could recite the stations. They have good place names in that part of the world, easy to romanticise. Like in Scotland, they get wilder as you approach extremity. I liked to imagine the submarine cables emerging onto the rocks at Porthcurno, connecting this island to the world. It made my skin prick – something about the inevitability of the tracks, taking me as far as they could before land fell into sea.

The man sitting opposite, where I'd wanted to sit, wore a Help for Heroes hoodie, unzipped to reveal an England football shirt. I glanced under the table to see a hybrid of hiking boots and trainers, a gold signet ring, a gold wedding band on the other hand resting on his thigh, a silver dog-tag-style bracelet hanging from his sleeve, a red poppy keychain fastened to his rucksack. He had the shining, ruddy skin of a younger man, his grey hair shorn in a military style. I looked into his eyes for a moment – large and black with no discernible irises. He reached down into his bag, pulling out the same flask Luke had, drinking from it then folding his arms, staring directly back at me.

I wondered now if I had the wrong seat after all. No. I knew I was being paranoid again. I switched my gaze to the window. A wide brown expanse slanted with boats at low tide. The view for that part of the journey is how I imagine Doggerland.

Occasionally I caught the eye of the woman at the opposite table, which she shared with two children and a man. I guessed from the proximity of their legs that they were her children and he was her husband, but in the five hours until they alighted at St Austell, I never saw one of them look up from their screen. She was conspicuous for not having anything to occupy her attention and her pale skin seemed to be lit by a different source, belonging neither to the train nor any of the worlds in which her family were separately engrossed.

When our gaze met at Dawlish as the train grazed the sea, I sensed something strange in my vision. The speed of the train seemed to accelerate, dizzyingly, like we might reach the horizon. Looking at her, it was as if either she or I weren't really there but regarding the other from another point in time.

Later, as I stood between carriages in preparation for my stop – the last – I remember thinking: I'll be alright if he breaks this off because I'll still have the PhD to finish. I'll crawl deeper into that black hole. The more dependable institution. The hammering in my heart again, the war drum starting up.

*

He was waiting beyond the railings. He wore an un-familiar coat. I didn't recognise him until he got out and signalled from the door of his dad's car. The sticker in the window – Kernow, with the white cross on black. Even then I saw him as a stranger. This was a phenom-enon I recognised when we spent time apart, but the physical attraction now took me by surprise.

His mother often said Luke had been a late bloomer. He'd been substantial as a child. Durable, like the white goods that come with five-year guarantees. You could see the evolution in her framed photographs – which were everywhere – how he'd whittled into his present form, head separating out from neck. Lately his newfound fanaticism for running had made him sinewy.

I dropped my bag and held out my arms to what was left of him. The yellow diamond flared. Luke kissed the top of my head and pressed me into the thick, fan-shaped muscle of his chest. I reached inside the strange oilskin then withdrew, holding him at arm's length. He had the beginnings of a beard.

Hello . . . ? I touched his face and then the coat.

It's Dad's.

I felt him take in my appearance now, worrying I'd applied too much foundation. He hated make-up, and then when he commented on it, I'd feel the self-con-scious urge to wear more.

I felt nervous, I said, on the way here.

Me too.

Driving down or coming to pick me up?

He took my bag but did not answer.

How are they?

Fine.

Listing Luke's good traits, filial duty went near the top, but I'd never felt closer to him than during the previous summer, when he and his parents had fallen out. They had said it would be *suicide* staying in Europe, while Luke thought that word would be more apt if we left. Sorry, he said after, I only meant –

I assured him I didn't mind. Being taken into his confidence, listening to him rage behind their back, had produced a mirage of married life which lasted the duration of the rift. From the referendum until his mother called to check we were still alive when concrete barriers were installed on London's major bridges.

All arguments about sovereignty were suspended after those attacks. They asked if he wanted to move back. Now he minimised their estrangement, and seemed to resent me for what I remembered. I couldn't understand what had gone on between them, he insisted.

I'm sure his parents thought that I had been the cause of it. The cosmopolitanism I'd tried so hard to cultivate did not succeed at charming them. We had a row about it, maybe the closest Luke and I ever got to a real fight. He characterised his parents' aversion to the bloc with ever more left-wing arguments, which I could not dispute although it was maddening. If I ever mentioned the conspiracy theories she bought into now, he leapt to her defence. If her trust in institutions was disintegrating, he said, it was even more important to hold her close. I knew that this was his way of reconciling his parents with his own world view. It was commendable, in a way, how he, a scientist, modified these facts out of loyalty. He'd been doing this ever since he went to university it seemed. Despite what Luke did for a job, his mother did not believe the world was warming, and her resistance had only grown alongside her son's expertise. I'd wondered if it was a reaction to it, as if she had to compete with science, but actually it had started long before. She had refused all vaccinations for him growing up. The way she'd told me this, proprietorially, made it clear his body would never belong to me.

I climbed onto the passenger seat, held up my newspaper, its front page still on fire:

NEW DEATH TRAPS FOUND

Good to get out, I said.
   He glanced at the photograph.
   Of the city, I mean.
   OK, how are you?

I realised my error – talking about Cornwall as an escape irritated him.

Fine.

He claimed to have poor reception when he went home. He called it home though he also used that word for our flat. His flat. The flat his parents bought. Whenever he went to Mousehole, I expected minimal contact, so that when we were reunited, there was usually a period of adjustment, of having to make small talk as strangers might. Luke inscrutable, me eager and puppyish, sniffing out each interstice.

This separateness could last for hours unless we had news to tell. I thought back over the past week. I'd spent it eating leftover chicken pho, digging through fat which had solidified a greenish grey, leaving the flat only for small intervals of sun or to work in air-conditioned cafes or the British Library, alone. I'd achieved nothing. Several versions of a diagram, the tensile limits of my cables.

When Luke was away I could turn feral on my own. I tried to think of something to tell him as he edged out of the station, but as I opened my mouth he pressed resume. The timbre of the podcaster familiar.

I've done a lot of driving, he said noticing my look. It's different when I'm alone.

OK, can you fill me in?

You'll catch up.

I was sensitive to that tone. I inferred from the tight-ness in it, like a wire stretched from the wall, that he'd reached his conversational limit during the week and had taken refuge in the solitude of the car before I'd broken it.

I kept my eyes out the window, on the stream of moss-covered roofs, drystone walls, dark slate. One of the hosts thought the murderer was not a monster until society had made him one, the other took a more 'Hobbesian' view.

Outside the town, the trees on either side of the road interlaced their branches to make tunnels. The roads became narrow lanes with fields either side of tall hedgerows. Then something one host said made me open my mouth without thinking.

Any infestations I should know about?

He was silent long enough to unnerve me.

Not in the house.

The first time I'd visited, a swarm of bees had exploded from the attic and the bluebell patch his mother culti-vated was under threat from badgers – leaving me with serum sickness and the confused impression that badgers went out at night to gather bluebells. I heard Luke refer to me, upstairs, as the convalescent. I wasn't *listening* – I'd been afraid of drifting off in case my mouth fell open. I was terrorised by small creatures. When I caught something scaling the wall, I left it dashed there as a warning until Luke had said there'd be other things that came now because they were *attracted*.

What does that mean, not in the house?

He stopped the podcast, softening. Moles were tunnelling in the front garden, he said. His father had abandoned the roller, conceding the area in the hope they'd be happy there and call it a day.

But moles *like* tunnelling, he went on. It's not a war you can win with them. They swim through the earth. If I was blind I'd do it too. But obviously my mother is losing sleep over it.

Anne hated the idea of losing control of her property, whether to me when I tried to help her with domestic tasks, or to the moles, the crowning glory being the lawn at the back which she mowed in stripes sitting on top of a large machine. When she was not mowing she gazed at it from the kitchen window or watched protectively from the door.

Luke had found a vibrating device that claimed to deter moles, believing it was better to use preventative measures rather than combative ones. He suspected his mother still kept a supply of strychnine, despite it being outlawed.

Outside the breeding season, he continued, moles live alone and defend their tunnels aggressively. Maybe several will inhabit the same area, but each makes a separate system. She goes after them when she's mowing but they burrow right down and instead she kills everything else in her path. Frogs and voles get spattered everywhere. I've convinced her to let me use a scythe for the long grass, that way they have a chance to escape.

He began telling me about his rewilding plans to convert one part of the garden into a meadow, and I stopped following him.

Some of the times I felt most sure of Luke involved watching him free wild animals. In France he'd saved a small green frog from the bath by throwing a wet cloth over it and carrying it outside. The frog kept coming back. It did not want to exist in a state of nature, preferring the cool sarcophagus of the bath despite our looming presence over him. Maybe, I suggested, it felt safer there from other predators.

Around the time I moved into his flat, a bird fell down the chimney and beat against the window. Luke guided it down to waist height with the soft end of a broom. I stood dumbly by, conscious my ovaries were pulsing. When I couldn't turn the window locks, he made me take the bird. I was afraid to touch it, and the fear only intensified when I did, the throb of tiny life, the crush of feathers ossified inside my hands. I didn't mention my father's nets, hung in trees so we could catch birds like it to eat.

He punched the horn in warning as we approached a bend.

When we started seeing each other, I'd asked him just to drive me around. He said I was likely the only person aroused by authority in the form of the highway code. I'd made a joke (auto-eroticism) but he'd looked blank. Now I imagined him driving other girls for whom the car itself was the fetish. I saw him going faster along these lanes, someone's sandy foot, toe ring on leather, blonde hair furious in the wind.

Did you ever surf? I asked suddenly, interrupting him.

He paused, narrowing his eyes. Why?

No reason.

We'd once pulled into a disused quarry somewhere not far from where we were, and I'd tried to persuade him to fuck me against the car. In the end he let me go down on him. It was the first time he'd allowed this and I remember his visible shock when I swallowed the mouthful like seawater. I'd sensed that I'd misjudged him, or misunderstood something much greater about that act. Before we met I'd always been looking to please this way. Confusing the desire to please with my own pleasure. But as we drove out of the quarry, I saw him revising his understanding of who I was also, and felt as if something solid beneath me had given way.

As we got closer to his parents', the cat's eyes began to shine from the road, the headlights making a pale wreath ahead of us, illuminating the side of a cottage daubed with the words ENGLISH OUT.

We passed the church where Luke's parents got married, which I knew would be the theme of our weekend. Then, at the end of the tarmac, I touched his hand. I had the feeling, close to homesickness, of longing to be there even though I was. Finally, the garden wall covered in lichen, the barking of the dog.

As a child I'd fantasised about a low-beamed, thatch-roofed cottage from British children's books, and no matter how many times I arrived, it still felt like stepping inside that fantasy.

We entered the hall as, from the back garden, Anne came in, carrying a torch and covered in dirt. Her grey hair had turned white in the sun. She gestured to her smock and gardening gloves, then walked toward the sink with her hands up as if I held a gun.

Michael appeared behind her. He had to stoop, and from this posture, the tic of rolling his shoulders and his beak of a nose, I'd always associated him with a large bird. More blood vessels had broken across his face, darkest on the chin where white tufts of hair also sprouted. When he leant toward me I saw the deep folds of skin that intersected at his neck. His scalp was mottled brown. I tried to imagine Luke at that age.

Train OK?

Fine, thanks.

Luke got you OK?

Yes.

Given that we were both standing there, I wondered if this question was meant to draw attention to the fact I was reliant on him to drive me, as well as everything else.

Oh I nearly forgot. Congratulations!

Well, he corrected himself, it's Luke who is lucky.

I appreciated this. Any indication they did not view me as a parasite, looking for a fold in their family. I made that sound that is laughter without smiling and placed the hand with the ring on Luke's chest, leaning into his shoulder in a way that was supposed to be a parody. It had made his friends laugh but Michael only nodded.

Upstairs, I unpacked and Luke sat on the bed, leaning back on his elbows. A book had been left at an angle on the desk. I turned it over. A volume of poetry by a Cornish poet. This was Anne's mode of diplomacy. Not poetry as such, but objects she thought I'd like left out without explanation.

Luke pulled me onto the bed. The distant look was gone. He climbed over me and I smiled. I felt powerful and steady and stopped his hands in their tracks.

We should help your mum.

He froze for a moment, then groaned, pushed his erection against his stomach with his waistband.

Anne gave me a pile of new napkins to put out instead of the ones I'd used to set the table. They were decorated with little blue pictures and accompanying Cornish nouns.

There's a picture in their downstairs toilet, a framed photo of their whole extended family, all smiles except Michael, mid-soliloquy. They're standing by the monument to Dorothy Pentreath – supposedly the last person who conversed in that language.

When the table was done, Anne gave us beans to shell. My way was to split their seams gently and slide them along, Luke's was to snap the pod in the middle and press, so they shot out like bullets, ringing against the pan.

Anne stood at the sink peeling potatoes until I noted a small yellow fly on Luke's shirt and she spun round, pointing the peeler at me.

There were so many bloody apricots over the summer I had to make buckets of jam. And then the flies came. They were *out* of control. I had to make a trap – she indicated the counter where a glass bowl was filled with liquid – using vinegar. Not as good as the sticky paper but we ran out. Chaos. I tell you now, I nearly lost my mind.

She flushed, pinged the elastic of her neckline and blew back her white fringe. Luke bent over the bowl, wrinkling his nose, and I came closer too, thinking of bleeding apricots. Some flies had drowned but many more sat on the rim, watching their friends sink into amber. There was something languid about the scene, like the aftermath of a wild party.

The first meal I had in that house I realised that the plates we were eating off were the exact same as my aunt's when I lived with her in Glasgow. In Glasgow, I'd felt the same sensation, seeing that my aunt had the same lace crochet table runner as my mother – an uncanny effect of making me feel less at home. Every time I sat down to a meal Anne had made, I had the urge to comment on them. I stopped myself. Other than being dull, I worried it sounded like I was trying to prove something.

Anne took her seat finally and said, Well. She wanted to discuss our wedding. I tried not to look at her crowded little mouth. Full of overlapping teeth like a shark. A bone from the fish pie stuck in my throat, scratching it, so that I kept trying to clear it even after it was gone. Each time I did, everyone would stop talking and look at me expectantly and I would have to wave the conversation on. Luke seemed reluctant to engage so his mother couldn't get very far with her questioning.

Here, Anne said as I cleared my throat again, eat some bread.

Michael changed the subject to their war with some neighbours. Second-homers who'd complained that the trees in Luke's parents' garden obscured their view.

A petition was sent. Anne didn't recognise *any* of the names. Now two trees had fallen within weeks of each other, though there'd hardly been a breeze.

They know we know they poisoned them, she said. I suppose we're lucky they fell toward the road. But there might be more any day now. Or as we sleep. We could all be killed. I've asked Paul to have a look.

Until the first – and only – time I saw his parents in London, I'd thought they had no fears. Then Anne said she had heard my university was a hotbed of terrorism and she seemed eroded, standing there in our kitchen.

She had once been in the news, I remembered as we cleared the table, with the headline BRAVE LOCAL WOMAN SURVIVES COLLAPSE. While walking the dog along a cliff she'd spotted something strange – the land moving – and filmed the moment when a section of cliff collapsed onto the beach. In the interview with a local reporter she says that the sea, which had always seemed to her like a defensive moat, had threatened to eat her up. I searched for it again. There were now links to other reports about sea defences, a story of a man in Southwold who was fighting both nature and bureaucracy at once, and a scientific study which claimed Cornwall had at one time formed part of France, owing to a clear geological boundary.

*

After dinner we sat in front of a documentary. A penguin couple arched their necks in a synchronised, hypnotic dance. The ritual helped the pair to bond, the voice-over explained. Luke, lips dark with wine, provided meta-narration based on the extent to which the programme anthropomorphised its subjects.

I liked the superimposed narratives. The animals wanted the same things I did. We learned that puffins die at thirty, have one offspring at a time, and mate for life.

I don't believe it, Luke said, they must get divorced.

But even he was transfixed by the bowerbird. Michael liked the way it could shrink and expand its pupils to seduce. Anne admired its thatch of orchid stems and neatly planted lawn. Luke said the way the bird accumulated and displayed treasures in its theatre reminded him of someone, meaning me.

What's the opposite of anthropomorphise? I said.

Dehumanise, Michael said, unaware, again, I'd made a joke.

Zoomorphism, Luke corrected.

I'd watched a lot of TV the summer my sister and I arrived in the UK. I sat indoors with the curtains drawn watching Home Front when it was still hosted by Tessa Shaw. After that came Changing Rooms, Better Homes, Grand Designs. We hadn't been able to watch TV for months at a time so my aunt allowed it at first.

It was perhaps the easiest way to deal with me. Then she let it go on as it became clear I was gaining a precocious vocabulary: *feature walls*, *imitation mahogany*, *local vernacular*.

By the time I started my new school, I felt a primitive desire for accumulation. I lusted after swag curtains and ornaments visible through the windows on more affluent streets. I stole small items from children in my class. The first was a gaudy tassel from the skirt of an armchair which I stored in a shoebox under my bed. It had relieved the tight feeling in my chest for a few days.

After the main programme ended and the bit about how it was made came on, Michael returned to his crossword.

Shibboleth, he barked suddenly. Five letters.

We were silent for a while. All I could think of was Doris Salcedo's crack in the Turbine Hall floor.

I wish they gave clues, I said at last.

His eyebrows jumped and then the three of them burst into laughter. I smiled though I didn't get the joke, then for real as I understood, and then, with a radiating warmth because Anne had put her arm around my shoulder in a clumsy way – a hug, in essence – and I felt as if I'd finally stepped over her threshold. I had a vision of the four of us in the cottage, seen in cross section. Miniature figures, like in a doll's house, moving between scenes. I saw us from the other side of this vertical plane, from where I seemed a part of it.

Upstairs, undressing, I held him off again. Then I lay back to read the poetry book.

The poet was deaf-blind, the foreword said. People wrote on his hand so he could communicate. He was also a self-proclaimed *sex mystic*.

Have your parents read this?

Luke, his face now deep in the pillow, was unresponsive.

I tried to feel my way into the deprivation of those two senses, to step into being deaf-blind like an analgesic suit. I imagined it like a special power of concentration.

The poet wrote about the landscape of china clay mining. I'd seen some of what remained: the scars, the quarries turned lakes. Luke had taken me to the Eden Project – built in reclaimed china clay pits, now home to a transplanted forest. It had been the first time he talked to me in any detail about biodiversity – his field.

I remember first explicitly wanting to marry him that day, moved by how much he seemed to care about future lives. That went on my mental list with filial loyalty and the way he liked to do repairs, or own things that needed constant maintenance. All things which suggested reliability.

I put the book down, turned off the light and lay my head beside his. A rush of warmth spread across the pillow. The bead of water that had rolled into the canals of my ear on the last day of our French holiday had tormented me at first, but by then, two weeks later, it must have travelled to a sanctum so deep inside I'd ceased to feel it. Now it was gone, I felt rehabilitated. I lay on my side, holding him from behind, imagining the day when this house would be ours.

The water cooled beneath my cheek. I could feel the whirr of sleeplessness accelerating. I tried to imagine us living in a simpler time. In the time of china clay mining. I could see myself with an auburn dog and soft-bellied children: blob-like shapes, legs blotted with pink bruises. They ran around and splashed in the craters filled with turbid water.

I did fall asleep but had one of my recurring dreams in which I can't. These are almost exact replicas of the nights in which I lie awake. The night sky is always a saturated yellow, like there will be a storm but there never is. The window is broken, or I can't close it, but there is a metal bowl beneath a drain pipe, catching rainwater for someone to drink. The drips ring out, unpredictable, all night. I try to focus on falling asleep. Then, with the effort of doing so, I wake.

3

In the middle of the night – the real night – Anne flung open the door. She was the kind of mother who refused to knock. A fan of borders but not boundaries.

They've dug up *all* the courgettes, she said.

The moles?

Much worse. Forget the moles.

Neither of us moved.

Come on – she flipped the lights – we're being besieged. Get a shovel. Anya you can hold a torch.

Michael refused to be routed. I heard him insist Anne respect his sleep – she was more than intimidating enough to handle marauding boar.

Outside, we took in the destruction. Mounds of earth uprooted, shredded plants, craters, gougings and tracks disfiguring the lawn.

Monsters, she spat.

It's not their fault, Luke said.

Whose is it then?

They were hunted to extinction then reintroduced. Deliberately. By *us*.

I never introduced pigs to my garden.

They were here first, then we killed them off and got nostalgic for it.

Luke. I'm an animal person so spare me the sermon, please. But this – she gestured around. This is ridiculous. They go after dogs. They laid waste to Pem's farm. Last time I heard one run along the decking I leant out the window and shot it. It was like a bomb going off. All the mud and dust. Took four of us to put it in Pem's truck. Very good meat, so it was probably worth the carnage, in the end.

Luke stopped digging, closed his eyes and exhaled.

Your mum's – she seems manic, I whispered. Do you think we – you – should make her lie down?

He mumbled something about going to get a glass of water but never came back. I finished our end of the trench alone.

After several hours digging, erecting fortifications using upturned chairs, I realised I was enjoying myself. I felt useful working alongside Anne, and it reminded me of my childhood, when anything could be reimagined into something new. Shoes became firewood, sheets became windows, my brother's skateboard became a water cart.

But the objects I gravitated toward aesthetically now, I realised as I positioned two dining chairs like coping stones, all had an underlying stability. The sculptural things I collected maybe did have emotional resonance then, in that I couldn't imagine them transmuting into anything else.

Finally Anne surveyed the barricades. Seagulls called overhead and I followed her gaze to where the perimeter disappeared into the dawn mist and then the creek.

That should do it, she said. For now at least.

I crept back into bed beside Luke and admired the crescents of black dirt under my nails. I kissed the warm skin at the back of his neck. Then I remembered the poisoned trees.

Luke drank several cups of coffee at breakfast, rubbing his face and the back of his head. I was used to surviving on no sleep, but he needed at least eight hours to make any conversation. I loaded the dishwasher and pretended not to notice as Anne restacked everything.

I thought, she said slowly as she closed the machine, we'd take a walk to the church.

We put boots on and followed her and Michael along the road past the Spar. Another new house had been built, its glass front loomed behind a row of white saplings, spectral as a mushroom. Like the others in their vicinity, it appeared to be empty.

Can't understand why anyone would want to live under *glass*, she hissed. The few times I've actually seen someone in there, well, you can see *everything*. At night especially, I can see all its insides, like a jellyfish. There are more and more, they attract each other, these planning notices – she pointed to one pinned to the gate – like a swarm.

I imagined Anne standing outside the house in the dark. I agreed it was out of place.

We passed the disused garage, overgrown by weeds. Here Luke, an only child, had founded his own clubhouse after reading *Lord of the Flies*. Still his favourite book. And of course, as Anne was fond of pointing out, another Cornish author. There was still genitalia-themed graffiti in the basement and a shrivelled buoy hung from a steel joist to make a swing. On the upper level, where cars were repaired, there were stepped walls on three sides like a theatre, which must have lent gravity to meetings. Luke confessed they used to defecate in the long grass behind rather than return to the cottage where his mother remained in charge.

I followed Luke's gaze toward it, it was clear he wanted to go inside.

Go on ahead, we'll catch you up, he told his parents.

I didn't like going in there, but I liked it that Luke wanted to go in. It suggested a continued wish to escape his mother's influence.

There was no glass in the window frames and it smelt of decay. Sometimes I seek that basement smell out precisely because I don't like it. It's still familiar. Cold concrete and earth.

In the graveyard, Anne took me through her thoughts on floral arrangements. I looked in Luke's direction, wondering if he would mention the idea we'd come to the night his friends had interrogated us, of having a non-religious ceremony with Christopher as our celebrant. I knew the only gay men Anne had ever knowingly met were two Canadians. Rather than say the word she now referred to all gay people as being *like the Canadian men.*

Michael pointed out the usual headstone belonging to their family. I spotted a magpie dart away beyond it and looked for a second. On a similar walk, long ago, Anne had stopped abruptly before one and saluted him in the middle of the road. Not understanding, I'd reacted with nervous laughter. That Christmas she gave me *A Pocket Guide to the Superstitions of the British Isles.* They're othering you, Christopher had said. Give her one for the Balkans next year.

The church was dismal. Michael disappeared and a few electric lights came on. I sensed Luke waiting for me to say something before he would. Then into the resonant silence, Michael's voice:

Not much trade except funerals these days.

Luke appeared to be avoiding eye contact with me now and I panicked.

I love it here, I lied.

Wonderful, Anne said, that settles it then.

Going back, we took a longer route off-road. Gradually the path narrowed so that we walked in single file. I felt myself detaching, following Luke's calves, letting them get further ahead until finally they were gone.

When I arrived back at the cottage, they were seated in a ring on the lawn which still bore the scars of the previous night. Luke was describing our holiday and the town of Sanary where many artists and writers had exiled themselves as Hitler rose to power.

Aldous Huxley, Thomas Mann, Bertolt Brecht, Stefan Zweig, he trailed off.

Sybille Bedford, I continued.

Don't know her, Anne said.

I said I would give her one of Bedford's books. Maybe *Quicksands*. I realised I did not want to share with them her impressions of Yugoslavia from *Pleasures and Landscapes*. Though much of it was admiring – the mountains, Venetian architecture, translucent water – I'd experienced the familiar contraction around my chest as I read her descriptions of the terrifying roads and wild children on the ferry crossing:

> What one wonders about is the future. Will it be a graceless, stark new world?

And finally of her time in Sarajevo,

> nothing ever, perhaps, quite safe, quite clean, quite straight . . .

Bedford, I told them, lived out the Holocaust in Sanary, later California. I heard my words echo what I'd read about her, sounding fluent. I understood her ambivalence at having spent so much time reading in comfortable places.

Anne and Michael wanted to see my photos. Luke had told them I'd taken several hundred. This was true. He rarely recorded anything on his phone except runs and photographs of plants.

They admired my pictures of the villa, the pink oleander, the view of the bay, Luke's kitesurfing technique, the harmonious blue of the water, tasteful market stalls, a fish we ate at the Hôtel de la Tour that had baked inside a white salt crust and was then exhumed for us at the table.

Doesn't look as flashy as you'd expect, Anne said, approving.

If their family went to restaurants, she would instruct everyone to order the same thing, since that way it was more like being at home. It was one of the things I felt I offered Luke, permission to indulge his yuppie side – to go out and order whatever he wanted.

Luke said there were no gin palaces in the harbour, a section of which was occupied by traditional fishing boats. He said there were few tourists, other than French from the north, and it was, compared to the surrounding destinations British holidaymakers had heard of, unspoiled.

Then he told the Bedford anecdote I'd relayed to him, concerning the Huxleys' arrival. Looking forward to the anonymity of a foreign place, Maria and Aldous had pulled up at their new Belle Époque home to find VILLA HUXLEY painted in bold lettering by the well-meaning decorator on the front gate. I knew why this resonated for Luke, who was horrified by the idea of public spectacle. It was something we'd discussed with regard to the wedding, he wanted the minimum possible number of guests. I was fine with that. Relieved, actually. It was easier to describe a wedding as intimate than find the words to explain why no one from my family would be there.

Anne held out my phone. I felt her gaze linger on the ring as I took it back and felt hot as if I'd stolen it.

She offered around segments from a clementine which I declined, though not before Luke could remind her of my hang-up.

The excuse I usually gave was not a lie, exactly. I *had* been eating plums gathered from the base of my grand-mother's tree as a child. I *had* accidentally picked up part of a bird, ripped open, the greasy remains now heaving with life. I *had* been horrified by the sticky mess, its texture in my hand, the apprehension of anarchy.

The sight of some fruit can affect me like an animal whose fur is rubbed against its growth. Perhaps reason-ably, given the nature of his work, Luke found this fact exasperating. Even *seedless* grapes? he would ask in perplexity as I declined to follow him down certain supermarket aisles.

As a child I dreamt about exotic fruit I knew only from cartoons. Sometimes we got parcels with excit-ing things and we'd make them last for weeks. Other times we got biscuits from WW2 and we'd feel resent-ful of the kids on other streets. I wanted Coca-Cola so badly that I hate it now. The same thing happened when I finally tried tinned pineapple and choked on the wet, syrupy chunks. In my mind, the longed-for fruit had the texture of human flesh.

The smell is fine. Maybe I've been desensitised by synthetic fruit-scented things. I can even enjoy fruit flavours, as long as there is no remnant of the original texture there. But the thought of biting directly into a tomato or unmediated slice of orange makes me gag. The various sensations that combine in the average piece of fruit! Seed, liquid, flesh, skin . . .

In the afternoon Luke caught up on sleep, forgetting to take the meat for dinner out of the freezer as he'd promised Anne to do. I remembered too late, and had to massage it beside the fire while he slept and his mother was busy somewhere in the garden. I was still attempting to defrost it when she came in and saw me there, crouching. When he came down I was silently angry that he'd left me open to his mother's suspicion of being a barbarian, and as we finally sat down to eat, much later than planned, we seemed to be engaged in another psychic war. I did not know why he was angry at *me*. I had saved the day. I remember hoping those vicissitudes in personality were chemical. A lighthouse whose beam disappeared only to come back.

Normal people argue, I said once, and then we had a very quiet argument in the garden centre, beside an LED Buddha fountain and a sign that read TRANQUIL OASIS. I felt such relief despite the humidity, the claustrophobia, the smell of rabbit hutch. His moods would shift abruptly, and at times I would find myself having crossed an obscure boundary into a strange place, a territory which only minutes ago had not been there.

The change could be even subtler. A shadow over the sun, a cold spot in water. Swimming as a child, I remembered turning onto my back, putting trust in the sky, imagining I swam in that element instead.

Luke could be two people as distinct as these elements, just as he had two names in my phone. Real name to indicate company mobile and pet name for personal. Depending on which he called from, our conversation would be altered.

At first I hadn't noticed the second person. I began to, soon after I moved in. Around the time things started to go wrong in the flat. The bath plug lost its suction. I couldn't fill the bath with water unless I kept it running, and even then, it would only reach my hips. A shelf came off the wall. A chair back marked another with a groove. The tap – which Luke had never had a problem with before – now leaked, heavy and staccato through the night. A gas ring refused to ignite. Clicking over and over without producing a flame. These went on a list of things to be fixed, and everything else on a list to break.

After dinner we watched the news and the mood lifted. They liked working out the BBC's more obscure visual puns. A story about pressure on primary school places was accompanied by seemingly unrelated footage of rowers, then canoes, and then the Queen's barge moving down the Thames. The connection between these images and the news story remained a mystery until the reporter ended with the words: The race is on.

Ho ho, Michael said.

Luke held my foot under a cushion then took one of my hands. They were covered in soot after poking the fire to thaw the meat, my fingers stained purple from chopping red cabbage. I'd removed the ring to prepare the food – an absence he mutely noted as he examined them. I tipped my head back to indicate where I'd put it. Then the news came to Brexit and I felt the room contract.

His parents knew which way I'd voted, but we hadn't directly talked about it since. They didn't know I'd exchanged insults with strangers on the internet late into the night. The 'real' people, with whom I'd argue until confronted with my own unreality, my own irrelevance. It was not the specifics of opposing arguments that upset me, but that the things I held on to, which kept me from being sucked back into the past, were coming loose.

Because my aunt was not my mother, when I'd had disputes with her children, they felt she was biased toward me and I felt she was biased toward them. Her son Nikolaj was a compulsive liar who had a problem with authority, except where it gave him power. He hated me not only for being clever, despite the language disadvantage, but because I'd experienced things he had not. I didn't understand then that he felt threatened. Not just by having to share his family with strangers, though that didn't help, but because in comparison to mine his life story was a domestic drama. He'd take great pleasure in warping events with unnecessary lies so that our referee, his mother, would eventually wave us away: *carry on for all I care, just stay out of my kitchen.* My sister Daria left for university a few months after we arrived, and then I had no one to confirm what I'd seen or heard versus what he then said had happened.

Why did I want things to stay the same? Christopher, who'd spoiled his ballot, asked me. He has an anarchist streak but somehow ended up a lawyer. A human rights barrister, more accurately. Law was what his parents had wanted him to do, and perhaps because of his ability to stand outside or above any such man-made edifice, he was very good.

I didn't have an answer for him. It was an emotion I couldn't put into adequate words. I remember right before the referendum, another wedding, this time Luke's non-Cornish cousin's, on Michael's side, I'd been seated next to a man I didn't know. One of the groom's parents' friends. He didn't know *anyone*, he claimed, which initially seemed the reason for our pairing. Then he said he was a poet, as well as a writer of thrillers for which he used a pseudonym. He pointed knowingly at my surname on the place card. He asked me about my parents, their ethnicity, and I said I was the child of a mixed marriage. In his capacity as a poet, he had travelled to the Balkans, and so for most of the reception, wanted to talk about the war.

I detected that tone I so often encountered then. As though such chaos could never occur within his island, whereas in the Balkans it was inevitable. Luke had later sympathised when I complained about my table, saying he understood how maddening it was – in the context of anthropogenic climate change. He called it the blind spot of any culture – the inability to conceive of its own destruction.

Occasionally I'd made attempts to engage the neighbour on my other side, an elderly relative of the bride's. She'd blinked at me kindly and said it must be sad when your country no longer exists, then returned to pulverising her asparagus. The need for discretion removed, the poet began to list his top ten most harrowing sights. His lips were wet. He topped up my glass and said that history must not repeat itself. That though the EU was imperfect, like Yugoslavia, like any marriage in fact, British people valued what it represented. Membership, he mused as a server took our plates away, was probably my homeland's only hope. We had better get a move on with integration.

A year on, if someone raised the subject in my presence I felt myself shut down. I couldn't bear to meet people's outrage or smirking faces, even their shock and grief. If it was mentioned at a party, whether or not I'd had anything to drink, I would simply walk away. Now I felt myself sliding into apathy.

On Sunday morning Luke kissed my shoulder tenderly then got up, pulled on his shorts and went running. I stayed in bed, the windows open, listening to the gentle call of a wood pigeon. The room flooded with light and a breeze came in off the creek. I'd had my first unbroken sleep in weeks and the combination of breeze, sunlight and memory foam gave me the sensation of gliding. Suddenly I heard the strains of what I took to be a recording of a piece of classical music. It began with tuning, but then, from its occasional repetitions, stops and starts, I understood that it was live.

I guessed a group of students were rehearsing, but I'd never seen any young people when I'd stayed before. My only explanation was that one of the elderly neighbours, or maybe the very rich one who poisoned trees, had convened a small orchestra, not for any reason other than enjoyment. Something about this idea seemed incredible. Though I did very little in the way of making money – did very little generally – I found it hard to think in any other terms than productivity.

As the communal effort of several brass instruments sailed into the room, a feeling of contentment and security verging on euphoria coursed through me. I stretched my limbs toward the four corners of the bed and felt a desire that I'd forgotten. I wanted to have sex with Luke.

I remained in that position for several more minutes with my eyes closed, listening to what I guessed was a cello, letting it merge with the wind, the heat of my skin. I sensed this was a moment I could have only once. When it stopped I'd never know what the piece I'd been listening to was. I thought of its transience, of using it up, like precious water running.

The solo ended and the silence which followed sounded entirely different from the silence that had preceded it, as if it was now part of something else.

I didn't know much about classical music and wondered if I should admit to this in order to ask Michael if he'd heard and could identify the piece for me. To risk being told it was something obvious.

He had extensive knowledge of all genres. The search function on iTunes had proved endlessly absorbing. He spent hours on these voyages of discovery, back and forth in time, through world music, thrash and elec-tronica. He'd made Luke four CDs composed of songs with American cities in the title for no reason other than the search function made it possible. They had been good for long car journeys before we discovered true crime. Some were classics, others by obscure heavy metal groups we knew to skip past.

He had unofficially taken charge of wedding music and given us a list that included a Cornish folksong arranged by Holst. The lyrics describe a woman released from bedlam by her lover who has returned from being at sea. I wondered if Michael had recalled the part about it being the man's parents who'd tried to keep her institutionalised.

I rolled over on the bed to the window, pulled myself onto my knees and crouched forward with my elbows on the sill to wait for him, watching the Optimists sail past the mouth of the creek, remembering the time Luke had insisted on taking me sailing. They could not believe I'd never been before, until I got into the boat.

Now I heard Michael's voice. He and Anne were standing below the window. I shot back, covering my chest. Thinking they must've heard me, I prepared to call out a greeting, but a prickling heat rose across my skin and I closed my mouth again.

I've looked. Nothing comes up. Nothing I can make sense of anyway. I really think it's odd Luke's never met them. I know he says they're just not close but I'm beginning to think it's more really.

Snip.

More than she's let on you mean?

For a few moments I was paralysed.

. . . contribution . . .

. . . never . . .

. . . marquee . . .

Snip.

If that's what he wants.

Snip snip.

. . . clever seating plan . . .

Sometimes I could hear whole sentences very clearly, other times only random words as they moved with secateurs along the trellis against the wall. They must've assumed we'd gone together – but would see when Luke came back he was alone. Given the open window, it would look like I'd been listening, and I knew I wouldn't be able to pretend I hadn't heard.

I put my hands over my ears, then pulled the covers over my head but could still detect certain words. I longed to close the window but forced myself to be still.

Savages,

If they come,

Children,

Communists,

Christmas,

I told you,

Stuck with it darling.

I pressed harder into the pillow. Trapped there, with my eyes closed, I could almost see the words as illuminated streaks firing through the window.

When Luke got back I said I had a headache and needed to stay in bed. I gave the kind of vague explanation

– fine, tired – he always gave that drove me mad when I knew something else was wrong. I didn't come down for lunch and saw Anne and Michael only to murmur bye and thanks as we put our bags into the car.

On the motorway I was silent, listening to the murder Luke put on – a woman who'd stabbed her fiancé in the heart with a steak knife – until we stopped for fuel. Luke bought food from Marks and Spencer which we ate across the dashboard. When we'd finished, I slotted the oily containers one inside the other, and asked if he still wanted to meet my family.

SPLIT

4

You can't fly direct to Sarajevo from London. We decided to take a connecting flight on the way back (using Luke's preferred calculator to determine the carbon footprint and how much reforestation would offset it) but on the outward journey chose to fly to Split instead, where we'd rent a car and drive along the Croatian coast for a few days (what Luke called a holiday and Christopher called assimilation), then head inland to stay with my parents.

The night before we were due to fly I crawled out of bed, staggered to the bathroom and lay with my cheek against the cold tiles before reaching my arms around the toilet to be sick.

When I stood, the walls disintegrated and I was sick again, depositing, into the basin this time, the little food I'd eaten. I stared for a minute, then tried to wash everything down, succeeding only in blocking the pipe. The sink began to fill. Sensing the end was far away, I hobbled out for a bucket and rug, teeth chattering, then sat back on the bathroom floor to ride things out.

When Luke's alarm sounded at five, I felt too weak to call between rooms, so stayed there on the floor, waiting for him to find me.

What are you doing? he said, reaching over me for his towel.

Sick, I whispered, jaw rigid.

My mouth barely moved but still the effort produced another spasm. I raised my hand in warning. I thought of that gesture in religious paintings. *Noli me tangere*.

Luke said we didn't have to go. Or didn't have to go that day. I hadn't slept, the flights were cheap, we could always catch another. I said I suspected I'd feel the same way until I got there. That though I still felt nauseous I'd passed the bile stage and didn't have anything left inside me to eject.

I'm not prone to action, but once I do commit I find I can't change course. I'd consulted Christopher about the trip. It might be good to make things normal, he'd advised.

We had to leave the blocked drain for when we got back.

Luke got an Uber to take us to the station and from there we boarded the airport express, where my ashen face did not stand out from the other passengers headed for early flights with other budget airlines.

He got me a seat facing forward and began to make a circular stroking motion on the back of my hand. I shook him off.

He nodded and turned back to his phone while I sat, straight-backed, taking small sips of water.

At the airport he checked in our shared suitcase and I responded to Christopher's chirpy *bon voyage*, thumbs shaking. *Already a nightmare*, I typed.

After security we navigated the speciously winding path through A WORLD OF BRANDS. Salespeople in black menaced us with perfume and Luke steered them away protectively. Ahead of us a figure in an unidentifiable animal suit lurched toward small children and their parents, listlessly waving a Union Jack.

Waiting on the transit bus, I studied faces. Some were young couples going on holiday, familiar in that they looked like us, but then I noticed others, perhaps returning. Strangers with faces I somehow knew.

Our seats were in the middle of the plane and as we shunted past each row, the sight of so much irradiated human flesh made me convulse again. Luke gave me his aisle seat so I could make a swift exit, just in case, and he took the middle one. When the seatbelt signs turned on we realised no passenger had claimed the window so Luke shifted over, leaving the seat between us empty.

I placed my water, phone, book and A4 thesis note-book on the empty seat (with the fantastic notion I might feel better and want to work) until a steward-ess told me to hold or stow all of these away. I knew I couldn't tolerate holding water as it sloshed about, and I couldn't face bending over or standing up again, so placed the items inside the leather pocket in front. I remember telling myself not to leave them behind, which was something I usually told Luke, who was always losing things. The stewardess then asked if we were aware that ours was the emergency exit row, and whether Luke was prepared to open the door in the event of emergency.

Her make-up sat thick and matte over her face, while the back of her neck and behind her ears, where her hair was pulled tightly into a doughnut, was pale and shimmered with blue veins. It seemed less like make-up than an actual mask. I imagined that behind it she despised her job, which involved making so many life-saving announcements and yet never being listened to. She carried on down the aisle. Whether they knew it or not, the surrounding passengers, like myself, now had no choice but to place their faith in Luke. The idea distracted me a little from the nausea. I glanced at the rows of waxen faces, strange companions in this aluminium tube, with a new feeling of shared destiny, or powerlessness.

Then it occurred to me that any one of these captive strangers might yank the emergency door in a suicidal act. I closed my eyes and felt the plane start to roll away from its moorings.

When I opened them again Luke had started reading my copy of the Rebecca West. He'd asked if he could borrow it, if I thought it would be good to read, and I'd said yes without admitting I'd never read it. I'd filled whole shelves with books about the Balkans but couldn't bring myself to open any. I'd told myself that on my thirtieth birthday I would finally begin to read them as a symbolic transition into adulthood, having respectfully observed something like a governmental thirty-year-rule. I was thirty-one then.

I felt the ground begin moving, vibrating through my feet. I had to lift them off the floor but that also made me dizzy. An acrid taste coated my throat as we rose up and into the air.

I fell asleep at some point and woke to find the cabin peacefully aglow. The stewards were making their way along the aisle with the trolley. I looked at Luke, still absorbed in Rebecca West. The sun shot through the window, bleaching the fibrous edges of the page. His face, where he hadn't shaved, was haloed with white fuzz. Beyond him the sky. Our plane was its sole occupant, and I felt my stomach relax for the first time since the pain had woken me in the night. By keeping my gaze steadily on the blue, its refuge at once a private and unbounded space, it was possible to forget the confined one in which I sat, the proximity to treacherous neighbours.

Then I heard a small thud. My feet felt the reverberation too. I started and looked down. A dark, compact object had appeared beneath the seat in front. Unwilling to risk renewed nausea by bending forward, I watched as a woman's arm emerged, followed by her upper body which bulged around the armrest before becoming trapped. A hand groped on the floor beside her for what I now saw, with horror, was a navy plum.

The woman was too wide to extend far enough out of her seat to retrieve it, and the seatbelt signs remained lit. The plum rolled toward my foot. I felt the muscles in my stomach tighten. As the plane turned slightly, the plum rolled hopefully toward the stranger's hand, then back again toward my foot.

Luke, I murmured, unable to raise my voice above the engine and the rushing in my ears.

Luke – please –

He appeared not to hear, or maybe he just ignored me. I couldn't look away from the plum, throbbing on the floor like a grenade.

Sometimes language helps in these situations. Not articulating what I'm feeling, but putting the scene into words as if I was transcribing it, separating me from the experience. I put the different elements into separate lexical sets. The plum rolled against my foot. An explosion. Seeds, skin, liquid, flesh. I thought about the etymology of *grenade*. In French it means pomegranate, after which the explosive is named.

A slow tear slid around my cheek and without warning, I saw the toe of my own shoe kick the plum away from me.

A gasp.

A pause.

Then the plum owner's eye emerged in the slit between the seats in front, swivelling from Luke, hidden behind the enormous book, across the empty seat, to me. It narrowed as she took in my appearance, calibrating her response.

Well thanks, she said at last. Thanks *very* much. Can't fucking eat it now, can I?

Luke shot a hostile glance in my direction but otherwise pretended not to know who I was.

A muscle in my eye quivered. Since this was out of character my brain could not admit guilt. I took a deep breath and shut both eyes until the woman stopped speaking in my direction and began complaining about our disintegrating social contract to her neighbour.

Everyone just looks out for themselves now, don't they?

I went back to my view, but another plane was visible now. It hovered like our plane's shadow on a bright blue floor. This changed the way I'd interpreted the scene before. Now the emptiness felt exposing. I was desperate to get off the plane.

The second, miniaturised one changed the nature of our aircraft as well as the sky we travelled through. No longer containers for human transportation now, but sentient beings almost. The pair seemed conscious of each other, and not merely in that they registered on their respective radar screens.

I wondered about the people on board the other. What, if anything, any of them made of us. But then the second plane rolled away or ours veered slightly to the right and in an instant the sky was empty. Once its wake had dissipated, it was as if neither the slow, synchronised dance, nor it, had ever existed.

At Split Airport, Luke walked up the jet bridge to the terminal ahead of me, carrying my small bag as well as his backpack. I stared at his back with a feeling of tenderness. How well I knew it. Watching his long, purposeful strides I felt unusually light, carrying nothing in my hands or on my shoulders, and optimism swelled inside me.

I watched him move through the double set of motion sensor doors that sealed the terminal from its points of entry, and followed him through, enjoying the way the two panels pulled apart in quick succession with a curving mechanism. The moment I passed through the final doors and heard them swish behind me, I knew I'd forgotten the items I'd stored in the seat in front of mine.

I stopped abruptly. My whole body seized up. The person behind rammed into me but I stayed rigid. I called to Luke, who continued marching ahead, before I took a few reluctant steps toward where he was already rounding the first bend of a ramp to immigration and connecting flights. I stopped again and turned back toward the doors, above which were written, in several languages: DO NOT STOP, DO NOT RETURN.

I waited for a few minutes like a cat, watching people pass through, judging the brief pause between the first closing and the second opening, looking for an opportunity to push back through, the precise manoeuvre such doors are designed to prevent.

Then I felt my arm restrained above the elbow and Luke appeared at my side.

My book's in the seat, I said, stumbling. And my phone. Which has everything. But the book has *everything*, everything. Everything for my, every – all in there. Actually – too – but mainly—

Luke patted his backpack, I've got the book.

I was confused for a moment.

No. The other one. My thesis.

Oh that.

He sounded irritated. I stared past him in disbelief. How could I have done this?

Well the phone's backed up right?

I don't know.

How can you not know?

I don't even know what that means.

His thumb dug painfully into bone, pulling me away from the people trying to get by. There was no way he was letting me try to get back to the plane. I'd get stuck, or shot, he promised, looking warily around. We'd be better off presenting ourselves to one of the kiosks beyond passport control, getting them to call someone on the plane. I kept staring at him. He stared back. I thought about pulling my arm from him and making a run for it but my legs were rooted.

Come on, he said decisively, the irritation checked. It's not lost, OK? We'll get it back.

I pressed the heels of my hands into my eyes and stood like that for another minute, then let myself be guided down the ramp.

I could count three times I'd lost anything of any value through my own carelessness. My first mobile phone – taken from a leisure centre in Glasgow. A twenty-pound note – escaped from the back pocket of fitted jeans while protesting war against Iraq. A cache of used film – when my bag disappeared at an airport. Each a devastation.

I didn't understand how some people seemed to lose things so often and hardly react. Because I was the kind of person who did not lose things, on the rare occasions I did, I too felt lost.

You're exhausted, he said. You were up all night. It's not your fault.

As we stood in line to show our passports, I raked a nail along my jaw as he told me about the doorway effect. Moving to the kitchen from another room, we forget what we were looking for as we pass through the door or open a cupboard. Our brain is wiped clean in that new place. What had just happened to me was the reverse, he said. It was passing through the door that had unfrozen the memory of what I'd left on the other side of it.

Everybody loses things on planes, he concluded as our passports were handed back.

Well I don't, I said, forcing myself to stop scratching at my skin. I never have.

And you haven't now, I mean. We're going to get it back.

The man behind the glass at the counter for airport enquiries and lost property was dressed as if he took his role extremely seriously. His hair was slicked back and a tie clip glinted on his narrow chest. I hadn't been prepared for this conversation, and when I opened my mouth no words came out. Without the lost things, or in this place without them, my brain seemed to be malfunctioning. I pulled my hands slowly down my face, digging into my cheeks. Tears came but I didn't cry.

Officially, the language I was trying to speak no longer exists. Now there are four names for four dialects, though anyone who speaks one can understand the rest. There's a meme of a cigarette packet that bears the words SMOKING KILLS. Twice in the Latin script and once in Cyrillic. The spelling is exactly the same for each.

Breathe, Luke said.

Sorry, I said, observing the man as he made some new calculation as to who the young woman before him was, speaking rusty Serbo-Croat.

I handed over the stub of my boarding pass and watched his expression change and then change again as he called the aircraft. I understood that he spoke with a woman who had gone to check my seat. I held on to the counter to stop from scratching at my chin.

She says it's not there.

I closed my eyes.

Anya, you were sitting in my seat, did you give them my seat number?

Yes, I said irritably, realising I hadn't.

Luke gave me a suspicious look as I added this information.

Not there either, she says.

I placed my hand over my stomach.

Tell her . . .

No phone has been found.

I clenched my fists.

Tell them the book is black and smooth, very smooth. It would feel the same as the magazines and . . . cards. She has to open it, the seat pocket, and look.

He spoke further with the voice on the other end, looking at me, then hung up the receiver and shook his head.

Please fill out this form.

I wrenched the chained ballpoint and tried to contain the urge to scream. In that moment, it seemed preferable to be trapped in limbo between the two security doors than here, free, without the lost items. I felt betrayed by Luke's caution, wishing I'd followed my own rash instinct to run back.

What's that supposed to be? Luke said, peering at my cross-hatchings.

In addition to filling out my details I'd used some of the blank space to draw a picture of my A4 notebook. The drawing described the situation in three composite ways. Appearance (black, rectangular), silhouette (black, rectangular), absence, and my feelings about that.

What was in your book? the man asked with new curiosity.

I gave him the form, blotting my eyes with a sleeve.

Everything, I said. My life.

He slotted the form into a folder – whose flap I could make out said LOST.

I pictured the little beige counter this man presided over, with his shiny hair and tie, his hitherto indifferent manner, as having been set up at the end of the car hire and currency exchange kiosks not as a place to retrieve physical belongings (which evidently was not its chief success) but as a means of rehabilitation to the state of losing things.

I thought about how recovery is the opposite of loss, and how the word, in my adopted language at least, contained the two senses – to have returned and to heal – often, though not always, one and the same thing.

It also occurred to me that it might have been the first time I'd seen Luke at a disadvantage. He did not have a mother tongue with which to exclude me now, except in the native language of his body. Here the scales had tipped a little. It was a new sensation, to know he was reliant on me.

It now seemed impossible that at one time I could barely speak his language. Long before I met him. Still a child. Or more childlike. I had made learning it the focus of my life. I said so at my undergraduate interview, going full tilt.

Why English?

The professors were too awkward to ask much more than that, but I know my English teacher, who'd encouraged me to apply there, must have told them something in her reference.

Luke went to get the car and I waited for our shared black case. The same bags came past over and over. Round the carousel in a figure of eight. I felt the tiny surge of semantic power extinguished. My thoughts kept looping back to the lost items, regretting having come, then a self-loathing that energised me briefly, before remembering the purpose of the trip. In essence, to ensure life didn't turn out like this: a lone woman waiting, unable to pay proper attention, her personal property slipping from reach.

At last our bag dropped down the chute. I made a pact with myself not to bore Luke about the missing things, aiming for temporary amnesia until we made it back to London. Only once I'd decided this did the practical consequences register. I didn't know my parents' or sister's number by heart, or even their address. They'd moved again, apparently, this time back to our old neighbourhood.

I joined Luke, still negotiating car rental, and asked to borrow his phone.

Why?

My parents' address.

What for? We're not going there now, first, are we?

In the car, he keyed our Dubrovnik address into the map. I said I was feeling more normal again, nausea-wise, and so we decided on the scenic route that twisted round every bay along the coast. Once our route was decided, he passed the phone to me but I couldn't log into my email. Luke, ever security conscious, had insisted I activate Google's two-step verification, which required inputting a passcode that was sent to your phone.

How else can we do this? he said over the satnav's voice. Is the address written some—

He was about to suggest my notebook but stopped himself in time.

We did a second tour of the roundabout by mistake. The obvious person to call would have been my aunt, but again – no contact for her without my phone. I thought about trying to reach one of her children on social media. Luke had quit all his and had pressured me into quitting too, but I knew they could be reactivated.

The idea filled me with dread. As far as I was aware the two daughters, Diana and Tamara, lived in Dubai these days. Nikolaj, or Calum as he went by now, either did not have Facebook or never sent a friend request. I shrunk from the thought of having to explain myself and why I did not know my parents' address. Why I was coming back. I didn't want them to know anything about me. I didn't want that part of my life to know Luke existed. I thought of his reluctance to hand his phone over again and felt the familiar tug of possessiveness.

What about friends?

I blinked and looked down at the phone.

I could sense the realisation dawning on him that the minutes we'd spent digesting this administrative problem, broached on a Croatian dual carriageway while our overlord barked NEXT EXIT, had occasioned greater insight into my past than we'd managed in the most intimate conversations of our relationship over the previous five years.

For a long time my sister and I couldn't go back. First because war was still going on, then so as not to jeopardise our status. My parents became voices inside a beige receiver. One time after I spoke to them, I heard my aunt suggesting to my mother that they join us in Scotland. This was something I'd asked them to do, twice, in a letter and in a phone call; both times it had been dismissed, but hearing it in her mouth made me realise it was a valid question.

I don't know what my mother said, but from my aunt's side it was clearly unsatisfactory. Think of your children. Of Drago. Those people are not your family.

You don't owe them this loyalty. My mother must have said something harsh in response, because the pleading tone changed and the conversation ended.

By the time I arrived at university, where everyone was away from home, I could imagine it no other way. We continued phone calls – a monthly check-in as unremarkable as menstruation – meaning only that nothing there had changed. I asked them the same litany of questions and if they started to veer off script, I would find a way to cut the conversation short, citing an essay deadline or lecture, some shiny facet of my new intellectual life – the bourgeois exile they'd arranged for me for all their talk of *brotherhood and unity*. Sometimes I was callous. I didn't want to hear anything that would make me feel bad. Sometimes I said things to estrange them purposefully, like wishing them a Merry Christmas.

Mira! I said finally, startling him after a long silence. Mira.

Mira. OK. Who's that?

He turned to me expectantly, but I was busy searching her name.

Mira was my brother's girlfriend, his fiancée in the end, and the last time I'd seen her was at his funeral nearly a decade ago. 2008. I was curious to see how things had turned out for her since that year of turmoil. She'd been his age, twenty-six. I was approaching my first graduation and remembered how she gripped my hand as she told me her plans. She was going to move to Belgrade. She had completed a Masters, spoke three languages, but was working as a nanny. I avoided talking about my brother. Her grief felt private, removed from our shared history.

Her family lived in the same apartment block as mine when the only people we could stay in touch with were our immediate neighbours. Everyone else might as well have been on another planet, though there were only streets between us. We played games in the basement and the hallway when we couldn't go outside. That group of kids we were part of – all ages – had become family.

Like my brother, I'd had a crush on Mira. I gave her my last piece of Čunga Lunga, only to discover it had made its way back to him. When I cried he gave the gum back to her, and she to me, telling me I should savour it, divide it into pieces and chew each one until all the taste was gone. I was ashamed of crying and I wanted to show her I could be defiant, reckless like my brother who liked to tease the snipers. I remember her eyes flashing as the bright blue square disappeared inside my mouth.

She started calling me her sister after that. A ten-year gap meant my own regarded me as a burden on her free-dom. Mira, who had no siblings, derived great pleasure from me – braiding my hair and helping to furnish my dolls with clothes – and I preferred to be infantilised by her rather than act grown-up for my actual sister. We played marbles when Drago was reading Alan Ford.

They began calling themselves boyfriend and girl-friend although they were only eleven. It seemed intoxicatingly mature to me, and at first it had strained basement relations with her parents, hers being less permissive, but Drago was so devoted to her through-out that period, and after as far as I know, that soon they too were in love with my brother.

It was very chaste, but I heard my mother caution him that she'd had Daria by accident too young and Drago had looked horrified by the insinuation.

My parents weren't married when they had my sister. But when Daria was four, Mum proposed to Dad – not long before Tito died. The day after their wedding was spent reading the newspapers and following his state funeral in a stupor. Drago used to remind us both with a haughty look that while Daria and I were mistakes, implicitly the product of erratic lovemaking, he – the halfway mark between both errors – was the only child they had planned, which was somehow less horrifying.

The marriage had been open, though not without jeal-ousy. Even before the siege I'd got used to waiting with increasing foreboding for one or other of them to come home, or being bundled out of bed still in my pyjamas. My mother would take us to one of the neighbours and disappear into the night, or, worse, bring me with her so I could press the buzzer and ask for my father back. One of my earliest memories is coming into the living room in the night only to find a strange man on the sofa with his trousers down, my mother kneeling. Me and my siblings were the go-betweens, delivering entreaties or threats, depending on which of us was enlisted.

I knew from rare conversations with my sister that Mira's Belgrade plan had worked out, but still I was surprised to find that she was the first search result returned for Mira Panić. The one I clicked on first, halfway down, produced a Bad Gateway, but her company profile listed a work email and a direct line.

Calling felt intrusive. Unnerving for me, too, with Luke sitting there, even if he couldn't understand. Instead I wrote a short email from Luke's account before I had time to overthink it, then fell instantly into a deep, remedial sleep, rocked by the winding road.

When I woke Luke was tapping my shoulder. The car was stationary.

Passports.

He looked agitated, indicating a checkpoint several cars ahead.

We're about to drive through Bosnia for six miles, he continued as I came round, then out again. I think.

He cocked his head at the map. We were indeed about to pass through the tiny stretch of BiH coast. Those twelve miles now separate the northern part of Croatia from Dubrovnik.

On leaving Croatia, the Bosnian officers gave us a cursory glance through the window and waved us through. Luke shifted in his seat, peering at the terra-cotta roofs and identical sloping foothills as if trying to detect some slight variation. Minutes later, we arrived at the checkpoint to re-enter Croatia again. The Croatian guard solemnly inspected our passports and the details of the hire car for several minutes before allowing us to continue. As we pulled away Luke checked his rear mirror and said:

That was mad.

Just symbolic.

He turned to me, eyebrows raised.

And mad. Of course.

Then his phone vibrated.

I'd forgotten the email I'd sent before falling asleep. Mira was *delighted* to hear from me. My heart thudded. She explained that she was currently in Belgrade for the book fair that took place in the city every October but would be visiting her own parents (who I may remember had moved to the coast) in two days' time. Since I'd mentioned that we wanted to travel as far as Kotor, would we consider meeting her for lunch in Sveti Stefan on Sunday? There was now a good restaurant on the island.

Stefan? OK. How far is it?

From Kotor? Forty minutes, I guessed. Less.

I was keen to delay.

Well . . . sure, I'm up for that if you are.

After a while we were directed onto the motorway. I prefer a straight road to avoid travel sickness, but also the certainty of it.

When we stopped for petrol, people asked me for directions, which at first seemed a good sign but then depressed me. Maybe our route was the same as when Daria and me had been going the other way. In the convoy of tourist buses commandeered for evacuations. Most of the passengers were unaccompanied children. A white UN truck like an egg carton had escorted us. When we got to Split there was a ferry waiting in the port.

Ancona, then England, then Glasgow. 1994, just after the World Cup, the summer the Channel Tunnel opened.

A woman who met us asked us if we were happy as I unwrapped her crayons from their skins. My sister translated. I had said no. Daria was embarrassed. Though everyone insisted it was not the case – that it had more to do with the cost of the tunnel passes and the need for men, the impossibility of abandoning their neighbours – my mother's decision to stay behind with the rest of my family, the suddenness of our departure in the middle of the night, the severance from our basement community, had felt more like exile than escaping.

I don't know what she told our distended family about me and Daria leaving, but the first time I came back, that gang of children seemed even closer to one another, and united in punishing those who'd left.

Luke complained he was hungry. I said I might be able to eat something too now the nausea had subsided, but it was already three and most of the restaurants in the small seaside village we stopped in were closed.

Guess it's out of season, I said.

We found a bar still serving, though its umbrellas and terrace tables had been folded. Half the dishes on the menu were written in English, enclosed inside quotation marks.

I just feel like they'll turn out not to be what they claim, he told me, studying it.

He'd relaxed his pescatarianism since visiting his parents, so I ordered him what promised to be ćevapi (a skinless, garlicky sausage), a basket of bread and a Coke.

Thank you for driving, I said as the waiter retreated. And sorry, obviously.

What for?

For being sick. For blocking the sink.

Yes, that was quite shit.

Seeing me cringe, he laughed and leant in, kissing the skin below my eye.

That last bit was pretty white-knuckle. Good you were asleep. The drivers here are mental. Cliff one side, sheer drop – his hand sliced down – Adriatic the other, and the truck right in the middle of the road. On a bend.

The waiter returned and ceremoniously laid out cutlery and glasses. Luke thanked him at each stage of the ritual until he went, then asked me to teach him phrases (hello, thank you, goodnight, beer) and in some ways, it *was* like a holiday, because seeing things through his eyes (the karst mountains and pine forests, the shining path of the sun on the sea) made me feel as if I'd never been to the region and had simply read a crude entry in a Lonely Planet guide.

He had claimed his main reason for wanting to visit Dubrovnik was that it was a World Heritage Site. I knew what he meant was that the medieval walled city was used as a location in Game of Thrones. Saying he might watch an episode of GOT, as opposed to one in the rotation of series we watched together, was a cue for me to entertain myself, preferably in a different part of the flat.

As we waited for the bill he asked me about our destination and I reminded him I'd never been. Instead, I took his phone and read from Dubrovnik's Wikipedia entry.

In 1991, after the break-up of Yugoslavia ...

I paused, unwrapping a boiled sweet Luke had saved from the rental desk,

> ... Dubrovnik was besieged by Serbian and Montenegrin soldiers of the Yugoslav People's Army

I glided over the blue hyperlinks as if they were merely waves moving in and away on a shore.

Back in the car I asked Luke to open the windows which were child-locked, and the smell of the pine, the past, hit me full in the face.

5

We reached Dubrovnik at sunset. Its aura sunk beneath the roofs of the Old Town, rendering the limestone walls gold then pink then grey. We found the Airbnb easily enough, an apartment in the eaves of a neat, white building with notepads and water glasses arranged on each side of the bed. It was obvious real people did not live there. The man who met us with the keys seemed like an estate agent, indicating a plate of complimentary halva before leading us out onto the small roof terrace to hear the bells that were now chiming. First on one side, then the other, the rhythm of the second becoming tangled inside the first. The first light and quick, the second deeper and portentous. They looped and took after each other like swallows, then began to fade, slow and dissonant.

Luke showered first, emerging head-shrunk and sleek with his towel around his waist. He stood dripping onto the floor, browsing restaurant recommendations on his phone. I washed my hair, put on a single coat of brown mascara and the one nice dress I'd packed. Looking in the mirror, I saw my colour had returned. That dress gave me something approaching cleavage. I knew Luke liked it, or the way it split the white meat of my breasts so I gained the little V-shaped shadow.

I leant closer so that the fur along my jaw glowed beneath the spotlit mirror. I licked my lips. When I came out of the bathroom I tried to hide what I was thinking, but Luke pulled me onto the sofa with my wet hair on his chest. He stared into my face as if he'd asked a question. My response was to bite. Sometimes I need to sink my teeth. I was ravenous suddenly, but Luke said we would be late. That's how quickly it happens, the power shifts.

We ran down the stairs and onto the street, my hair still heavy with water, the complimentary shampoo not quite rinsed. There was a chill now, though earlier in the day autumn had felt inconceivable. The limestone paved the streets as well as the walls of buildings. Worn smooth, they shone in the lamp-light like trays of melting ice. The streets were fairly empty, and we held hands, following the blue dot.

Luke described my appetite that night as carnal. I ate a whole schnitzel, took food from his fork, pretending to *bite the hand that fed me*, and drank most of a bottle of red wine. I let him catch my foot, which was cold, under the table, wrap it in the stiff folds of his napkin, then feel his way along my leg. Not having my phone, I felt anxiety but also freedom.

We shared a tiramisu and he shoved in beside me. I thought: How did I doubt him? And then: Here we are. No longer he and I but us.

Luke was drunk, and the conversation became more word association. He insisted on paying the bill as if I would argue with him over it. My treat, he said.

That morning I'd had a crust of vomit in the corners of my mouth and then he'd let me snore in the car most of the way here. *My treat* went back to an earlier stage, before he became my benefactor.

I was an indigent student, *art historian*, he continued, slurring. I should let him get this. He might have added I had minimal self-respect, for I had little desire to break my bondage.

The funded PhD was part-time, and so I made some income transcribing audio, mainly for a medical company, which I could do from home, writing dissertations for one of those essay mills (of which both Luke and Christopher especially disapproved) and tutoring – which also made me ashamed. It meant travelling all over London and into people's homes, often seeing how very wealthy people lived and how I helped perpetuate that wealth by getting them into elite schools and universities, even winning them scholarships. Among the children I preferred were the ones who could not have afforded those places otherwise, usually first or second generation immigrants. It weighed on me that their parents were throwing all the money they had on private tutors. Of these, my youngest was working toward the seven-plus. Her family had recently arrived from Bulgaria. The father was a cardiologist and had moved the family to an apartment in a high-rise near Canary Wharf without ever having seen it. They seemed pleased that someone like me had ended up at such a prestigious British university. I was, they said, a good role model for their daughter.

It made me feel good about myself certainly, but I also liked that child. I admired the way she approached verbal reasoning. Such as: should parents and teachers treat boys and girls the same? Answer: no, because you would not hug and kiss your teacher and your parents should not be too strict.

She was the age I was when I found myself transplanted to Mosspark Primary, learning to recite poetry by Robert Burns. That was where my desire to study humanities came from, I used to say on those personal statements and funding applications where you were asked to explain such things. I could have talked more truthfully about what Mira had read to me in the basement, but instead I cited the first Burns poem I'd learned. The one he addresses to the mouse – whose home he's just destroyed with a plough.

Despite what I wrote, it had not affected me because of 'the power of language' (I had barely understood it) but due to a physical experience. As I read the line: *Thy wee-bit housie, too, in ruin!* I had my first experience of what I later understood to be vertigo. The room spun violently to the left. Panicked, I tried to move with it, or rather against it, hurling myself out of the small plastic chair and onto the floor of my new classroom. In shock at hitting the ground, I began to sob uncontrollably.

For a few years, I'd also earned money working at a bookshop, but this coincided with the online rating of the bookshop going down. It was clear, Christopher said, from some of the customer reviews, that I had been the cause. One simply read: the girl at the counter is elitist.

When the waiter came back with the card reader, Luke returned to his side of the table and handed over his card. I reached my hand across and he held it while the machine whirred, looking, I felt, at the ring.

Let's go, I said. Let's walk.

But walking took too long, and I started to feel the good mood draining. I ran ahead, pretending to be some-one free-spirited. By the time we reached our doorway and he'd fumbled with the key, which required pulling the handle toward you with exactly the right force, we'd separated again. I wasn't sure whose fault it was, whether I'd created the tension with my false gaiety or simply detected it and then tried to paint over it.

Upstairs, I undressed, the way I would alone, not willing to give up though not willing to take the lead. Sometimes I worried my body had grown too familiar to Luke, and that was another good reason to keep it from him – the laws of supply and demand. But after a moment of stillness, Luke stayed my hand, slipped from the edge of the bed to the floor at my feet, pulling my underwear to one side and lifting his tongue into me. To steady us, his other hand travelled behind my thighs. I leant against the wall, tipped my head back, raised a heel onto his shoulder.

He was never rough. I suppose he thought I was extremely fragile. I faked a climax every time, hardly even aware I was doing it. If I did think about it some-times, remembering my only boyfriend at university, I felt frightened. As if there was a dark void I might fall into without warning. But when I opened my mouth just then, the shuddering sound was something different.

I looked down at the top of Luke's head. I put my hand on it to check that he was really there – my surround-ings in the strange room now surreal. Far away from where the day had begun, the night spent on the bath-room tiles, the acid taste of bile. His head tilted so that his eyes met mine and I found the door to the place I usually only find as everything's ending. Normally that feeling means I start to back away, pretend I've already come so he'll move on and concentrate on finishing. This time I didn't. I couldn't stand any longer and moved around him, lowering myself onto the bed, unsure of how I wanted the next part to go. Something like this, like the music heard through the open window – this other, unmapped level of the game – would turn out to be illusory, or happen only once, which was the same thing really.

No, he said. Not that.

No, I repeated.

I lay back and felt myself shrink beneath him. The shine of his collarbone level with my eye. Bird-boned, the same dizzy lightness I'd had all day but good now, spreading.

Inside me, I commanded.

As he pushed inside I went through another door, and I found myself smiling at how fast it was happening, how easily, as if I'd expected it to be locked but in fact it was open. The room began to turn. Rippling like it was fabric. Not a void, but I felt hollowed out, so that I became the air in the room as well as both bodies in it. The feeling was of expansion, lines melting away rather than emptiness, like I would black out if I stopped thinking.

I reached my hand around his arm for its solidity, the stability of him generally, and again, from some deeply worn groove, the reflex for thought over annihilation.

But just as I pulled back, I felt his body respond, his chin turned in, lifting off a little so he could see into my face.

I love you, he said, you know that?

I'd woken up first. From the short coma that follows sex if you haven't had it for a long time. The thud of sleep like a rebound that comes before real sleep. Waking in confusion to a room with the lights on.

His arm was wrapped around me but I needed to pee. I lifted the arm and slid out from under then scuttled to the bathroom, breaking into a run. Though it was a half-level down from the bedroom and sound barely carried, I reached forward and ran the tap out of habit. I towelled the insides of my legs, brushed my teeth, removed the smudges of brown mascara under each red eye. Staring at the face above the sink, thoughts returned to me. Like: I'd missed my pill that day. The previous day's was likely purged in the sink at home.

Fuck, I said to the mirror. *Fuck*.

When I woke again just before dawn, the room was dark but for a blade of light which marked the doorway and a blue line at the bottom of the windowpane. I'd been having a complicated dream and my first thought was to write it down as I usually do, to separate it from reality. Then I remembered the black rectangle that signified the missing notebook. I groped for the complimentary pad beside the bed and felt my way outside the room, closed the door gently and turned on the light, writing up the main points of the dream while standing naked in the display kitchen, pad pressed against the wall, until Luke gave a moo of irritation.

Back beside him, I couldn't sleep. My brain had returned to its fractious state.

It's the rich food, he said sleepily. We ate too late.

I thought of Luke's blood sausages and potatoes fried in oil.

I lay there and pretended to be sleeping but then a repulsive memory surfaced. The memory of my mother in a strange bedroom I'd been put to sleep in when I saw, through the slits of my eyes, her climbing astride a man – my father? – him pushing her away.

In the morning he sat half-dressed, the same corner from where he'd watched me undress the night before, now searching for a pharmacy. I paced the room then went to the fridge and ate both pieces of halva. He called out an address.

What time does it open? I called back.

Oh, wait, no. Ignore that. This one's old . . . Like a seven-hundred-year-old-apothecary. But we could go there? After. Might be fun? *Europe's third-oldest working pharmacy . . .*

At the counter I spoke in English. In case the pharmacist turned out to be religious I thought it would be
better to feign ignorance. He looked confused. I took
out the Airbnb pad.

Woah, Luke said, woah, woah. What're you going to
draw this time?

I ignored him, forging a condom in one smooth
line, then adding a jagged one to indicate a split, then
a dashed, determined one, heading toward a circle. I
crossed through the dashed line with a flourish.

Noli me tangere.

The pharmacist's posture stiffened but he went
into a back room and returned with a silver packet of
Escapelle, putting it straight into a bag for me. Luke
handed over 200 kuna from a plastic wallet and then
we turned, mission accomplished, pushed the door and
walked briskly toward the steps of St Blaise.

While I sat on the top step and waited, Luke went to
buy a bottle of water. I opened the box and toyed with
the contents – a silver spaceship-like dish in which a
single white pill had been sealed as though it might itself
grow into an alien baby. My hands itched, I realised, for
my phone. I toyed with the blister package.

I wondered if Christopher would be worried about
me. Though I'd only been without it for twenty-four
hours, this was perhaps the longest we'd gone without
some form of contact in several years. In many ways I

already had a husband, the kind Luke would never be, and I wanted to tell him about the previous night. The possibilities it had suggested.

Sitting on the church step, waiting for Luke to return, I relived the moment we first met:

After the ceremony. The glare of white stone. Us sitting on the wide, shallow steps leading to the church. The square before it a relief after the alleyways, dead ends and sudden drops. Neither of us really knew anyone. I had been struggling, feeling low in confidence, and we were waiting on the edge of a gang of braying family friends for the last boat in a wedding flotilla. No cars meant we'd started out even, at least in that regard. Neither of us knew it was bad luck to go to Venice together before marrying. I don't know if it's the same if you meet there.

When the boat arrived, a boarding school clique in damp linen suits crushed together. There wasn't room for the last four of us so Luke hung back. The other couple said they'd had too much sun anyway and would see us at the reception. We sat on the edge, spray from the Adriatic against our legs, looking at the deepening green of tide bands on the stone beneath us. The step's heat seared through the silk of my dress. I cast it in a circle around me. When he asked where I was staying, I laughed and said the cheapest hotel from the 'cheap' section on the website. That was our first joke. The wedding website. The *cheap* section. It kept us going in the early weeks, evolving quickly into shorthand. When something was unreasonably expensive it was *from the cheap section*, and when something that was supposed to be simple (like planning where to meet) got over-complicated, that thing got its own website. I did not realise then that he had his own flat his parents bought him. Luke did not think of himself as wealthy because he had some working-class relatives. His dad was self-made as he often told me. Besides, he was not a banker and had gone to his boarding school on a scholarship.

Later we saw the seating plan had us together again. Diagonally across on one of the long tables under strings of orange paper lanterns. As the sky turned green they glowed like sea creatures. A conga line started. Rowdy but affectionate Italians. I assumed Luke, who'd so far operated on the fringes, whispering savage commentary into my ear, would hold back, but he pulled me into it. Then, once our section came loose, I guessed the idea had been to reduce the intensity of our sudden pairing, to make ourselves available again to other people at the party. I thought we'd maybe circle each other awkwardly then lose each other half-intentionally on the dance floor. But soon I found myself hanging limp with my arms around his neck, both of us swaying gently.

In the boat going back from the reception, I watched how the dark, compact seaweed that hung from the walls of the buildings transformed in our wake, expanding, floating upward in bright clouds of green from the submerged brick, drunkenly convinced it was the perfect metaphor for our meeting.

The next day we nursed each other, eating only gelato. Hips pushing against the clicking turnstiles, my stomach fizzing and empty, head an ecstatic balloon. We tried to follow the blue dot but there was a delay, so following the map only sent us down wrong paths. There were no right ones it seemed anyway – everything was crooked and led back to the same square. I didn't care where we went, I said. Whatever he suggested was what I wanted. Pliable instinctively but also because the whole place was something to see, wasn't it? I'd studied its artefacts as a sixth-former but never in person. I hadn't understood, in the physical sense, that the city was stone on water, a sinking museum. I was mesmerised by the erosion of grandeur – monumental palazzos where the doorways had rotted and the rising water left the ground floors uninhabitable. To save battery, Luke had a book for learning Italian that had been free with a newspaper, evidently from years ago. It followed an English couple, Tom and Kate, around Italy, and referred to prices in lire. Tom worked *with computers* and Kate had been a teacher for three years but now worked for Rover. We quoted the lines they spoke to each other before painted altarpieces in dark churches. These were not the stock phrases I'd been expecting, but how a real, intimate couple would converse while navigating acqua alta. It was intoxicating, role-playing Kate, with her nice English boyfriend and middle-class tastes. I kept everything, every souvenir. All the tickets bearing reproductions of tiny details from paintings of heavy-lidded saints.

Noli me tangere, Luke read aloud, is the Latin version of the phrase spoken by Jesus to Mary — touch me not — when she recognised him after the resurrection. The original Greek is better translated as *stop clinging to me* or *stop holding on to me* — the attempt to stay joined together as an ongoing action rather than a single moment.

We stared at the returning Jesus, brushing away his mother's arms.

At sunset we went to another island. I was keen to let him know I was reading Jan Morris. That I was considering a masters in Art History.

I started to tell him when we sat down. Talking fast, my eyes darting up to his face. Falling for him already. In those days my brain was always brimming with real things, facts, and I had to find ways to halt its progress for an audience. I found it so much easier to concentrate, to retain information. To use it to my advantage somehow. How the monks were expelled from their monastery by the Turks, then granted asylum on this island. How Venice was founded by refugees, forced to become seafarers. Half western, half eastern, half land, half sea.

On the morning we were due to fly home – separate airports, one expensive, one *cheap* – I'd woken to Luke's first disappearing act. From the open wardrobe, I heard the empty hangers sounding in the wind like church bells or far-off goats. I realised I was alone in the bed. I felt the damp air rising up the staircase and knew the door to the room was open. I aimed my gaze at the ceiling, lay still as if I'd been stabbed. The heavy yellow plaster sagged between the beams.

I got up and sat with my back in the sun on the small Venetian balcony. A couple, Italian, were arguing in a narrow street below, beside the canal. The woman was becoming hysterical. I leant over between the laundry lines and terracotta pots and saw them. The woman had sunk to her knees and the man was trying to pull her up. She seemed to be in shock. He tried to drag her along the street and she would not let him, but when he tried to walk away without her she screamed at him to come back. Finally, he gave up and walked away and around a corner so that she cried out again, louder. I'd closed the window, there was something about the scene, her helplessness, that had made me imagine her body, or the discovery of it, drowned. I remember thinking I would never let that be me, that woman and her body, her loud, inhuman screams.

Luke returned to the church steps holding a glass bottle and unscrewed it for me. I sliced into the silver foil and gulped the emergency pill down with ice-cold water.

6

Early on Sunday he went running. When he got back we
drove from Dubrovnik to the Bay of Kotor, a place I
knew I had once been to from a hazy memory augment-
ed by photographs. The last holiday as a family, though
we didn't know it then. Dan Republike. Daria, Drago
and me sitting on an upturned fishing boat and beyond
us the water, which I'd thought of as a lake but was actually an indented part of the sea.

Luke and I sat in a square with small glasses of bitter
coffee. I wasn't in the mood for walking or looking at
Venetian fortifications anymore and drew my fingernail
back and forth along my chin. He took out his phone
and started registering me with a company that special-
ised in locating personal property lost in international
airports, asking for the details he needed in the same
coaxing tone he used on animals he was trying to move.

The Escapelle had left me feeling unstable, or that
was what I'd said, and I knew he was being kind to me
because of this. After a short wander which made me

worry we'd run out of things to say already, we drove on, arriving at the restaurant before Mira.

The hotel occupied the whole of the island, tethered to the beach by a narrow stone causeway. It had been a fishing village – simple stone buildings with red-tiled roofs, white shutters, cypress trees and pines set on top of the rocks. A woman at the reception desk escorted us along narrow cobbled lanes which climbed toward the centre and a table; the only one laid in an otherwise deserted courtyard presented to us as *the piazza*. Mira, the waitress said, had requested this specific table.

It was smarter than whatever I'd pictured. We scanned the menu, presented to us in English, Luke laughing at *forgotten vegetables* and deciding it must mean heirloom.

I like it, he added thoughtfully, looking around as if surprised. Here, I mean. Mira must be doing well for herself.

My head began to hurt – a sharp and insistent pain. I put one hand to my temple.

What does she look like? Mira.

Most of my childhood memories had her in them. I searched for her adult face and found it at the funeral; the doll eyes dead, face white and wet, but even then Mira was beautiful. Her face was like the Fornasetti woman's. She was the type Luke found most attractive. Dark hair, thin arms, oval face, no make-up.

On an early date, I'd asked him about his type and he'd claimed he didn't know or didn't have one. I'd pressed harder and he'd said: just not an English rose I guess. Foreign-looking, that was his thing. He looked at me as he said it, shrugging. My infiltration of his browsing history contradicted this.

As we waited I felt increasingly nervous, as if someone might be playing a massive trick on me, my headache getting steadily worse. I got up to pace around, saying I wanted to look at the view from the other side of the square, away from the shore, and found a tiny chapel tucked away there.

What about here for the wedding? Luke was suddenly behind.

I didn't turn around. I doubted he was serious anyway. The way he'd said *here*, I decided, was as if he'd used quotation marks. Since Cornwall, we'd not mentioned weddings.

A woman's voice could be heard talking animatedly and we returned to the table. Mira was there smoking, seated in the only chair not in full shade. She wore dark trousers and a black sleeveless tunic so that her bare, brown shoulders were flecked with sunlight beneath the trees. She turned to us, smiling, stubbing her cigarette in the ashtray as she rose to her feet. Slowly she came toward me and gripped both my wrists, staring at me with her large eyes for a moment, then pulling me in to her chest and whispering things I couldn't entirely make out so close to my ear.

It's lovely here, she said, reverting to the English of our emails as she shook hands with Luke.

It was jarring when she first did this, a betrayal of our former closeness somehow.

And you have to imagine Tito's poodles trotting around.

He laughed.

Yes, she said seriously, nodding as she lit another cigarette. He came here. Lots. And now they've made it smart again. It's very popular for weddings. Djokovic, you know the tennis guy? He got married here.

Oh!

She spread her hands to where we sat on either side of her – I must give you my congratulations!

This was the first time anybody had said this and I hadn't felt like I'd been caught out in a lie. But I felt another kind of guilt. She wore large, chic rings on most fingers but Daria had never mentioned Mira getting married.

Luke pursed his lips and rounded his shoulders in a self-effacing way, looking from Mira to the table.

Did this belong to him then, this island?

She gestured behind her in the direction of the beach. That was his summer palace.

Not bad for a communist.

The waiter came and stood rocking on his heels to list the dishes of the day. Mira asked for a bottle of wine by name, without deferring to Luke as I usually did, then removed a pair of angular black glasses from her bag and began to read with great attention. With the glasses on she looked older and I realised she must be thirty-six or -seven now, if I was thirty-one. The age my mother was when the war started.

She told us her father had briefly worked on the island after Tito turned it into a hotel. That hotel predated this one, she explained, but it had, many years ago, been full of Hollywood stars.

Then, of course . . .

She made a swooping motion with her cigarette to suggest a steep decline.

He was an assistant to the manager, I think. That's why I like coming here. When he went back to Montenegro with my mother, ten years ago now? No. More. It was just when the owners had leased the island and were having it restored. He's pleased with the refurbishment I think, though he can't afford to come. They've redone the rooms inside, or made under, as you say, very monastic, much more basic than they were before and so naturally more expensive, but outside all the details are the same.

I looked at Luke, who looked at Mira with rapt attention.

I worked in a hotel once, she added. A horrible one in Belgrade, when I first moved there. I worked nights. On reception. Not for long. They fired me after I placed a wake-up call to the wrong room. I remember the man answering in a panic and apologising for having been asleep. Then of course he came to and was very angry with me. I've never been good at them, she laughed, wake-up calls.

The waiter returned. Mira asked if we would like her to order for the table and we agreed. It was exhilarating to see Luke's usual dominance checked as she pointed out antipasti and several mains. My headache was subsiding.

I remembered, she whispered with a confiding smile, still speaking in our language. No tomatoes.

I was moved by this, but also embarrassed that she could still recall the tinned pineapple incident. Whenever my aunt told me to think of children still in basements dreaming of tomatoes or cultivating them on balconies, keeping me at the table until every last one had been eaten, I would think of Mira. Having logged so many hours slumped in my chair after my cousins had left the room – trying to think of good places to dispose of them – tomatoes, then all fruit, became the manifestation of my survivor guilt. To avoid tomatoes, which felt childish, I now claimed to be allergic to nightshades, but then I had to be devious about potatoes, which I love.

The waiter returned with the wine and another came with fancy varieties of bread. Mira poured the oil into a dish then added an apostrophe of balsamic to it. It floated for a second, held in tension, before settling as a black dot on the bottom. Everything she did was mesmerising, and I saw Luke grow less reserved. It suddenly reminded me of spending time with her and my brother.

He asked her about Belgrade.

The book fair's where I've just been.

She smoothed her smart black clothes.

It's always stressful there, but this year . . . she exhaled . . . more so. I wanted to get out of the city and come here, see my parents, you know.

There was a long silence. Mira pressed her bread into the oil and the black dot exploded.

This year's fair had been decisive for her professionally, she explained, as well as significant in her personal life. One of her authors, a journalist she represented, had written a fictionalised account of the war drawing heavily on her own experiences. Many of the pages dealt with a man whom foreigners knew as the *butcher of Bosnia*. She'd give us a copy if we wanted, there were dozens in the boot of her car.

I felt Luke's arousal at the mention. A year ago we'd listened to a series called 'Most Wanted' which had featured a few crimes from my part of the world.

Mira fell silent again, chewing her bread with concentration.

Is he the, er . . . the one they found guilty in The Hague?

She continued to chew, her gaze steady on Luke.

Was that last year? He posed as the therapist? Or he was one, first, but then . . . The new age healer, I mean, or – no . . .

He trailed off, self-conscious again.

You've read the Edna O'Brien?

He's seen *The Hunting Party*.

She looked blank.

With Richard Gere and Jesse Eisenberg.

Oh. Well, you're thinking of the other butcher. Incidentally that one, the one you mention, yes, he posed as a healer, with his own well-being website and everything as you say, but he was also a poet. She inhaled deeply, reaching for another cigarette.

Karadick! Luke shouted, startling us, his spit landing on my cheek. That's it. I remember reading about him in the *Guardian*.

I shut my eyes. The evening before our flight, I'd found him watching a YouTube film set to Max Richter's 'Sarajevo', the same, trance-like expression he got listening to 'My Favourite Murder'.

Karadžić, I corrected.

He came from here, Mira said gently. From Montenegro. He only moved to Sarajevo in his teens. There was a lot of snobbery about him in the city. They dismissed him as a nutty peasant from the hills.

She gave a dry laugh.

A sheep-fucker, my father used to call him. People said he turned up in the city wearing pointy peasant shoes.

I had heard this from my parents too. Kulturni versus nekulturni. It was one of the few elements of their early conversations about the war I'd understood and absorbed – that this man did not come from a city, and that made him somehow less threatening to us.

Mira looked over my head toward two hotel staff members and back to us before lowering her voice.

It was Belgrade writers, literary, academic types, who came up with the ideological underpinning for what he did, Mira continued. And even when he was one of the most wanted men *in the world*, he published his novel and it sold at the fair in Belgrade! That was before my time, of course. I came the year they finally caught him. By then he was writing under his guru name, with a monthly column for *Healthy Living*. Promoting vitamins, crystals, and cleansing *auras* rather than whole villages.

But anyway. The other one, the other butcher – she looked around again – they haven't sentenced yet. They expect to next month I think. That's another reason it's all so fraught right now . . . the conclusion of the Mladić trial, the publication of the book . . .

She sighed and folded the fabric of her napkin into a rectangle, then a square.

I've had threats at the office. My home address has been put online. It's not out yet, the book, but I've had things sent to me. Awful, disgusting things. My mother had her email broken into, which she doesn't ever use so there wasn't much to find in there, but they sent out a load of messages pretending to be her, denouncing me. For a moment . . .

She broke off, raising her eyes to the swaying canopy overhead as the wind picked up, brushing her hair away from her eyes.

Well, I thought the email from you was something to do with it. That morning my assistant rang to say we'd had another phone call calling me a traitor.

Luke was shaking his head, and I reached out and placed my hand very delicately on hers.

But what are *you* being targeted for? he asked.

Oh, she exclaimed, brightening, for doing my job!

She held up her wine and tapped the glass.

For representing a very talented, very brave young woman.

She tapped again.

For defending her against the trolls who still believe it's an international conspiracy!

Then blinking hard, as if to correct her vision, she put the glass down and pressed her fingers into the table, nodding slowly to herself.

On the tram, when I got your email, I got this creeping feeling. I had this very real sensation, this hallucination almost, just as the phone buzzed in my hand, that a bullet or shrapnel or whatever had come whizzing into the back of me. I even put my hand there, on my neck. It was like I could feel something hot, like I'd been bitten.

She shuddered and took up her wine again, extracted another cigarette from a new pack.

I'm sorry, I said.

Don't be, she looked at me, switching out of English, it's so good to see you.

Both of you, she switched back again, rending the intimacy between us. Here. Nothing could be bad. It's only . . . a shame, that's all. To still be stuck talking about this. Even some of the publishing people I know say we should move on, stop making art about it, they say we're in paralysis, which is true, politically, economically, everything. That the worst books coming out of the Balkans are the ones still going on about war. They're as bad as the old stories, the folklore, which makes war seem inevitable. But it seems impossible not to talk about it when these people, these revisionists, still exist, even if we'd prefer to forget it.

The food arrived. Conversation turned to her non-work life in Belgrade. She had a nice life there, she said, a new apartment, nice new friends. I wanted to ask whether she still saw the old ones – the ones from our building, all adults now – and did they still call one another *comrade*?

She told us that until recently she'd shared a flat with a not-so-nice boyfriend, but thankfully he was not around anymore.

My stuff's only just come out of storage again. I wore this uniform every day at the fair, pretty much, because right now everything is everywhere – except for what I *need*, which is nowhere.

She laughed.

I just want to throw it all out and start again, really. It's not until you clear out rooms you've lived in for a number of years that you start thinking about – or begin to come to terms with – *how* you've been living, you know? In what filth and confusion, in my case. How did I function with all this *stuff* everywhere? And beyond that, you think about the choices you made – when? How did it all get here? Greed? Distraction? Did I carry it back bit by bit or did others bring things for me? Either way I want to be rid of it. Even my books mostly. I'm done with them. I need a change.

She flicked her hand as if knocking something off a shelf and into oblivion.

The world just becomes this mystifying accumulation when you start seeing things that way. Of people and street names and, like, all these buildings and political parties and front doors and plastic cones, all these posters that are ripped down and then pasted over. Putin, by the way, stares at me from every billboard in Belgrade right now. There's one eye level with my kitchen. Everything razed and then repaved, so that after a while you don't even recognise where you are anymore. But someone must know! Who is putting all these things everywhere in the first place and where, in the end, does it *go*?

Mira turned and signalled to the waiter. Luke widened his eyes at me and made a gesture against his nose, which seemed to mean *is she on coke?* I ignored him and returned my gaze to Mira, fixing it there, willing her to go on.

The other day I was sitting on my old sofa in the new apartment when I felt something sharp, sticking up through my tights. Guess what! It was Andrej's – my ex – his toenail poking right into my thigh. This thick, calcium . . . what's the word?

She made a motion like the Grim Reaper.

Scythe, Luke supplied.

That's it. I thought about putting it in a little clear bag, you know? Like with evidence from a crime, and sending it back to him with all the other things I keep finding that aren't mine. Whenever I change my sheets, I find little curls of his fucking hair. Woven into the duvet I mean. From his body. Not even his head. They've got themselves into the static. I thought to myself: for fuck's sake, get out! And I set about unpicking them until I started to get a pain in my neck from crouching over like some old spinster. I always say I'll stop and finish another time, but the task is never finished. I should keep them all and make some kind of quilt. Did you see the tapestry in Kotor? A medieval woman made it with her hair for her lover who was at sea.

She looked up at the trees for a while.

I think I'd like to be at sea maybe.

The waiter arrived with more wine and poured two large glasses for me and Mira. Luke put a hand over his.

It sounds like you're better off without him, I said.

Mira rolled her eyes. That's why I hate breaking up. It reduces everything to this single, frozen moment when it ended, and everyone picks sides depending on the version of history they heard first and who told them.

A young couple emerged from one corner of the piazza, holding on to each other in a way that suggested they were on honeymoon. Mira watched them and took out another cigarette, then offered the pack to each of us. Luke declined. I declined, then accepted, letting her put it to her mouth and light it first.

How come you broke up? I asked as I took my first drag, feeling an immediate rush.

Luke looked around then abruptly left the table. I assumed to find a bathroom, but there was something about his gait that made me watch his back as it retreated.

I couldn't sleep, Mira finally answered. I had this techno track going around in my head all night. It was driving me mad. I don't even know who it's by or what it's called, so I can't listen to it and scratch the itch, so to speak. There's no lyrics, so how could I find it? It's literally stuck in my head. And then, when I couldn't bear the broken record anymore, I'd switch to rearranging the furniture in the flat, mentally, imagining Andrej had moved out and I could put things wherever I liked with all the new space he'd left. Then when I couldn't rearrange the mental furniture anymore, I'd switch to the techno again. It fried my brain.

I haven't had that, she hesitated, since . . .

And I knew before she said it that she meant since Drago died.

She blew smoke up into the air and I felt the wine tip a scale in my head, the smoke clouding, something dilating.

After he'd died I'd had dreams in which he hadn't, in which I couldn't understand where I'd got that macabre idea, had worried there must be something wrong with me. That's when I started recording my dreams — as a rite like confession.

I hate giving up, Mira continued, so it took ages, and after I ended it I kept going back. Then that cycle . . . I just went back and forth in these figures of eight when I lay in bed at night with him snoring, weighing things up again, subtracting, starting over as if I'd missed a decimal somewhere. But each train of thought came right back to where I started. I tried massage, yoga, acupuncture. All to get rid of this compulsive self-narration I can't help. The dissociation – do you get that? And I did lie there and try to think about where my pelvis was poised in space – but in the end I decided the only solution was to explode it, otherwise I was going to spend my life that way, missing my exit, my opportunity to escape. So, here we are. Thirty-six. Single. Great.

Luke had been gone a long time. I remembered the weekend we'd memorised each other's numbers in case of emergency. But I couldn't remember the number now, only the fear.

With my friends I found myself defending him, Mira continued softly. They'd give their pseudo-psychological diagnoses. Then I'd be with him, we'd argue, inevitably, and I'd find myself agreeing with my friends.

Luke came slowly back toward the table, looking warily from Mira to me. The sky was darkening as if for rain.

You must be tired from driving, she told him. I only want a coffee but you two should try something, they have an excellent pastry chef.

She insisted on paying for the meal, since we'd driven out of our way to see her, and then, once she'd paid, suggested in her irresistible way we come with her after to her parents'. They would be overjoyed to see me, she said. Surely Luke would not want to drive all the way so late. The roads, as he must know by now, were lethal and it would get properly dark very soon. It wasn't an easy drive by day. He must've noticed not many companies would insure us. Why not spend the night in the upstairs apartment her parents kept for holiday lets?

I wished I could sound so self-assured when I wanted Luke to stay with me. He looked too tired to argue anyway and I was eager to further delay the drive. I called my sister from Mira's phone to tell her we'd now be there by tomorrow evening, not tonight. I could hear her daughter crying in the background which always took me by surprise — I had a niece.

Fine, was all she said.

7

The sun was setting as we tailed Mira. Luke pointed out the horizon of motionless cranes. Most buildings seemed to be under construction or arrested construction. Unclad, unfinished storeys of brick and concrete balconies without railings, already trailing black vines. Every other yard was littered with mounds of soil and sand, blocks of concrete, pallets, rubber coils, and every so often an old woman stood still as a statue among them, as if lost in her own front garden.

Spooky, he said.

What is?

This mania for building. With no one really here and nothing finished. It's like some great sickness hit.

We parked and stood waiting for Mira, who was re-organising items in her boot. The sky had turned a queasy orange, too warm for October.

It's like last week, I said to Luke. Do you think it's the same thing?

The week before we'd flown to Split, people stopped in the street and took photos of the sky. Storm Ophelia had brought dust from the Sahara and smoke from European wildfires. The sun was an apocalyptic red. The news reported birds swirling mysteriously. In Lancashire, where Michael's family came from, an entire town was covered in foam. In Cornwall, Anne told us, there had been beach invasions by Portuguese man-o'-war — also known as *floating terrors*. They looked like blue plastic bags on the sand, sometimes pink or orange. Rather than propelling themselves, they used their gas-filled bladders as sails. The high winds had blown them out of the water.

Extremely poisonous, Anne had captioned the photo she sent to their family thread. *Can't walk the dog!*

In Scotland, aged nine or ten, I remember taking part in a disaster relief mission on a beach somewhere when all the children came together on the sand to save a swarm of stranded jellyfish. A teenage boy, who did not help but stood around and watched as we dug a channel to the sea, told us in poetic terms all the information he had somehow learned about them. These milky, almost invisible creatures had no bones, no heart, no brain. They were 98% water in fact. This kind couldn't even pulse. They were at the mercy of the ocean, or they were the ocean, depending on how you looked at it.

Up until that moment I'd been taking part in the rescue mainly because of the sense of occasion, the urgent solidarity among the children. I hated jellyfish, ranking them alongside wasps, maybe worse for being inconspicuous. I'd imagined their sting to be vindictive – less a defence mechanism than a calculated marking of territory where happy children dared to swim. But listening to that boy, I'd felt my animosity draining. In that moment they were the most vulnerable creatures I could think of, entrusting their lives to total uncertainty in exchange for locomotion, moving wherever the moon, the wind, the water drove them. Venom was their one protection, the only thing they could control.

Luke studied the orange colour of the sky for a long time without responding to my question. Then, as we walked from the car park, Mira explained to him that construction work was not allowed in high season. It was all condensed into these months, when there was often bad weather.

The other thing, she said, letting Luke take her heaviest bag, is if they don't finish they don't have to pay tax. There's a whole Russian village up on that hill, completely empty. They just build these fake castles then leave off the roof.

We took back alleys, ducking under washing lines heavy with carpets and towels, before coming to a yard.

One wall had been sprayed with two words. FUCK LOGIC. In English.

This is the back entrance, Mira said. Safer. In case we're being followed.

She guided us past an improvised trellis with the fruitless remains of a vine.

Then again, as my friend Neda says, safety is a trap!

She laughed to herself and began coughing, a hacking smoker's cough, guiding us between two leopard-print towels and a number of real pelts, strung up beside her parents' door. Her father liked to hunt, she said. Luke would have to excuse them as their English was limited.

He stooped nervously in the low-ceilinged kitchen while the rest of us embraced. They'd aged since the funeral but said I had not changed. We sat at the yellow Formica table where the two of them had been eating, and Mira's mother passed black plums round with a bottle of slivovitz – the plum brandy, which, unlike the fruit, I liked.

Her father wore a green gilet with a hospital logo, though in my memory he'd worked for a tobacco company. He talked about moving to Montenegro partly because of more religious people who'd come to Sarajevo. They were more traditional, not socialist, he said. They feel about Erdoğan the way Serbs do about Putin. Like he's looking out for them.

They took the jobs too, his wife added before Mira chided her.

It's all changing.

But not enough, Mira said.

There are now new shopping malls everywhere, he continued. Shopping, only shopping. Like America.

You're obsessed with America, she groaned.

We discussed Trump, the pro-Trump fake-news sites set up by Balkan teenagers as a way of making money, and then Croatia's rising nationalism, with the opposite nostalgia in Sarajevo. When he asked how my father was I said it sounded like he spent most of his time, when he wasn't looking after my mother, in a Tito-themed cafe. He said he knew the one. Near that ICAR statue they had erected. A monument to canned beef with a little EU flag – an ironic gesture by the Bosnians to show their gratitude for what the international community had done for them during the siege. I looked at Luke, wanting to explain the joke in English, but I saw that he was looking at his phone.

Mira began helping her mother make a stew she told us we could have later if we got hungry, slicing mushrooms against her thumb, a motion which made me wince but somehow compelled me to watch her too, then she excused herself. A few moments later, from the hall, there was a strangled sound and then a cry.

I wondered if one of us should leave the table and go to her, but her parents sat still, as if nothing out of the ordinary was happening.

When she returned, her eyes were watery and unfocused, her hands shaking as she lit a cigarette. She spoke so fast I barely caught what was being said. Luke looked from me to her, as she paced the tiny kitchen before sliding to the floor and weeping as freely as if her tears were laughter.

I think, I said quietly, leaning my head toward his, Mira's author's dead.

Long after her parents went to bed, the three of us remained around the table. We sat there until my eyes were raw from smoke. Luke's became narrow slits, but he did not seem to want to go to the upstairs apartment unless I came with him, and I did not want to leave Mira.

It was unclear whether the journalist's death was a suicide or only staged as one. Mira was at first sure of the latter, but then went back and forth. I couldn't stop looking at her hands. They moved as if possessed, making it difficult to put the cigarettes between her lips.

Sometimes I wonder what good it actually does to *bear witness*, I remember her saying. That the whole world was fixated on us and all we got was Vietnam leftovers. Canned beef. We're supposed to be grateful they tuned in to watch us dying?

At some point I got up to get some water and as I moved my vision blurred. I stayed a while at the sink to steady myself, letting my glass overflow, pouring it out, refilling, listening to the low murmur of Mira's monologue. Coming back, I saw a framed cross-stitch I remembered from their old apartment, which at the time I could not read. Now I saw it said, in English NO PLACE LIKE HOME.

I returned to my chair, turning these words over like I'd never heard them before in my life. Mira was telling Luke, now sunk deep into the sofa, why she'd really left Sarajevo. Ash flaked from her cigarette. I felt my eyelids shudder from the effort of keeping open.

They don't see a future, many of my old friends. I don't know what to say when I see them. I have this guilt, so now I try not to come back much. People like you though – she pointed her cigarette at me – I mean, I guess if you left as a kid, watched it on TV and not in person, only came back every couple of years, then everything reminds you of it.

This stung. I didn't say anything. It was true. But I'd been thinking how much this evening reminded me of being together with the others in our old basement.

The last time I went there was winter and the air was so toxic I could barely leave the house. I know your parents won't leave – but Daria could. She has a baby.

I nodded silently.

My mother wants me to have one. She says we should be replenishing the population. They're just as nostalgic as yours by the way. It's a kind of collective psychosis. I'm always saying what about press censorship? What about gay people? What about Goli Otok?

Luke frowned and mumbled something. Mira didn't seem to require anything more from her audience; her eyes wouldn't focus and she carried on, her words unstoppable as if it might kill her to fall silent. I felt hot. Excruciatingly hot all of a sudden. I pinched my earlobe. Her eyes finally locked on me and her hands dropped to her lap, still at last, silent, shoulders limp, the frantic energy now spent.

I think of him constantly, she said.

In my dream, I woke in the back of my parents' car still under my duvet but now across my sister's lap, my brother in the front where my mother usually sat, my mother in the driver's seat. No Dad. She rarely drove after dark and claimed to have poor night vision. As it was pitch-black on the road, I assumed we were on a mission to find my father and shame one of his girlfriends. No one would say what was going on except that we were going to grandma's to sleep over. When I woke a war had started. Shots fired on a wedding party that had been waving flags after the referendum. I remember this shocked me most because it involved a wedding and I could not connect that idea with death.

Early the next morning we said sober goodbyes, and Mira promised to be in touch when she next came to London. We picked our way back through the ghostly fairground of cranes and abandoned diggers, a green-house with weeds pressing against the ceiling, plastic chairs and low-hanging laundry lines. Luke kept looking over his shoulder. He seemed more vigilant.

Christopher says if you have to have a difficult conversation, walking or driving works well. That is to say side by side, in motion with a changing view. Luke found it easier for any conversation. For our relationship in general, sitting face to face across a table induced a hostile charge. But as we drove inland, I felt a new tension between us. I stayed silent and kept my eyes on the landscape, devoid of people, where life had apparently stopped.

What did you think of Mira? I asked finally.

Interesting, he said after a long pause. Very interesting woman.

Interesting, I repeated. OK.

Forthright, he added. She had opinions. Seemed very sure of herself.

I said nothing this time.

Very direct. Not like this route you're taking.

We'd chosen a winding one to avoid the motorway the satnav kept insisting we join every few kilometres. Mira had told us there was an old road through the mountains, tracing with her red fingernail the line on Luke's satellite image. You'll just have to watch out for landmines, she deadpanned, pinching the screen and handing it back to him.

The old road lived up to its name, moving us back in time and becoming increasingly pockmarked, passing abandoned homes with cows that wandered in front of us, disappearing again into ruins whose remaining walls still bore anti-NATO graffiti. There were no other cars, and as the road climbed swiftly higher, white mist occasionally surrounded us, blotting out all visibility. The houses became fewer and further, their aspects more hermitic. Occasionally we'd spot a miserable-looking donkey or dog chained up, or a lone figure would appear at the window. I had the feeling they could see something we couldn't – invisible but right in front of us.

We carried on past them until, up ahead, I could see what looked like a stone in the road. Slowly I realised it was moving.

I shrieked. Something prehistoric maybe. It was a tortoise creeping across the tarmac. Luke swerved, just missing it. The road had abraded as we'd climbed and where the brown shell edged along, veins of scrubby grass grew from fissures. He whistled slowly.

No car's come this way in a while.

A dog chained to a dilapidated building began to bark and then a man came out and stared at us as we passed him.

Do you feel like we're not supposed to be here? I said quietly.

For fuck's sake Anya, how am I supposed to know? You're supposed to be navigating.

We carried on for several minutes in silence. I could see the pulse in his neck. I told myself he was in a mood because he'd missed his run, but soon something else, black shapes just visible beyond another band of mist, stretched out across the road ahead.

What are *they*?

I shook my head.

He slowed our speed to a crawl and I sat upright in my seat, gripping the door.

Several tyres were strewn across the middle of the road, rainwater collecting in their cavities.

He clenched his jaw but made no comment. I thought of asking whether he thought we should turn around then but I didn't want to be responsible for any resulting decision.

The car made a strange whine, weaving between the tyres until the road was clear again and we reached the next ridge where Luke sped up, clearly desperate for the journey to be over. I pulled up the other route on his phone again but the dot pulsed frantically on white, the markings of the map wiped clear.

No reception up here.

Great.

I think if —

Jesus Christ

I lurched forward in my seat with the force of the brake but managed not to scream this time. Luke shot out his arm, too late to stop me flying forward.

I was expecting another animal or strange object, but only a few metres ahead the road ended.

Just stopped and disappeared. It fell away into thin air.

Don't move, he said, his voice shaking.

I'd never heard him be afraid.

We sat in stillness for a few seconds. Then Luke turned the engine off and gently opened his door, as though trying not to wake something.

Look that way, don't look forward, he said.

He climbed very slowly out. I followed, terrified the car would roll, moving my eyes in spite of his warning from the chasm where the road vanished — to the stub that remained on the opposite side. There was no sound except a distant roar of the motorway miles below.

Safely back from the precipice, Luke put his hands through his hair.

Why the *fuck* didn't one of those village *idiots* say something?

Maybe they thought we knew what we were doing. Our plate's Croatian, remember?

Where was the fucking warning saying the road literally cracks up and falls away?

I guess the tyres were the warning.

He kicked a rock over the edge. It fell soundlessly.

Well I'm not going back that way. No chance. I don't want to see those bastards gawping at us again.

I saw his hands were trembling now, as well as his voice, whether with rage or fear I wasn't sure but it was certainly *emotion*.

There was a dirt track back there, self-control returning as if aware of what I'd been thinking, we'll see where that takes us.

He got back into the car carefully, reversed a little way to let me in, then drove too fast down the steep dirt track as the tunnel of branches whipped against my window.

8

We parked near the Latin Bridge and Luke sent a photo to his family thread of the stone marking Franz Ferdinand's assassination. The result of their driver taking the wrong turn, or the right turn according to the original route.

With Luke beside me now I saw everything in high definition. Like the time I'd put on my first pair of glasses and looked up at a tree. The scars on the facades stood out more, as did the darker patches where they had been rendered over. I saw his gaze rest on the pockmarks concentrated around most windows and so I noticed them again as if they were new.

He wanted to get presents, including for my parents, and we wandered through the narrow streets of the bazaar. *Pazite, Snajper!*

Luke pointed silently to the rusting sign turned fridge magnet, waiting for my translation.

Sniper, I said flatly.

Who's this for? I wanted to snap at him, amid rows of souvenirs outside a shop called NOSTALGIJA.

He eyed up a pepper pot made from shrapnel, then settled on a copper serving dish.

The call to prayer sounded. It was getting late. We returned to the car and drove up the steep hillside. I noticed I was sweating.

He asked me about the last time I'd seen them in person and I lied and said I couldn't recall. That was my mother's way of dealing with things she didn't want to discuss, but I could remember it perfectly. It had been a weekend visit after my niece Hana was born. While my sister slept, I'd taken her baby for a walk in Veliki Park. There were lots of women pushing prams, but I held Hana, about six months old, tightly to my chest, stopping on a bench. Her little hand caressed one of the rotating memorial cylinders that bear the names of children who died during the siege. I realised I was gripping her too tight. Protectively. She began writhing so I loosened my hold a little, but when I next looked down, I saw a leaf disappearing into the dark O of her throat. She must have plucked it from a low branch over my shoulder, and now she began to choke.

I held her upside down and beat her violently until it came loose. She started screaming and would not stop although I reassured her, and myself, this had been an act of love.

When we arrived in my parents' neighbourhood, Luke's expression was that of a child who realises he has followed the wrong figure in a crowd. He looked at me as if I was a stranger.

It hasn't aged well, I found myself saying. It's different from the Austro-Hungarian stuff.

What are you getting defensive about, brutalism?

It's supposed to be about collective living.

Relax, you're making me nervous.

Sorry. I'm sorry.

So, he rubbed his hands, Elena and Jusuf?

He said it once more under his breath as we stood waiting for someone to buzz us inside the building.

And she's a teacher?

Yes. Was.

I'd not told him she'd been sacked for teaching *Macbeth* to her class and setting them the task of writing a suicide note.

And your dad?

A writer.

Like books or?

Sort of . . . bits of journalism. For a local paper.

And your sister's name again?

Daria.

And her husband?

Boyfriend. He won't be there.

But his name?

I, I actually can't remember.

My sister answered and told us which floor to come up to. In the lift I took his hand and watched his face, half in shadow in the mirror, his expression set. But I'd noted his disorientation before he caught it. As the lift rumbled upward, smelling of stale smoke, I slid the ring on my finger around to hide the yellow diamond.

Hana answered the door. She wore a translucent night-gown like some gothic heroine, and a chalky substance on her skin that smelt medicinal. I bent to embrace her but she took a quick step back and held her palm up to stop me.

Chickenpox, she said with the dignity of someone terminally ill. I'm off school. Have you had it?

Oh. Yes.

Noli me tangere.

In that case, she submitted graciously, we can touch.

The calamine smell was overpowering. Luke looked on bemused, waiting for an explanation. Hana glanced at him shyly, then waved us both through and ran out of sight, leaving us standing in the small corridor.

She has chickenpox. You've had it right?

No, he said slowly. I don't think so.

Oh. Well this probably isn't the right time to be exposed to it.

I don't know. I'll ask my mum.

He retreated to the doorway and took out his phone. I studied what was visible of the apartment – I didn't know it but I also did.

The little ghost returned with a glass bowl of bright orange crisps in one hand and a bag of peanuts in the other.

This way, she said primly.

She wanted me to see a house she'd made for wood-lice on the balcony, though all the lice must have recently escaped. Luke joined us and stood gazing at the view. The hills dotted with white tombstones.

It was a relief to me that we'd been met by Hana, who appeared to harbour no discernible resentment, though I'm sure Daria discussed her own antipathy toward me in front of her daughter.

How old are you, I asked, as she crouched down to shut the sliding door again behind us.

I'm six now. And three-quarters.

The sun was nearly gone and I began to feel cold. Luke had seated himself in a plastic chair and was still scanning the silhouette of the hills as the sky turned swift-ly violet. Setting off the geraniums growing in the red slouchy boots that were actually terracotta pots. My father adored these – one of the few things we still had from the first flat. Or he might've bought a replica. I

guess that makes more sense. I felt Luke throbbing beside me, as if he was about to go on stage.

Actually Hana, I'm a little cold can we go back inside
now?

She took a crisp from the bowl as she led us back
again, the white gown floating behind her. It had been
my mother's, I now realised. I motioned to Luke to sit
down.

She set the crisps down on the table. I noted her downy
moustache and seeming unselfconsciousness. I thought
of myself, two years older, on my first day at Mosspark.
I'd spent hours that morning tugging at my fur with my
fingernails, pulling it out in clumps. All I'd wanted was
to be blonde and otherwise hairless with a name like
Amy. While it was not that remarkable to encounter
foreign surnames on a class register in Glasgow, mine
glowed radioactive in the nineties. Certain teachers
looked up from the list in horror – as if I myself was
violently disintegrating.

And then, on that first day, I was one of two who
couldn't make it to the top of the rope to ring the bell
in Gym. Hearing the screams below to GO GO GO, I
panicked. Unable to go on or to let go and fall to the
mat, though the rope cut into my hands as I clung to it.
Suspended there, halfway between the peeling paint of

the ceiling where the brass bell hung and the baying mob below, I noticed new growth along my thighs. Gradually I understood what they were chanting in syllables. Hair-y An-ya. Hair-y An-ya. That night I got hold of my aunt's foul-smelling depilatory cream and nearly burned my skin off.

Mummy's helping Nena. Daddy's with Deda. Out.

She says Daria's helping my mother get dressed and my father's somewhere with her dad.

Luke eyed the little ghost warily as it offered him the bowl of crisps.

Tell them to get comfortable Hana, a voice – my sister's – called, then, switching to English, I'll be out soon.

By the time I left Sarajevo, I knew lots of English words already from school and subtitled films. Even during the siege when schools had closed, Daria would read to me from what books she still had, books that had not yet been used for fire.

When are you going to tell them? Luke muttered. He seemed unsure if Hana could understand him.

He'd been the one to suggest we do this in person rather than before we arrived. That's the kind of thing his parents cared about, along with thank you letters and other arcane formalities I'd come to excel at.

I'd wanted to do it in an email ahead of time. I'd written long ones, which I'd cut down to short ones, then hadn't sent. I knew we would have to do it on the first night, get it over with, and that then there would be the question of whether they would come, with the answer being that of course they would not.

Dinner, I replied.

Now Daria emerged. I noticed, with some satisfaction, that she'd gained a bit of weight. Her skin looked grey, her dark hair was scraped back from her face.

Zdravo, she nodded.

Turning to Luke: Hi.

Her eyes barely met mine, surveying me briskly and shaking Luke's hand, explaining my mother still wasn't ready to greet us. I was sure even Luke could pick up on it.

So, you found us. Eventually.

She had a way of making statements so that I sensed she was actively avoiding posing questions to me. Making a point of her lack of interest in my life, in case I mistook curiosity for envy.

Minus a near-death experience, Luke said, reddening as the words left his mouth.

Daria's eyebrows raised a fraction.

We'll eat at nine, if that's alright with you.

Of course, I said, we had burek half an hour ago.

Daria went toward – but not onto – the balcony and lit a cigarette. She did look much older. Our aunt had stuck her Bristol graduation picture to the fridge, saying she looked like Olivia Hussey. None of us had heard of her. But when she put on the VHS of Zeffirelli's *Romeo and Juliet*, her daughters and I were furious, though I was proud as well. I hadn't realised how beautiful Daria was until I saw her likeness on a screen. I have a similar thing when I look at photos of Luke. Without being there, without it being the real him, he looks completely perfect.

Mira says hi, I said, switching out of English for a moment to be conciliatory as I came toward where she was looking for an ashtray. It was nice for us to see her. Her parents send their love.

Hana arrived with glasses and a jug on a tray in the same style as the copper serving dish. I noticed Luke fiddling with the gift at his feet while we spoke our language. His eyes wandering again to the hills which were now blue, as though they'd moved further away into the distance.

She found the ashtray and opened the sliding door a crack.

What was the *near-death experience*?

Oh, a road fell away, or had fallen, and there was no warning put in place.

My sister snorted and Luke looked awkwardly around the cramped room.

Doesn't *feel* smaller, this apartment. You said —

It is, she shot back, flicking the ash so it blew inside.

She nodded to the leather sofas crammed behind her.

And the building has a communal laundry instead of each apartment having their own machine. You get electric shocks from it so we wear rubber shoes to go down. You can borrow mine if you need to do any washing while you're here. However long that is this time.

I ignored the non-question.

Thanks. Where do we sleep?

Goran and I are going to stay with his cousin.

Goran, that was it. It means man of the mountains.

OK, if that's OK with you.

My sister shrugged.

Hana poured out glasses of lukewarm water then sat between us, eating peanuts from her white hand.

How long's she had it? I asked.

She's not infectious anymore. It's crusted over.

I had to wear gloves before, Hana piped up proudly, so I couldn't scratch it. But now I can use my fingers.

She wiggled them. I wiggled mine back, grateful for her presence if only as a buffer.

OK, I said, well that's good. Luke isn't sure if he's had it.

Luke? I switched to English, has your mum replied?

She hasn't, he said, looking up from his phone on the sofa. I don't think I've had it, but I'm sure it's fine. He smiled at my sister meekly. No problem.

Daria raised her eyebrows unmistakably this time. A voice called from inside and she excused herself.

That was the end of the universe, I said to Hana who had followed my gaze to the hills. Even now, I continued – surprised, feeling something like adrenaline coursing through me – when I see them, even though I *know* we just drove through them, it's like I'm looking at a photograph and there's nothing out there, beyond them.

I glanced at her and she nodded.

Can you show me to the bathroom?

I followed where she pointed, the door open beside the one Daria had just shut. I pulled the cord for light and a fan came on. The walls were peach-pink and peeling. I sat on the side of the bath and took deep breaths. A framed picture hung on the wall above the towel rail. My mother holding me as a baby, taken in our old bathroom, in our old bath. Her smile blissful, eyes shining, the skin on her naked shoulder shining too, her body curving around mine. It was so bleached by sunlight it looked almost artfully overexposed.

My hangover was maybe kicking in again and my stomach made strange gurgling noises. I reminded myself I always got this sensation of dread when I'd been drinking. Daria knocked to tell me Mum was ready. Looking in the door's direction, I noticed strange marks in the painted plywood where the light caught them, like someone had once struggled to get out.

The living room, when I returned, looked even more crowded and was now lit by some unforgiving ceiling lights. The two identical sofas faced each other with a narrow strip of floor between, the width of an armchair sandwiched at one end. Luke looked claustrophobic. My mother was now sitting in the armchair between the two sofas. She also looked very small and boxed-in. Her face unfamiliar thanks to the way her hair had been clipped back, and new white teeth that appeared when she smiled. They were too big, making her face seem even more shrunken. Under her eye, a delicate swell like an aubergine. A faint crust at the corners of her mouth when she closed it. The teeth pushing against the skin stretched over them. She stared at me placidly. Luke sat beside her as if waiting for someone to take a photograph, Daria took a seat opposite him. As I leant in toward her I caught the smell that had so disturbed me the last time I'd visited.

Whether it was really Alzheimer's or something more in her control, it began before the siege. That's when Daria says she first noticed something. Nothing dramatic. She would repeat or forget small things. Clear away a cup of tea that my sister had just put down, then if asked why it was missing she'd insist angrily that she hadn't touched it. If she'd just brushed it off as something she'd done absent-mindedly, Daria said, I wouldn't have thought anything of it. But she was often aggressive, saying I was criticising her and making things up.

During the siege, such symptoms barely registered. Depression, apathy, paranoia . . . these made her seem sane. She developed a slight tremor in her hands and said she felt weak, and that too seemed entirely reasonable. Then, to my father's exasperation, she began to act out her dreams, often hitting him squarely in the face.

When the siege was over, my father told my aunt she'd begun to experience hallucinations and would often seem disoriented, but many of their neighbours were experiencing similar things. It wasn't until after Drago died that there was a noticeable decline, though again the symptoms were masked by what was happening. She was only in her mid-sixties but had finally been diagnosed a few years ago, right after she had a fall. It became harder to speak to her on the phone after that. I felt even more self-conscious and my calls seemed to make her more agitated.

She appeared to confuse Luke for Drago at first, rubbing his arm distractedly. Then, from the greetings Daria translated, she seemed to decide we were being visited by another foreign journalist.

She wants to know if you know Christiane Amanpour, Daria said. She thinks you work for CNN.

I stared at my sister in disbelief. For years, until Drago died, we avoided talking about the war – quickly tiring of the same bad news. After he died, it was never spoken of at all. Daria stared back as if to say yes, this is what we are dealing with now, what *I* am dealing with while *you* are not here.

Luke smiled nervously.

She's been stuck in a version of the siege since August, Daria explained. Dad's convinced it's best to go along with it.

Around the time I met Luke in Venice, Daria had persuaded our father to try a home. She was supposed to be safer there, but she hated sleeping alone in unfamiliar surroundings. In turn she became unrecognisable. He'd told me the doctor prescribed her antipsychotics. She could barely move her eyes while she was on them. I remember getting a call saying he'd taken her out again and devised his own system for her care.

The idea was to embrace the alteration, as Daria said, like putting on a play. Resisting or trying to reorient her only got all of us more lost. You couldn't persuade someone back into who they used to be if they were dead set on living in the past. To find her we had to enter her reality, he'd concluded, and meet her at whatever landmark she'd found.

War metaphors were banned. Mum was not *fighting* a disease, there was no winning or losing. Nothing was invading her or taking over. When we spoke after the 2016 presidential election, Dad said the new guy proved what he'd always said. We lived in a demented society and everything was coming apart, so why not embrace the fragments like the pebbles on a beach.

Some things, he conceded, were harder to play along with. Letting her believe she had to keep away from the window – where until recently she had liked to sit – seemed cruel, for example. But as a result of his methodology, she'd passed from a state of anxiety into one of occasional euphoria.

I did not have the same abilities with her as Daria or our father, switching between these multiple worlds. I felt neurotic when I did, and afterward it was I who needed consoling. I longed for her to hold me. For her old smell. It felt like another casting out, this change, even as my mother's look charged me with abandonment.

Instead Christopher soothed me. Making up for husband *and* family. He said it didn't matter whether she recognised me now because I still knew who *she* was. I didn't say that I was constantly looking for ways to erase this knowledge. Because her deterioration had accelerated exactly when we started dating, each time I saw Luke with his family the desire grew sharper to escape mine. To learn to stop wanting something from them it was now too late to get. I was afraid that if Luke ever met them he'd recoil. Feel the sudden vertigo I did watching my mother grapple with reality. Without telling him things I was ashamed of, complex things, I couldn't make him see that coming back was no homecoming for me. That I felt surer of my place there if I stayed away.

On my rare visits, I'd attempt to do practical things for her instead, cleaning her teeth or spooning her food, but I could see she found me threatening.

It reminded me of our first reunion but in reverse. I'd been nervous on the journey from Glasgow, but assumed the feeling in my stomach must be excitement. Then when I finally saw her, something froze. I couldn't speak. She went to hold me and I felt myself go limp. My eyes rolled back and away from her. I shut my lips, clenched my arms, and would not submit even though she begged me.

Soon, if I was mired in my thesis or in a particularly vigilant mood, reading every unspoken message Luke sent me, I became terrified early onset dementia – out-of-mindedness – was happening to me too.

When memories from the past intruded (tunnels, basements, waiting for contact, certain foods) I would worry about it even more. Maybe they were not a sign of what I thought they were. I would focus on physical sensations of relief. The sun on my face. Finding a precarious spot to balance a glass in the curved slats of a bench, releasing my feet from their shoes or sitting when my feet were tired. Coming into the cool when I was hot, washing my hands when they were sticky, pressing my cheek into the sleeping heat of Luke's back.

Is it shelling? she asked Daria, the way you'd ask someone if there was rain.

Nope, all clear.

What network are you from? she said, sitting up and cocking her head at Luke suspiciously, American?

Reuters, Daria said quickly, passing him a pad and translating simultaneously. He's just going to write some notes, he wants to hear your point of view. Shit. I need someone to get a can of cream. You still can't drive?

No.

I'll go, Luke said.

No. Thank you. You stay here and talk with her. Entertain her. I'll ring Dad. He must be on his way back by now.

Listening to my mother speak then it was as though she was telling me a made-up story. The kind I'd once begged her to invent, not read from existing children's books. Then, in the middle of saying something, she stopped and looked straight at me. Not as though she was lost, but had detected something, like a cat padding along a path who suddenly freezes.

9

The first thing my father did after closing the front door was to pick up Luke's rucksack from the hall, walk gravely into the living room with it hanging from his index finger, and ask in a threatening manner if Luke knew that APC stood for Armoured Personnel Carrier.

At least that's how I translated it.

His sense of humour can be unnerving. In the last census before the war he'd circled his nationality as Pacific Islander. Apparently I'd scolded him. I was too young to remember – it sounds like me. Beating my puny fists against his shins from underneath the table.

Tell the truth Babo!

This *is* the truth Anja! His voice mimicking mine.

Stop being silly!

Babo's not silly, he protested, it's everyone else that's gone mad.

His jokes are not intended to make other people laugh so much as frighten or confound them, which makes him laugh. This tendency made his sublime tenderness toward my mother all the more surprising.

My father dropped the bag and his face creased into a smile. He was reassuringly the same compared to my mother. The very large hands and ears. I waited for him to address me individually.

Here's your cream, Daria.

Then looking around, What, can't this English guy take a joke?

No one translated but Luke offered him his hand.

Dad says it's good to meet an Englishman, I lied.

Thanks, Luke said, Well. Cornish technically. It's good to finally meet him, say.

Daria clicked her tongue as she got up to turn the oven on. I sat beside my father, opposite Hana and Luke, too close in a way that made it impossible to really look at or talk naturally to one another. My mother still in the central chair in the narrow gap, as if we sat around an open casket.

I had expected, I realised, the conversation to focus more on me, or at least *us* rather than Luke. I did do the majority of the talking. Filling in for him more than I usually did and having also the task of translation. He explained – then I explained – his job so that, at first, I managed to make him sound like a eugenicist before I tried again to explain bioscience.

The future is uncertain, I said, starting from the top.

My father nodded impatiently.

Crops get domesticated and can't adapt, so we need diverse seeds to survive climate change and other bad things we can't anticipate.

Before, I'd always applied these ideas about domestication to myself. The task of translating made me heed what he was saying in a more objective way, less encumbered by other interpretation. Hana seemed enraptured. My mother's mouth hung slightly open.

Do you know the story about Leningrad, Dad asked him, via me.

I said he knew about the siege.

Leningrad was the home of the greatest, most diverse as you call it, seed vault in the world. Nikolai Vavilov's. Stalin put him in a gulag. But his staff stayed at the vault, which became their safe house, though many of them actually died protecting the seeds. The curator of the rice collection starved at his desk surrounded by bags of rice.

He started cracking up at this idea before I'd finished translating.

In exchange for this anecdote, Luke described the vault they built in the Arctic circle. Though it was designed to be an impregnable deep freeze, it had barely been five minutes before rising temperatures caused the permafrost to melt and the entrance to the tunnel flooded. Both he and my father laughed at this.

People are in denial, Daria said. They are afraid of their own death, the end of civilisation.

The laughter ceased.

And what do you do, Daria? Luke asked.

I was about to translate again, forgetting Daria spoke perfect English.

What do I do?

She fixed her eyes on his as she spoke. She was using her lawyer voice. Hana looked from Luke to her mother, sensing danger.

I'm a mother, she said, eyes narrowing. And I clean the surgery.

She got up and excused herself.

Where's Daria gone? my mother cried suddenly. She hasn't gone outside?

She's just in the kitchen, making dinner, I reassured her. Hana, why don't you go and see if she needs help.

The high-rises all rely on electricity, my mother said, addressing Luke so I translated again.

The water is pumped, the lifts, everything. There wasn't a chimney. So we had to move into a place some-one we knew abandoned.

I left out the last part.

You don't think much about how everything works under the surface until it's broken – you just rely on each thing to do its job. Then you can't keep clean, you can't wash anything, when food does get through we can't eat it. Pasta, rice . . . everything requires boiling and we have no water to do it with. No heat. No electricity. So then we moved in here with my mother. But my mother is no Chetnik, you understand. She was AFŽ.

That's like feminist Antifa, I added.

The war is only between nationalists and those who are not insane, my father said, rubbing her hand in his.

Luke seemed to be finding the polyphonic, repetitive conversation difficult. I too was starting to feel quite mad.

What about her mother?

He asks you how your mother is.

Well she's deaf now. Can't hear the shooting, which is nice. But she can see how our faces change when it starts. She says the last war wasn't as bad as this one. My father fought against the Ustaše also. Did you know Sontag came here?

Not here, I said, not to the flat.

Would you like another drink?

Yes, please. Thanks.

Hana, go on, get him one. And help your mother like I said.

Mother? My mother said.

Yes, my father said.

Well, she was suddenly fed up, she knows all about wars. She predicted it. The women in this family have the gift of foresight.

This time it was me who laughed.

Some of the things she says, I said to Luke, aren't memories. Or they're not her memories. They happened to other people, or they're threads from stuff she read as a child, not always real. But now all mixed up as if they happened to her.

An acrid smell was coming from the kitchen. My sister called out that dinner was ready.

As my father told each of us where to sit, I shifted my gaze between my mother, my sister and her daughter. Memory passing down generations like water seeping through a multi-storey building.

At the table, he pulled the same trick he played on every first-time guest. It had been a while since I'd witnessed it and had forgotten the set-up until I heard him say slyly that Luke should be served first. I clenched my fists as Daria placed a plate of spaghetti Bolognese on the checked blue tablecloth before him and Luke raised his fork tentatively, sensing something was off by the way everyone was quiet and either watching or studiously *not* watching him. He tapped it suspiciously, then grinned.

My father slapped his shoulder, roaring as if this had never happened before, announcing, as he raised his glass toward him, that Luke was *OK for an ecofascist*. The ritual over, Daria set down plates of real food, less appetising than the resin version. Overcooked white fish, boiled carrots and buns not quite thawed from the freezer. The smell turned out to be rice she'd burned while trying to reheat it. In the oven. Daria was always a sophisticated cook so she did this to embarrass me.

She sat not eating, her elbows on the table, chin resting in her hands, so you could not see her mouth. I chewed the fish politely and tried to make myself swallow it, noticing an ulcer right between the skin and my bottom row of teeth. Throughout the meal I kept probing it with my tongue even though it made it hurt more.

It was too much effort to continually translate banal bits of conversation, and I let a lot of it go over Luke's head.

So you had a look around, Daria finally said in English. Even Luke must have sensed her sarcasm.

Yes, the old part of the town is great, he replied uncertainly. And the new bits are nice too.

What else did you see, the genocide museum?

No, I said curtly.

Maybe next time. What about the tunnel? It's very popular with the Chinese.

Yeah, I'd like to see that, Luke said.

I'm sure you would.

What's that supposed to mean? I said, switching out of English.

We had enough of people like him at the time.

Don't do this now.

Don't what? Hana said.

What's going on, Darko?

Nothing, my sister said. Who wants dessert?

After Drago died and Daria returned, my father had affectionately started calling her Darko. A boy's name. He joked she could live as a virdžina after he died – a sworn virgin – the old Balkan thing of allowing a daughter to live as a son. She could start dressing as a man, working outdoors, carrying a gun. The catch being a vow of celibacy.

Darko found herself a boyfriend but the name persists.

Clinton is the worst president we could have at a time like this, my mother said, back from somewhere else. He's like a president from a TV show.

Yes, Daria laughed, it's a shame.

Who's she, sitting there?

It's Anja. Don't you remember?

Sometimes it felt easier to hate my mother. Certainly less painful.

Oh yes, she said, a faint smile forming. Then her face fell and she pursed her lips.

It was hard to pretend after that and I kept my eyes on my plate as something black rose up inside me.

Daria watched me clear my end of the table before everyone else had finished eating.

You have weak wrists, she said, following me to the kitchen. You could never be a waitress.

She said she had wanted to do a dessert in my English boyfriend's honour, and returned to the table with an Eton mess. She had, she explained, given it a modern twist using some leftover food colouring in the cream.

Why green? I asked after a silence.

Experiment.

Then, to everyone else, in a more civil tone, At first, I only added a little, and actually too little is disconcerting, so then I added the whole thing.

When she did things like this I willed Daria to admit that she was bored.

How was Mira, my father asked. The first real question he had addressed to me. We miss her.

I noticed my mother sweeping the table with her palm. It was something I'd seen my grandmother do, and now my mother was doing it repetitively. When she noticed me looking, she stopped.

Happy in Belgrade, I said, then again in English.

I gave Luke a look I hope conveyed that he should not mention Mira's author.

But she was visiting her family, Daria muttered, I don't understand.

What, Daria? I sighed.

How can she be in another city and still find time to see her family?

I ignored her, turning instead to my mother. Mum, what about some chocolate?

No, Daria said, as she grabbed my mother's wrist, you don't get to do this, you can't waltz in and out whenever you like! I'm sure you think I'm a bad person, she continued, wresting the language back into English, and addressing herself to Luke. I don't know what she tells you, but it's lies.

Her voice was even and cold again, as if she'd been preparing this. I couldn't speak. Luke began breaking his meringue into smaller shards, as if this might defuse the situation. Hana and my parents waited for the translation.

We're getting married, I shouted.

My father looked astonished, and for a moment no one said anything.

We're getting married, I said more quietly in English.

His first question was whether I planned to take Luke's last name. I said I hadn't yet decided.

What's happening? Anja's getting married? When?

We don't know yet, I lied.

Don't look like that Anja, my father said. It's not your funeral. I thought marriage had died out though, I must say. Do people still have weddings?

Where's the ring? Hana demanded.

I don't know why women do it, for men it makes sense, Daria sniffed. They get unpaid domestic labour.

I unscrewed it from my finger so that I was left with a pale line, and gave the diamond to Hana who studied it. Then I took up a position at the sink, letting the hot water run to scalding. A cloud of steam rose, and still I held my hand under the column for as long as I could bear it, remembering when Daria and I got to Split and finally we had water, just running, running, running.

I put gloves on when the pain became too much. Inside gloves the heat and pressure were reassuring. Starting with the sharp things, moving mechanically on to the blunt, I let the oily water drain then ran the tap again, waiting for it to turn hot before realising – I'd used it all up.

From the table I could hear the conversation continuing without me. They had changed the subject from our engagement already.

If I'd directly asked for my father's opinion he would have told me that marriage was bourgeois. Only for women who wanted families. The family was also bourgeois. He should know. If I'd said I was actually doing it to escape, to make a bid for *freedom*, he would have said that this idea of freedom, which was Neoliberal freedom, was more bourgeois than the family and would prove to be just as stifling.

I wanted to see the photo in the bathroom again, as if that could confirm I'd once belonged with these people. I moved slowly and experimentally, as if each thing in my path were a tremendous obstacle.

I smiled exaggeratedly at Daria as I passed.

Hana's brushing her teeth, my sister said, you'll have to wait.

She got up, turned her back, went to the kitchen archway and calmly folded out the concertina doors behind so only her legs were visible. The overhead lights turned on. The candle flames bleached out. Things formerly outside the circle now emerged. The condensation on the windows, knives shining on the magnetic strip, a halo of needles around the potted cactus.

Tell Daria she mustn't go out or I'll kill her! Mum said.

You'll kill her? I heard my father repeat, I thought that's what you were worried about.

I worry whenever any of them go outside, she said to Luke. My eldest wants to study abroad and never come back.

This time I translated her faithfully. I was too tired to manage the situation any longer.

At least we have good views! A sly grin spread across her face and she waved her bony arm in the direction of the hills all around us.

All new windows since the shelling!

She laughed then broke into anguished, noisy sobs.

I sat in rigid silence with Luke while Dad shuffled her to bed and Daria put Hana to bed on the sofa, took her bag, and left.

Hana, with her mother gone, asked to watch a movie. My father sat in the armchair this time, and she wriggled between me and Luke with her feet tucked under mine. As the opening credits began she settled into a rhythm of gently rasping breaths.

I've watched *Home Alone* about ten hundred times.

So have I, I said.

I'd first watched it during the siege. It was the last VHS we bought before it started. I remember whenever the power came back on Drago would be watching it while rewinding another one with a fork. Then it was a Christmas ritual at my aunt's in Glasgow, but I'd never found it very comforting. Her kids identified with the boy's struggle to defend his home against the forces of destruction, whereas I could only think about the trauma of being left behind.

It was even worse watching it as an adult. Or watching Hana laugh maniacally as the invaders were repeatedly foiled. I felt myself leaving my body. Floating up toward the ceiling, into another atmosphere where sound did not carry. From there, looking down at the child in the white nightgown, I experienced that version of loss which is a casting out of subject rather than an object.

*

In Hana's narrow bed, Luke turned the lamp off and stars appeared faintly on the ceiling, adding to my sensation of floating outward into space. We lay in silence for a few minutes.

I want to go home, I said.

I knew he was awake but he did not respond. After several minutes, the glow of his phone. The nimbus around his back.

Serious question, I said.

What?

Nothing.

What?

Do you still love me?

What kind of question is that?

He removed his leg from where it brushed the edges of my body – so that no part of us was touching anymore.

I can't sleep.

Well me neither Anya.

It struck me then why it is that the English phrase – *to drive home* – means to make someone understand.

In the middle of the night I could no longer bear it and insisted that we leave without saying goodbye. We would check into a hotel before tomorrow's flight. I could not spend another second in that place without imploding.

Luke was half asleep at first and I had to shake him. We whispered furiously for a while. But when he realised I'd already packed up our shared suitcase, taken it out into the hall and was not coming back into the apartment, he evidently decided that staying without me would be even worse for him in the morning than this cloak-and-dagger disappearance overnight.

Back down in the lift, back into the car – parked on a steep incline – where Luke sat at the wheel for a minute with his eyes closed as if summoning strength, then to the only hotel I could, in that moment, think of, the big yellow Holiday Inn.

I locked the chain on our bedroom door. The bed was hard and low. Flyers for a 24-hour casino called NEW ERA and various strip clubs were fanned across the coffee table. Maybe it was the sight of these that made me think of tugging at Luke's waistband – to make it up to him, or to separate in his mind who I was now from the child I turned into with my family.

Immediately afterward he fell asleep and I got up and stood for a long time at the window.

As a child I would stay up watching the fires. Silhouettes of buildings, indistinguishable from the night except where they glowed. Their black geometry slowly folding. In the morning familiar places would look foreign, as if I'd never seen them.

*

I woke to three powder shafts of sunlight on my cheek. A line of moth holes in the heavy curtain shone white-hot like bullet holes. Leaving Luke to sleep I left the bed and tweezed two hairs from my jaw, crouching in front of the mirror.

The lights in the windowless bathroom went out midway through my shower and the hot water ran cold. In the pitch-dark I groped my way, dripping, to unlock the door.

Downstairs, the receptionist explained that the whole area had the same problem. Maybe workmen had cut through something – they were excavating under the roads all round the hotel. They had a generator but it was not, at this present time, working. One American woman who came to the desk behind me was outraged that she could not take the elevator up to her room. Was she supposed to walk up nine floors? My home had been on the tenth, I wanted to tell her.

Luke gave me the silent treatment all the way to the air-port. When I asked what was wrong he said: Nothing, but there will be if you keep asking me, so I stopped asking.

Our Austrian Airlines flight from Sarajevo Airport stopped in Vienna for an hour. Luke was miles ahead of me and I went through what turned out to be the wrong exit – for passport check not connecting flights. Luke had my boarding pass, so I had to go all the way through security again and back to the gate where he seemed to be in an even worse mood, headphones clamped over his ears.

Boarding again for the final leg, dusk shimmered over the runway and I remembered that first evening in Sanary. With a sharp intake of breath as if I was being submerged in ice, I realised I'd left the ring with Hana.

I couldn't bring myself to tell him what I'd done this time. It made me feel like my mother.

The cabin filled with the strains of Mozart. Conveniently, since we were ignoring each other, Luke was seated several rows ahead. I guess because he hadn't known how much time he could take off so soon after our summer holiday, he'd booked his own return some time after he'd done mine. That was the reason – but I kept looking up and between the seats to where I could see the curve of his ear, waiting for him to turn.

Poised on the runway, I looked over the tarmac. At the green lights glittering their messages across it in the dark.

After we collected the bags, and the train pulled into Liverpool Street, he finally took my hand.

The chokehold loosened. My words came out in a rush. I asked him again if he still loved me. Again he took his time to respond.

There was a lot of tension, he said finally. And I'm not used to that.

ASYLUM ROAD

10

It felt like returning to reality. London, but without a diamond flashing in my peripheral vision all the time.

Luke went straight to his office while I went with the bag to the flat. Entering, closing the door behind me, everything slipped back into place. I knew then I would never go back.

Luxuries I'd stopped noticing now seemed lit from within. The pressure in the shower seemed stronger. I stood under its cascade until I forgot where I was. The bathroom blurred and my breathing became shallow. I stopped the water and pressed my face into a heavy towel, its detergent smell, until I felt strong enough to tackle the blocked sink.

The various things I'd puked up had become one thick, primordial tar, but as the putrid remains began to glug away, I felt energised. A certainty came over me that order had been restored.

I couldn't bring myself to think about the ring yet. Instead I opened my laptop, emailed the lost property counter at Split. When the reply came that still nothing had been found, the feeling I'd had of something being stuck in my airways every time I remembered the lost items now dissipated.

That my confused thinking might ever amount to *a significant original contribution to knowledge* had seemed implausible from the start. It now struck me as ridiculous that I would have to have these same unoriginal thoughts all over again. To eke out the same niche and then defend it felt like the most futile thing I could imagine. Reproducing all those lost words (concomitant, coterminous, coeval) that no one would ever read and which could serve no real purpose to anyone.

University institutions had provided me with shelter and a certain amount of liberty, a veneer of cosmopolitanism, but I had not made many friends. By then I only spent time with Christopher, and sometimes his friends, or Luke and his. The two groups could not have been more different and they never mixed. I called the latter posh but Luke insisted they were middle class. Anyway, the correct word for truly posh people was *grand*, he said, and actually grand people were often broke.

Initially these posh friends of his acted interested in getting to know me. They made me feel welcome, if not at home. But five years on they rarely asked more than polite questions. How was your summer? How's the PhD? I realised they had only been starting conversations with me as a reflex of confidence, according to a code of behaviour they all knew. It didn't mean they were truly interested, just that they could speak to strangers with ease. In such an incestuous group they might pounce on one as a novelty – a *random* or a *fringe person* as they were known – but I was no longer new.

I'd made temporary alliances with some of them. New girlfriends mainly. This was how I'd made most of my friends – uniting with outsiders via a shared sense of exclusion. It could feel heady at first but that quickly turned to bitterness if they managed to assimilate.

I sent two emails with the same two words as the subject, ignoring the two warnings: *this body has no text*.

QUITTING PHD

I waited for two responses.

But you're so close, Luke protested. *It'd be perverse*.

Minutes later Christopher's:

Sunk cost fallacy. Where the fuck have you been? How was BiH?

I replied to Christopher's, explaining about my phone, the lost book, the desire to be free of it, and Luke's insistence I carry on. He said Luke's reservation would probably be that he thought I was looking to become even more dependent. You should tell him you'll get a job, he wrote. A full-time one, not more transcribing.

I tried to think of what else I could pretend to do while Luke went out to work.

Usually when he left the house I would listen for a few moments, imagining I might hear his key turn in the lock, footsteps bounding back up the stairs. Then I'd gaze at my phone's darkness, waiting for communication from someone. Once I was sure Luke was not coming back, I went round neutralising the absence. Closing things he'd left open or turning things off he'd left on. Replacing lids. Hanging up the wet towel, lowering the seat, picking up waste material.

The routine continued: check face, check chin, pluck renegade hairs – digging when they weren't ready, wiping blood from the blade. Brush teeth, wash hair, make tea, sift mail. Another flyer warning us we lived in a hard water area. Sort laundry, fill French press, find something broken, add to list, panic as the washing machine reached its frenzy.

If I didn't have a wash to do, the silence could grow deafening, waiting for him to make contact. Until he did, it felt as if I was very far from life and the outside world. If he didn't, my refuge could become imprisonment. To escape I'd close my eyes and see if I could imagine the future. Perhaps that's what my mother meant when she said the women in our family had foresight. Two more thoughts usually occurred to me then.

1   No one can give me what I need.
2   I need to need less.

I made quieter, smaller movements. Tried to take up less space. I once listened to an eight-hour YouTube video called Ambient Iso Binaural Beats and watched the sky pass beyond the window, imagining myself no longer *encircled by negative thoughts*. Still the unrelenting sensitivity as if my skin had peeled right off.

It was better if I wasn't already in the flat when he came back to it. Like a good exile, I began spending all my time in cafes. I felt better too this way, returning to the flat on a more equal footing. Like a dog that had taken itself for a walk.

Christopher called it limerence, the magical beginning I wanted back. When each hair I found after he used the shower, usually coiled in the grout between tiles, I gathered like relics of a saint. When I talked about him as *my boyfriend* and my heart had raced.

Luke had insisted we call his flat *ours*. In practice, both of us tended toward the evasive but definite article *the*. He had teased me, in the beginning, over how I couldn't bring myself to actually use things I owned, preferring to keep them for a future date. I used so little toothpaste, he said, it was unlikely my teeth were ever clean. I watched the smart meter he'd installed which told me how much energy I consumed each day I was alone there. It would go up dramatically in the morning if I had a shower or boiled an egg, and I would think that it was pointless to eat eggs. The benefit was essentially cancelled out by the energy and expense of cooking them. I started to buy food that could be eaten raw.

Still, it was hard to express my happiness then. There was no room. I remember it like floating in warm water. A weightless, all-over miracle, my body held by something that also ran through my fingers. I liked hearing the sounds he made getting ready for work. The shower turning on then its softening which told me his body was beneath it. The electric shaver, the kettle, cup down, the steam hiss of the iron. All meant progress underway, without me having to make any. I rarely had anywhere to be at that hour. And then, exactly twelve hours later, I'd assume positions suggestive of domestic bliss for the moment his key turned in the lock. Not bent over my notebook on the sofa but hanging washing, arranging a salad, or emerging from a bath to print my body against his shirt. Inhaling the smell of exertion, his fug of productivity.

Somehow I had imagined this state would be made permanent by the decision to get married.

Luke arrived back just before midnight. I was in bed, not wishing to give the impression I'd been waiting. Over the course of the day my optimism had begun to falter. I'd started to feel uneasy again. I'd gone for several walks, trying to rid myself of a burning sensation. Not hot but cold, deep in my chest, like smoking a menthol cigarette. Shrinking, twisting blue, crushing in on itself. It grew painful as I heard him unlock the door in the hall and climb the stairs. I'd draped a drying sheet over the banister – a white flag of surrender.

When he came in he sat on the bed, began to untie his laces without greeting. I waited as long as I could bear the silence.

Are you OK?

A longer silence. I began to vibrate in the dark. He got into bed and sat with his back against the wall.

Luke?

I'm trying to relax.

OK.

A longer silence still, in which I turned to face the other way, then turned to face him again, the coldness spreading out now from my chest into my veins.

Luke?

These pregnant silences drove me mad at first and then I tended to panic as if I was being strangled.

I don't know what to say, he said at last, staring at the wall.

I realised I was panting and tried to take smaller breaths than I felt I needed.

It's not working, he said then, in an unfamiliar voice.

What isn't?

I tried to swallow but my tongue felt swollen, blocking up my throat. By now my whole body shook, as if something inside – a whole other person – threatened to break out of it.

Well, I said brightly, aren't we going to talk about this?

I was determined not to behave in a way that was hysterical or backed him into a corner. That, as Luke had taught me, is when even docile animals lash out. It was better to sit with the uncertainty than provoke a reaction I didn't want.

It's late, he said with a shrug of resignation. Talk tomorrow. I need to sleep.

Yes, I said, as if this had been what I'd suggested, better to talk about things in daylight.

I lay awake all night again, listening to him sleep, but must've dozed sometime after five because I woke up to find him gone. Immediately the adrenaline returned. Then I heard him on the landing.

Where are you going? It's Saturday.

Work.

The word landed on me in the empty bed like something insignificant dropped from a height. Then a zip closed decisively and he returned, giving me a conciliatory pat. I said nothing, moved my chin a centimetre, offering him my mouth.

I haven't brushed my teeth.

I persisted and he submitted to the kiss, which made it worse.

You can't work here?

I left my charger at the office.

OK, well then, I'll see you later?

Maybe you should stay at Christopher's tonight.

OK . . . that's a good idea . . . right then, I'll do that.

He picked up his running headphones. I hid my face in the pillow, arm at a strange angle, unable to breathe until the front door had shut behind him.

I spent the whole day with the sensation that the floor beneath me was giving way. Nothing I came into contact with felt solid. Nothing could hold me. From the bedroom window I saw that a neighbour's roof had been removed and was now covered with plastic sheeting that moved like a lung in the wind. I watched it for a while, breathing in and out in sync. As one magpie sailed past the window I shut my eyes. When I opened them I saw it had been joined by what I assumed was its mate and felt this to be a good omen. Then I saw it was in fact cannibalising a pigeon and I reached out and struck the window.

Luke emailed in the afternoon just as the light was fading.

I think it's best if you stay at Christopher's for a couple of days.

I lay on the carpet until its weave was printed on my skin, trying to get rid of the falling feeling, interrogating the phrase he'd used. Couple of days. Couple. I often used that word interchangeably with *few* and *several*. Did Luke's couple strictly mean just two?

I could not think of any responses so I didn't send one. I'd communicate with potent silence the way he always did, saying only what was absolutely necessary and factual.

I emailed Christopher instead who said he would order an Uber for me. Twenty minutes later I got in with a bag – mostly the same things I'd taken to my parents'. The luggage tag from Split still attached. I kept my eyes out the window but the driver seemed anxious to make conversation, presumably not because he had much interest in his passenger but so he would get a good rating. He tried to catch my eye in the mirror. A cherry air freshener swayed beneath it.

Going on holiday? he said.

Yes.

The shop window below Christopher's place was daubed with the words FINAL DAYS.

It's a break, I said after he'd held my body for a long time, very tightly.

He'd taken the afternoon off work to sit in this alternate reality beside me. I wanted to express gratitude but could barely speak. I let myself be brought onto the sofa.

Do you want to take your coat off?

No.

Can I get you tea? Alcohol?

I shook my head.

I have a work phone you can borrow while you're here, he said, if you need.

I nodded, trying not to let his kindness undo me, and he nodded too, and then we watched nature documentaries. He didn't even comment on how relentlessly I traced my nail along my jaw.

Do you need anything? he asked when the third episode began automatically, I'm making dal.

I shook my head.

Would you rather listen to a podcast? What's that one you're —

I shook my head again, more firmly.

I woke up in the morning to find the sofa under me was moving. The place next door was a building site, I remembered. Someone must be tugging at the foundations.

Luke suggested we meet three days later, during his lunch hour, near his work. I told Christopher he had suggested a walk. I sensed his mother behind this idea, assuming being in public might stop a scene from taking place. Or so her son could not be trapped by me then held hostage.

On my way I passed a headline printed on a board: EXPERTS WARN AGAINST OPTIMISM.

His office was down a side street near the Heron Tower, shared with a few other green-investment-type companies. I was early, so I waited outside that building, rather than loiter directly outside his. The lobby was taken up by a vast aquarium which I knew Luke hated.

He knew I had no phone so I assumed he would not be late. At the appointed time, I stood waiting in the street.

He came out unhurriedly at last, wearing his suit. Looking more like a stranger than he usually did. It was more pronounced, maybe, in this world where I did not belong.

He directed us eastward and bought vegetarian gyoza for us both from a street food market. My stomach was tight as a ball.

He led me into a small park inside a square I'd never seen before. I remember the light gliding through the mulberry trees, down to where their bellies crept along the ground.

I watched as he tried his first real sentence. This took a long time. I formed what was supposed to be an expression of encouragement. A lack of reproach. Inside, the cold fire burned my chest.

At last I prompted him, *so is this over?* and he just sat there in silence again, before finally saying *I guess* – despondently, as if it was all my idea.

I sat for several moments, looking into the distance. Then, before I could stop myself, blurted out *is there someone else?* and he looked angry, as if I should know the answer to such a vulgar question, when I had no idea, any longer, what I knew.

What did he say?

That he has some stuff to work out.

He wants you to give him space?

Yes. That's all it is. I think he needs space to think.

In response Christopher emailed a link to a story about a lovesick Chinese woman who'd spent a week in KFC because she needed time to think.

Christopher invented the game What Can Anya Eat? The answer was usually one small plate of cucumber, thinly shaved.

He brought things to me for the first few days, then insisted I come to the kitchen, like a stray he was patiently rehoming. The game was satisfying, he said. It was satisfying for me too, to feel myself wasting away.

When he insisted I accompany him to the supermarket to guide him, everything on the shelves seemed useless, as if it was only packaging. I could not imagine what purpose any of it served.

Most nights I lay awake on the sofa reading old emails, comparing them to happier ones, putting words into the search box, as if this was a problem I could solve with research. When I did sleep, I felt as if I was still aware of everything, like the dolphins from the documentary Christopher and I had watched. They slept one brain hemisphere at a time, allowing them to swim continuously. I didn't dream, I just lay there in wait until the birds started up, as if nothing was out of the ordinary. When I woke, before I even remembered, there was already something pinning me down, a weight on my chest. It felt like waking inside a corpse. If I started awake in the middle of the night, I would imagine I was next to him as he whimpered. His shoulder would shine in the darkness and I'd say soothing things, tell him where he was. Wait for him to understand. Sometimes I groped for him in the empty space. My second thought on waking was that the day would end the same.

After several weeks I wanted to move. Not far from the sofa but in small circles around the room – joints swollen, head too light on my neck. My arms felt weightless, as if I'd just put down two heavy bags. This lightness sickened me, but I also felt disgusted by the more substantial parts, the way my thighs touched as I walked.

Soon I ventured up and down the street and to the nearest park. I felt myself to be allergic to strange bodies which were, and then were not, him.

I watched a skein of geese pass over me. There was, the formation seemed to say, safety in numbers, safer than within a single pair.

I thought of him out with his friends while I took my lonely weekend walks. Imagining the complaints he would have made about me, the assembled men revolted by my flagrant needs.

Out of nowhere, I began to run. No one was chasing me, I just felt myself speed up. It gave me a brief feeling of control, of self-direction.

December came with no word from him. Though I barely left the house except to exercise, I'd inched closer to the borrowing limit on my credit card. Christopher tried to make me come to *gatherings*, which I knew really meant drug-fuelled parties with hundreds of people. I said I couldn't bear the idea of strangers, when I really meant the smell. There were new proportions to smell now, I noticed. Sometimes I caught a sweet smell of rot when I was alone in my makeshift room, its origin unclear.

How much sooner I might've realised if I hadn't been used to near-permanent nausea.

At first, when it had been too long since my last period, I put the absence down to the Dubrovnik Escapelle. To the upheaval. The shock. Over-exercise. Near starvation. Then one afternoon I gave in and bought a pregnancy test.

As I waited on Christopher's bathroom floor, I studied myself in the mirror for the first time in weeks. I had muscles everywhere. Hollow cheeks. Rough, red patches on my palms. More blue veins in my wrists. The test turned positive. I stood rooted, the slight weight of it in my hand, wishing that every time I'd had a fearful instinct to confirm, I could have peed on a stick.

Until I'd quit, the plan had always been to finish the PhD before considering a family, except at certain points when I'd thought it would be easier to have a child. Luke was ambivalent too, for environmental reasons, but also knew how that would go down with Anne.

Now I found I did not want to evict the seed-sized thing, and nor did I want it to grow much more. What I wanted, if I wanted anything then, was to stay in pregnant limbo for as long as possible. To be pregnant was to be shielded by other, non-pregnant people.

I didn't tell anyone. Even Christopher. Every day I opened the cap to check the fibrous pink of the test until its validation faded. When it did, it felt like harbouring a criminal, both intimate and alien.

I had the sense that when I moved I glided. My breasts became two live creatures. They prickled against shirts.

My sister emailed about the ring Hana had finally turned in but I could not bring myself to answer. Something about the email, however, or just what it reminded me of, decided the question of the pregnancy.

The hold-music on the phone was relaxing at first. But after ten minutes it transitioned to electric guitar. By contrast the waiting room, when I arrived at the clinic, was very quiet. The sonographer moved along my abdomen, frowning at a monitor I could not see. I watched her face instead, deciphering the mystery of my insides in aseptic black and white. I imagined my womb like a dark basement.

Your bladder is full, she said.

The first time I'd been present for something like this had been in Glasgow. My aunt had given her teenage son a pet chameleon for his birthday. We were disappointed that his colouring never seemed to change. In the light, he did get a bit brighter maybe. Nikolaj, who was not yet Calum then, had christened him AJ. Who knows why. It made me think of AJ from the Backstreet Boys, and there was a similarity. But after only a few months, AJ grew gravely ill. He sat in a corner of his cage and wouldn't eat anything he was offered. My aunt put us all in the car and took him to the vet, who took an X-ray and announced that AJ was full of rocks. Why's he eating rocks? we asked. My aunt said she didn't know. She had to syringe feed him, and at first he seemed stronger, but then he stopped swallowing that too.

My aunt got a second opinion. The second vet said AJ had stopped eating as her belly was full of eggs. He, my cousin said, correcting her. No, she. AJ was a female chameleon, she repeated. This was a shock, and then we tried to understand how she'd managed to get pregnant too. The vet grew more stern with us, irritated by our ignorance. She's not laying the eggs because she hasn't got a laying tray. Female lizards need a tray. She pointed at the scan, her pen circling where the mature follicles clustered like grapes.

Discovering his pet was in fact a girl, Nikolaj immediately lost interest.

In the wild she'd have dug a deep hole, the vet continued, but she can't do that in captivity. Or not in this cage. She's holding them in until she can nest.

AJ died that afternoon. I helped bury her under the hibiscus.

On my way back to Christopher's, I took out my credit card and bought heat pads, eye pads, sanitary pads, notepads. White socks, white shirts, not, in the end, white underwear. Seeing some of this spread out on the floor when he came home, Christopher stopped and surveyed the scene, but he did not say anything except to enquire what oligarch's child I was now tutoring.

For my last trip to the clinic I wore a supersized pad in preparedness. The new doctor spoke very fast, almost slurring while explaining the various elements of the procedure in so much detail that she must have found the repetition monotonous and I found her incomprehensible.

I lodged the first tablet against my gums, which made it hard to ask questions anyway. The nurse insisted that if no one was collecting me, I had to get a taxi, could I give her my home address? Initially I gave the wrong one out of habit.

The roads were blocked with traffic. I began to feel hot, then faint. I thought again of the chameleon. My ears started ringing. Loudly. Suddenly I needed a bathroom. I have to get out, I said. I have to get out of the car. I stumbled the last few streets, tried to open the front door. I can't see, I said, now to nobody, and spat the remainder out.

Somehow I got the door open, ears still ringing, mouth foaming, and then there were rooms of pain. My vision swam. In and out, black spots, intense heat and then a chill, and then a kind of equilibrium where the pain subsided, before the fire returned, hotter than before. I felt it rising, moving up my body. Catching, rising upward, smoke. In my ears now, something hissing.

I woke and Christopher was there. I don't know how I ended up on the sofa, lowing like a cow. The jumbo pad crackled when I moved.

Do you want anything?

I shook my head.

Did Luke contact you?

Yes.

He looked at me for a beat, unsure if I was telling him the truth.

I woke up in the dark and knew immediately that I'd bled through. Returning to the sofa from the bathroom, I unzipped the soiled coverings from the cushions and reached for my laptop, then felt my stomach lurch. An email from him. Blank, but forwarding one from Mira, addressed to us both, apologising since she only had Luke's address. I read her words over several times, wondering how Luke would have experienced reading it.

She no longer felt secure or like she could achieve what she wanted work-wise, while living in Belgrade. She'd thought about moving to the Czech offices but that probably wasn't far enough. She was considering Berlin where she knew one or two people, and London, where she knew us and some publishing friends. It occurred to me Mira would've used the threats as her excuse for leaving to her mother. She would be in London before Christmas, at least until January to have meetings, scope things out, hopefully find a place to live, might she stay with us? If not, no problem, she could sort something else. She signed off with love and hoped our wedding plans were shaping up.

I knew Luke would not respond, but I kept putting off a reply. Then a few days later, Christopher said one of his commune friends was looking to sublet. Cheap, in your price range, he added. They were looking for someone long-term, in case, he softened his voice, that ended up being my situation.

Christopher stayed with his mother in Manchester for two weeks over Christmas every year. I was welcome to remain on his sofa, but what did I think about the room?

It was true I had a deep pain in my lower back, near-constant behind my kidney, from sleeping on a sofa bed which had lost a wheel so that, unfolded, it tilted toward the floor. But the idea of moving into a commune, however temporarily, during the time I was most tempted to become a hermit, was unbearable.

When I finally replied to Mira and explained the situation, I'd meant to put her off. Instead she said she would love to share the sublet, what a perfect solution that was. She'd arrived a few days ago and was staying in an Airbnb on a noisy street, having no luck on SpareRoom. Presumably my friend wanted their sofa back and she'd take the flat long-term.

I arranged to meet her in a restaurant I'd found near where she was staying in Shepherd's Bush. It was too far to walk and too cold. On the bus heading west, I sat on the top deck. I still felt nauseous, still had a too-keen sense of smell, but now I felt my body humming with concentration. There was a clap of thunder and the glass became wet with rain. A woman seated alone a few seats ahead threw back her head and crowed:

Pussy HOLE!

Then again, more insistently.

PU-SSY-HO-OO-LE!

The last hole had infinite vowels in it, like the blast of an ocean liner.

Normally this woman would have unnerved me, but just then I found I admired her.

When Mira arrived, I could tell she was disappointed.

Is this a chain? she asked over my Serbian greeting, I'm only speaking English now.

We left.

I don't really want to talk about it, I said as we resettled ourselves at a bar of her choosing. I'm trying to put it out of my mind. This felt as close as I could get to the kind of assertiveness that she had.

She opened her bag and handed me an uncorrected proof. I recognised the name.

Not light reading, she warned, but should be a distraction.

She told me the last time she was in London was five years ago, during the Olympics. It felt very different now, like the scales had fallen from most people's eyes.

How was it with your family?

Oh, I grimaced. A waste of carbon as far as Luke's concerned.

I meant how was it for you with them? Would Daria leave Sarajevo now?

I don't think so. No.

There's a whole Serbian crew that moved to Peckham, did I tell you? They squatted there. I met some of them in Belgrade. I told one guy the name of the road and he knew the place we're moving to.

I said nothing.

I think this will be good for you Anja. Independence.

But I'll be living with you.

I mean living for yourself – not pleasing other people.

It occurred to me I wanted Luke to hear I'd moved out of Christopher's. I didn't like that he could picture where I was while I had so many blanks for his activity.

The waiter arrived, his bald head glossy under a low-hanging bulb. I let Mira order. When he left again, she took out her phone, pulled up her photos and passed them to me. She'd been to see the commune that morning.

But that word . . . she rolled her eyes. A 'commune' is a stretch.

Listening to her as I scrolled through the photos I felt a surge of possibility. I noted the ease with which I could speak, or not speak, and have her instinctively understand my mood.

To us, she said, raising her glass. I still can't believe the road.

I'd let myself be copied into emails without reading them, choosing from the automated menu for suggested response.

What about it?

Asylum Road? By the way, you've lost too much weight.

I looked down again at my plate and pushed some chickpeas around it.

Anyway, next thing to sort out is getting your stuff back.

I nodded meekly.

She helped me compose a message to Luke that she would send, editing down everything I'd written to:

I'll be coming tomorrow for Anja's things.

Then she paid the bill for food only she had eaten.

Are you sure you don't want to come with me tonight?

She was going to a party with someone she'd met on a dating app that week.

I kept my mouth shut, feeling a tremor in my lip.

Well OK, I'll meet you at Luke's and we'll get a taxi from there together tomorrow. Yes?

I nodded again, unable to say thanks.

When I got back, Christopher was still at work and I started watching another documentary. So far I'd avoided ones with human beings as their subject, finding animals much safer, but this time I felt brave enough to try something about a once-famous folk singer. It turned out she lost her voice after her husband left her. I turned it off, reached for Mira's book and lay with it unopened.

Then a response from Luke arrived, forwarded by Mira.

Fine with me, let me know if I can help.

His efficiency was merciless. Google suggested three responses:

OK

Bye

Thanks!

When Christopher returned he sat on the end of the sofa and told me about a case that was going on. The defendant was representing himself and identified only as a freeman of the land. Freemen, Christopher was coming to learn, believed that laws only bind people because the state had issued them with a birth certificate. By this logic, if they rejected a state-given name, they would become free of the law.

How was your friend?

We're taking it.

The commune?

Yes.

Anya the anarchist!

I'm never going to be able to repay you, I hope you're aware of that.

Fuck off, he grinned. It's been nice to have you here. When you go I'll have to get a cat.

I woke up at four in the morning with a knife twisting in my side. It was hard to breathe and I worried the abortion had caused *internal rupturing*. I got up, put Christopher's parka over my pyjamas, and walked out into the night. Without knowing where I was going, I carried on for several hours and reached the Albert Embankment. The majority of tourists don't seem to know that those benches, on little individual plinths, give the best view of the Houses of Parliament. I was careful to stand in a non-suicidal pose, though there were few pedestrians in sight. Luke once told me the eels in the Thames were full of hormones and cocaine. I resisted the mental image but now I saw a roiling orgy of eels beneath the surface. Still, the walking had soothed my stomach, or the cold had numbed it, and for the first time since leaving Luke's, I understood that I was free now to do whatever I wanted. I wanted to be here, exactly where I stood, watching grey water moving somewhere.

A child's glove hung on the railings.

You're sure he's not going to be in? Mira said cautiously behind me as I stopped at the gate before the tiled path to Luke's front door. Painted the tasteful grey I'd selected before it became so prevalent in that neighbourhood, the typographic number in frosted glass above.

She was carrying several of those large, tartan-patterned plastic bags. The kind my mother had with the fraying plastic threads.

She looked at me, eyebrows raised, as if there might be an ambush waiting.

I doubt he'd do that.

Well, you know him best.

I wondered if I could really say that.

We climbed the steps and I fumbled with the keys, my fingers numb and inflexible, forgetting, for a minute, which way the lock turned.

On the mat there were notes from numerous parcel delivery companies. *We missed you. We missed you.* I'd always signed for his deliveries.

Luke had lined up some of my things in the hall. I walked past them into the living room. It was the sameness of everything that depressed me, as if my absence had left no mark.

It was only two in the afternoon but the winter sunlight was thin and Mira pressed down all the light switches but somehow that made it darker. Across the street I could see my former neighbour standing at his open window, watching us as if he thought we were intruders.

I looked at what Luke had left out. Mainly things from the attic and under the bed, in case I forgot them I guessed. There was something so final about this – so deliberate and determined that this was no longer my home to come back to, that I broke down for a moment. Mira squeezed my shoulder and I collected myself, noticing the roll of black bin liners in her other arm.

You look like you've come to rig the place, I said, wiping away tears.

Did you just make a joke? That's good. Tell me what you want to take and we'll get it over with.

I realised she'd switched out of English. We were back to our private language, which helped somehow in this familiar place I was now estranged from.

Who owns the plants?

He does, but I watered them.

So they come with you now. Same for everything else you took care of.

A defiant energy coursed through my body as it had the night before on the bus when the passenger ahead had screamed. Now he'd seceded, withdrawing protection, I didn't have to treat him or anything that belonged to him with reverence. I felt a flicker of temptation to break something. I wanted to do something rebellious, mainly to show him I was capable of doing it. As I took my pictures off the walls, I saw the nails I'd driven into the plaster and the black marks left by the frames. I scanned the rooms, the insides of drawers, picked up items at random. A lip balm bought in Copenhagen – a holiday tacked on to a conference he was speaking at. My noise-cancelling headphones – which I'd selflessly put over his ears to drown out the neighbours' parties. I put them down or resisted touching them altogether. Each banal object was a noose on the ground, ready to sweep me upside down with it.

Then I went into the bedroom. I stared at the crease marks like a sandbank in the centre of the bed. I tried to decide whether it looked like more than one body had been sleeping there.

I think the bed sheets haven't been changed since I left, I shouted.

Gross, she yelled back, then came upstairs to join me.

Changing your sheets alone is a struggle, she said dryly. You're lucky we'll be sharing a bed from now on. It made me feel so lonely the first time, and the weight of everything, all the thoughts I'd been holding off, suddenly dropped down all at once. I fell backward onto the bed in fact, with my arms and head inside the cover. Then I cried – the first time in a long, long time. I felt panicked, and sort of thrashed around trying to get out, and then I just surrendered. I must have fallen asleep. I think that's when the self-narration started, I had to talk myself out of there.

She asked if she could have a Fanta from the fridge. There were loads.

I'd never known him to buy Fanta and for a moment I lost my balance.

Sure, I said.

She went back to the kitchen.

I opened his bedside drawer. Looking for something incriminating I suppose, but the only thing I didn't recognise was a small blue book which I took and brought down slowly toward Mira.

I just found it in the drawer.

She took the Bible and turned it over, then opened it. Carefully, as if it might contain drugs.

I opened it already.

And this is a new thing? That you know of.

I nodded dumbly and sat at the table, digging into the base of my skull.

Well, she shrugged. That might explain some things.

I imagine it's his mum's. They're both quite into eschatology.

Do they know you're on a break?

I don't know what they know, they haven't been in touch.

It started to rain, a real rainstorm, drumming on the windows and darkening the cardboard boxes we'd already put outside.

She rolled her eyes and went to shield the boxes. Thunder and lightning in quick succession.

Whenever Mira stood beside me, I felt as if I might be better off in some essential way from now on. The minute she stepped out, this calm evaporated.

I wondered where to leave my keys. The kitchen table seemed too much like a message. I put them casually at one end of the sofa, then took them back again. I might still need them, I reasoned.

After everything had been gathered and stacked by the door, she ordered a six-seater taxi which appeared almost immediately so there was no time for any ritual.

She sat in the passenger seat and I sat in the only back seat not folded down, surrounded by belongings. As she confirmed the address with the driver, he turned and pulled a face. Asylum not as in lunatic, she explained, but almshouses before the welfare state. He laughed and said where we were going was no good.

Peckham is only bad people. Bad place, full of bad people. Always fighting each other. Like civil war.

Where do you live? Mira asked him.

Enfield. But I'm from Iraq.

I was not taking part in the conversation and did not want it to continue in this vein, but Mira was suddenly interested.

Did you move here during the war then?

He shook his head. After. I was an interpreter, for your country.

Oh, she smiled, we're not from here.

He was silent and I hoped he would not ask the obvious.

So, Mira persisted when he did not, they gave you asylum then?

He nodded, staring at the traffic jam ahead. Sometimes I wish they did not.

Will you go back there at some point?

He glanced behind him in the mirror.

No.

Mira looked steadily at him.

They killed my family who stayed, he said quietly. It took me two years to get out with my wife and children.

There, I am a traitor. I thought the English would have gratitude, but I have no more use to them these days. It's me who is supposed to be grateful. My children want to go back. We get everything here – school, doctor, so on – but they imagine Iraq as paradise. They live here since they were very small, but miss home more than me. They have a – a very idealised . . . image of the place. My youngest wasn't even born there but she knows all the old songs. She taught them to herself.

We settled into uneasy silence as the car slotted into more traffic on the Old Kent Road. It was dark already. My energy had waned and I slumped against the armrest with my forehead on the glass. The glass was frozen and the sensation was unpleasant – like a drill boring into me – but still I kept it there.

The rain slowed. I took in the neon glare of shop windows, Nigerian churches and floodlit retail parks. Their light and colour in the beads of water on my window. As we turned off at the forecourt of a shuttered Toys R Us, Mira reached round and squeezed my hand.

I forgot to tell you, she said as we parked outside. They have a mouse. But it means they don't have rats. We aren't allowed to put down any traps or poison they told me. We're just supposed to let it be. It comes with the territory, kind of like a pet. Maybe another reason why it's cheap.

I nodded, thinking about the set-up from the perspective of the mouse. Imagining her alarm if, with our arrival, she found herself unwelcome, having considered herself an established member of the commune.

Luke had once discovered a mouse making a nest underneath the floorboards. Making a nest, he said, meant she was having babies. It was sad. She was putting herself in danger just by getting on with her life because now she needed to be dealt with.

The interpreter helped us make several trips back and forth across the road to the pavement below a tall, dark-bricked house. Mira held the iron gate open with one of my bin bags and we carried everything up the steps. The cold, after the warmth of the car, was awful. I waited, stamping my feet while Mira tried to unlock the door, noticing that the ground-floor window had been covered completely with cling film, so that it sparkled in the glow of the street lamp.

We piled my belongings in the hallway first, to get them out of the wet. I hoped no one would come out to greet us. As if she'd read my mind, Mira said everyone was out for the night.

They invited us, actually. Some opening. An exhibition. So we have the place to ourselves.

She could still sense my anxiety. Apart from her, the nurse, and Christopher, I'd hardly spoken with anyone in weeks.

It's not like that. Really, nothing too intimate. Each flat's on a separate floor with its own door. Trust me it's nothing you can't handle after the basement.

The lights in the hall were motion sensitive. When they went out, Mira nudged against the dark to activate them and I followed her up the stairs to the very top.

Shit, I said. I left the pictures by the gate.

I ran down again, almost falling where the carpet treads were loose. My new forgetfulness was becoming habit.

Gone already.

When I came back up, Mira was unpacking for me. Putting my books beside hers. I wandered past her to the one other room which was the bathroom, the only place in the flat which afforded privacy through a door with a patterned glass window. I went in and shut it.

It looks dirty but it's not, she called after me. I tried to clean the shower and nearly fumigated myself. It's the enamel, not dirt – it actually makes it worse trying to clean it because then more gets stripped away.

I stood over the basin, waiting for a familiar wave of nausea to pass. When it had I came back to the window which overlooked the garden, now too dark to see anything except what looked like a chicken coup on a patio directly below.

Hens, Mira said. What were the names of ours again?

Agata was mine. I can't remember what yours was called.

Her father had sold things on the black market to buy them, but it was too cold for them to lay eggs. And, he told us sadly, they were very stressed. Mira and I would try to soothe them, warming them between our thighs, stroking their heads. Singing. I think it calmed us more than them. When the shelling's over, Mira would tell them, we'll go to the beach. Lie in the sun, swim. We'll all relax together.

I remember carrying one of the rare eggs to my mother with great ceremony, but my hands were smooth and numb with cold and the egg slipped as I tried to turn the door handle. The horror of that moment, as if I'd dropped a whole planet.

I saw now that Mira had taken Luke's juicer and an expensive set of Japanese knives. She winked at me as she put them on the kitchen counter then ordered us Vietnamese and two beers.

What does your ex think about you moving here? I asked her.

Oh – she waved her hand dismissively. I don't care what he thinks. He'd say I'm overreacting. He criticises people who move away from the Balkans.

She checked her phone to see how far off the Deliveroo was.

Every time we fight it's like I cut another thread between us. I get more and more detached and so he feels it more and more – how I didn't, don't, care. He's just so angry. Before I left I gave him a stone from my collection – sodalite – to help him unwind. Obviously, it provoked him. He insisted on coming back to my flat. To help me finish packing, he said. He put the stone back and sat on the bed and told me how worried he was about me – mostly the men making threats but also my mental state. Then he was the one threatening me. He's just insecure that I don't need him for my protection. When I finally managed to get him to leave, do you know the last thing he said to me? He told me I should get my ears pinned!

She pulled back her dark hair and bent her, admittedly prominent, ears forward. I smiled, finding it difficult not to feel envious. He was still trying to make her feel something.

When the bell rang Mira went down to collect the food, but after she shut the door I could hear her talking still.

Did you say you wanted driving lessons? she said when she returned. What about with the Kurdish guy? It's his car in the drive. He's an instructor.

Can't afford it sadly.

I'd told her I'd been using those online tutorials to distract myself and Mira had agreed I needed to have a self-improvement project to see me through this period.

I don't think I'm up for it right now anyway – I waved my hand – having to make conversation.

She laughed. You're managing.

I'd hated the real lessons I'd had, long ago, and even the few I'd done with Luke in the quiet roads near his parents' house. I'd been confronted with the uselessness of my qualifications when it came to learning something practical. My mind would not cooperate.

Mira had already finished her food and was staring hungrily at my untouched plate. I pushed it toward her.

He's quite handsome actually, the Kurd. Seems quite straightforward too. I need a simple man I think, but I know they find me difficult. And if they don't they're already married and looking for something very complicated. I met one of those at that party the other night. Actually, that was a funny story. There was no bin in their fancy bathroom, which I only noticed *after* I'd taken out my tampon. I thought, OK you deserve to have your toilet blocked. I was angry because the guy who'd invited me – I matched with him on the Heathrow Express – turned out to be married after all. Then I saw all these toilet books in the guest bathroom. It's the only rule I want to impose while we're here. No reading in the toilet. Anyway I wrapped the tampon and went to bin it, but one of the catering staff saw me with a wad of tissue in my hand and told me to hand it over like it was a spat-out canapé. I *ran*. Oh, let me show you something.

She got up and went to a chest of drawers then came back with a Cuban cigar box with drawings and stickers decorating it.

Open it, she instructed.

Drago's shrapnel collection. I quickly put it down and shook my head, blinking.

Waking, I got the lurching feeling in my stomach of being in the wrong place. Mira, I remembered, not Luke, was in the next room taking a shower. The windowpanes were covered in condensation. The misty skyline beyond that, back to front, now seen from south of the river.

She reappeared in a yellow silk kimono.

Have a meeting. Soho, she announced, an electric toothbrush in her mouth.

Applying her make-up at the table she told me about the other inhabitants of *the asylum*. I had imagined them all to be of a type but she said they were an incongruous group, like those motley crews of dogs led along by professional walkers, all yoked together in a faintly comedic way.

There was the Kurd driving instructor who was also a classical violinist. He tried to practise in the day, he'd said, which made her worry he mainly did it at night. The very tall girl with pale pink hair was, she suspected, his girlfriend. She was studying at Goldsmiths. She was not Kurdish – her family were from Wales – but she talked non-stop about the YPJ.

I looked blank.

Don't worry, she'll tell you about it. That'll be her boyfriend now.

She gestured below to the sound of a violin.

We listened, and suddenly I remembered what I'd overheard in Cornwall, the open window that led me here.

But I was spared that train of thought as Mira shrieked and pointed down beside her chair. I looked down to see a mouse. I bent closer. Even though I was so close I could have touched it, the mouse seemed unconcerned.

That's not normal, Mira said. Why isn't it running away? Aren't they nocturnal?

I shrugged.

There's a parasite, I said, remembering something Luke had told me. It removes their fear of cats. Instead of running away from the smell of predators, infected ones are actually attracted to it.

We watched as the mouse began to move, stop-starting toward the door. Mira looked up *mice that lose their fear of cats*, read a while, and nodded.

Toxoplasma can sexually reproduce only in the cat gut, and for it to get there, the pathogen's rodent host must be eaten.

It affects humans too – are you serious?

I watched the mouse come back again, then disappear behind a skirting board.

Mira continued in a voice of mock-cheerfulness:

In humans, studies have linked Toxoplasma infection with behavioural changes, risk-taking and schiz-ophrenia. One study found an increased risk of traffic accidents in people infected with the parasite, another found changes in responses to cat odour.

She rolled her eyes. That's why we aren't allowed to kill it. It trusts that we're not going to.

After she left, I dressed in random items pulled from bags, found my trainers and ran downstairs. I didn't want to meet anyone.

The temperature had dropped again. First, I ran the length of the road back the way we'd driven the previous evening, turning around at a church inside a commercial property called THE MOUNTAIN OF PERFECTION. I peered through the iron railings outside the almshouses. In the middle there was a chapel, surrounded by a lawn and low buildings. One side of the entrance I could see had been left open.

Inside, it looked like the building had been gutted by fire. Bombed during the blitz, as the noticeboard told me, it was now a wedding venue. Everything had been destroyed internally (except a few stone monuments) but not one of the stained-glass windows had shattered. I felt even colder inside, and desolate, as if I'd entered the depths of an aquarium.

I turned right then left, running until I reached the butchers and beauty salons of Peckham Rye, only stopping when I reached the park, then walking a bit further as my heart rate settled. The sun broke out from behind the clouds and I sat down on a bench. As I sat there, feeling newly calm, my breath rising up in clouds, another person joined me, and just as his presence and the silence was starting to make me feel I should continue, he turned his face to mine.

Hey, he blurted, almost aggressive. What's your story?

He was American, I couldn't tell where from exactly, but he sounded like he'd been practising with a pick-up artist. I tried to convey that I was not in the mood for talking, smiling then taking from my bag the book Mira had given me.

What's your book then?

I showed him the cover. He looked at the title, in Serbian, and appeared to ponder it. I held my breath.

You like reading?

I shrugged, keeping my eyes on the page.

What's it about?

Genocide.

OK. Any good?

Depends what you're into I guess.

Does it have a good plot?

It's non-fiction.

He laughed as if he'd finally got the measure of me. What's your name, if you don't mind?

I made a face like I did, but he continued looking at me with his light eyes.

Anya.

His eyes reminded me of my dentist's as they bore down on me from above the surgical mask. Whenever he had me in the chair and had begun to suffocate me by placing some kind of clay in my mouth, or probing me with his latex fingers while I lay choking on my spit, he would start asking me personal questions like *so when are you getting married?*

I reopened the book determinedly, deciding this was the right time to put my new, Mira-inspired personality into action. I had to save myself. My neighbour was not deterred, stroking his cheek as if to indicate that he was still turning my name over.

Well listen Anya, I actually came over to talk to you for a reason. You look a little lost, if I may say. He was getting smoother, more relaxed with me. Evidently he thought his strategy was succeeding.

I shrugged again.

Are you from here?

I hesitated. No. Not here exactly.

Where's home?

I could not yet bring myself to walk away.

Where are *you* from? I said, turning the question.

Nashville. He smiled like I was finally playing along. Now you.

Glasgow.

OK and where's that?

About as far as you can get from Nashville, spiritually.

Well, Anya, it's funny you should mention that –

I clenched my jaw. He was not a pick-up artist then, but a stealth-mode Jehovah's Witness. He reached into his jacket pocket and passed me a piece of paper.

GAME CHANGER, I read.

I'm just starting out as a life coach. And if you go to my website you will see I'm also a gardener. Do you know what life coaching involves?

I tipped my head to one side, not sure which answer would be rewarded with the shorter conversation.

The stories we tell ourselves, he continued, in a monotone as if reading from a script, are what make us who we are. They tend to become a self-fulfilling prophecy.

I gave him my old number so that I could leave, then forced myself into a phone shop where I got out my credit card again, bought the cheapest they had, and had at least some of my life restored to me.

It got dark quickly. With my new phone in a shopping bag, I found myself at the BMX track in Burgess Park. The helmets shone in the floodlights, swooping over the pale hills like starlings in formation. I stood observing them, alone. The lights made the sky feel very close. I sat down again on a bench under their brightness, took the phone out of its packaging and stared at it before doubling over and throwing up onto the frozen ground.

12

I bought another pregnancy test. The cheapest one that came as a single rather than a pair. The woman at the clinic had advised doing one again four weeks later and that, even if it was negative, I still had to be vigilant in case I needed an ERPC. When I asked what that was she told me it stood for Evacuation of Retained Products of Conception.

I swallowed several glasses of water and went to the bathroom. Almost instantaneously this time, I had another positive result.

As the shock subsided, I wondered what the tablet might have done. Whether, failing to abort, I'd only made it angry. Pulling myself up, I decided to go and buy another, more expensive test.

I called Christopher as I walked back to Tesco. He was on his way to a work Christmas party.

How're you doing? he said. You got your phone back?

The warmth in his voice had such a visceral effect I looked around me on the traffic island as though he might appear there.

Did you see my email about the reunion?

Suddenly the sky lit up as if by a silent detonation.

Are you actually going?

I can't but a part of me wants to. I think you should go.

Why would I want to do that?

Morbid curiosity? You're extremely morbid.

Ha.

I want you to tell *me* about it. I'm sure you know Eddie will be there.

As I reached the petrol station, I saw that the detonation had come from a rotation of advertisements on a huge LED screen. I was disoriented and had walked the wrong way down the road.

I'd rather die.

My phone buzzed against my head. I checked the screen — an unknown number was calling — and wondered if it was my new life coach.

Isn't it too late anyway? I thought you had to sign up.

They sent round an email yesterday saying there were still places.

I haven't been reading emails.

I know. But I think you should go. His tone was mischievous.

The last time I spoke to Eddie he was *lost at sea*. Literally. Somewhere off Corsica in a sailing boat. He had a fever and I think he thought he was going to drown out there.

At the time I'd thought this meant something, but then I doubted I was the first person he'd called.

You'd be a very comforting person to speak to in that situation.

Oh?

Definitely. I feel like you'd say whatever someone wanted to hear.

The flat reeked of smoke.

Look at all the ladybirds! Mira called as I closed the door.

I came over to the window where she was standing with an ashtray. There were dozens fluttering against the glass.

Must be attracted to the light. Or maybe the glass is warm.

My skin crawled. I pointed to a figure, dimly visible below, and gave her an apprehensive look.

I don't know, she said laughing, one of the tenants? What a nuisance. Shall we call the police to our communal property? Gentrifiers here, we'd like to report a neighbour in the garden. Actually I've just been listening to some depressing thing on the radio about how they're going to review security around all public spaces because of the terrorism threat now. To stop cars running people down and make us safer, ostensibly.

I felt edgy and went round shutting blinds.

I'd choose safety over terrorism to be honest.

I know you would.

Across the street, a man came to the window just as I did. He looked down at the road, listening to a phone in one hand and holding the other to his chest.

I'm being paranoid. Forget it.

Because people are after me?

Just the feeling something's about to happen, you know that feeling.

OK, she said, now serious.

Mira's family had a dog, but a sniper shot it when it transpired dogs could anticipate a shelling.

Now her phone rang. I went to the bathroom to do the third pregnancy test but could still hear her as she answered.

Daria! Yes, of course I can speak, comrade.

I was transported. I tried to pee very quietly, waiting for her to talk, but Mira was silent for a long time. Then as her questions came — when, where, how? — I realised something was wrong. I put my head around the door, watched her face turn to me with the phone still pressed against it. Her gaze full of pity for me. I knew already what had happened and went back in again. The positive pregnancy line had appeared and my mother had died that morning.

I held the sink for balance. I thought of the photograph of us in the bath, her shoulder, and then, for a split second I thought of calling her to be comforted, before it hit me – my mother no longer existed. I couldn't call to tell her this. It was total now rather than just symbolic. We were in two separate worlds.

That night I started dreaming again for the first time since Luke broke up with me. In one I was sat at a pot-ter's wheel, shaping with my hands a belly getting big-ger and bigger until it was bigger than I could control and caved in on itself. In another, my mother was in the commune, helping me assemble mysterious items of flat-pack furniture. We gave up trying to make sense of the diagrams and made them how we thought they should look. There was one box left. She was slow dan-cing with it – a very tall heavy oblong. The object inside the cardboard thudded against the side as she tilted and turned, dancing toward another wall where she leant it and took it back again on the same tender journey.

In another, from which I woke finally with a jolt, a man was in bed with me, not Mira. He was bearing down and I could taste salt on his lips, feel his chest under a loose cotton shirt. At first, I thought it was Luke but then, when I found his face, I saw the man was Eddie.

In the morning I found the emails about the reunion and replied that I would be attending.

After endless fields, she recognised the cycle track now running alongside the train, the science park, sixth form college, rugby pitches and tenpin bowling, the large industrial sheds. It felt like coming up on a strong pill, the connection to these nondescript places – places she hadn't noticed when she lived there. The train window slowed alongside the station sign.

CAMBRIDGE
HOME OF ANGLIA RUSKIN UNIVERSITY

Stepping onto the platform she regretted the shoes instantly. The pair pulled from a chaos of bin bags in the half dark that morning were heeled ankle boots. She'd forgotten they were painful. Worse, it would look like she was trying to impress people.

The area around the station was completely different a decade on from her graduation. There were new buildings everywhere – mostly tech companies and luxury apartments. Still, a wave of nostalgia hit her as she went through the barriers.

As a student there she'd never felt at home, but the sensation in that moment was that this was somewhere she had used to belong and *now* did not. Estranged, as if she'd been shaped by it, like an espaliered tree trained to grow up walls, in ways that were only sensible now she was back here.

It was always colder than London. More like Glasgow. The winds swept over from Siberia in winter, someone had told her once. Too cold to walk for twenty-five minutes in these boots. As she waited for a bus, her phone buzzed with another unknown number.

The bus was taking forever so she climbed into a taxi.

She wanted to drive around but the driver refused to drive unless it was to one specific destination. Because of *the system*, he said, passengers had to travel directly.

It didn't matter. Here, Luke did not exist. Nothing was tainted by association. Here, *she* did not quite exist either, a former life that had now been overwritten.

Collecting the key to her room for the night she smiled, not recognising the man behind the desk who signed her in.

Nice to be back?

Strange.

Did he know her, or did he just know what she had come for?

Well, he grinned as if he said this a lot, the past's a foreign country.

She was out of practice making conversation with strangers.

At dinner she sat next to a civil servant who looked vaguely familiar.

I studied SPS, he said, but they don't call it that now. I can't remember what they call it.

He was working on a Balkans summit, timed for when the UK left the EU.

It's all in limbo at the moment, obviously. But it's really a hole on the map. They feel abandoned by Europe, so it's Russia they're turning to. It's how people behave when they feel excluded, they don't necessarily act rationally, as we know.

Anya nodded, taking small, dry bites of potato fondant, wondering whether he was telling her all this so arrogantly, in great detail, because he knew who she was, and blushed when he said that of course he knew.

History?

English, she said. For undergrad anyway. Didn't you roll a disco ball back from a party – he laughed – only to discover it wouldn't fit through the door? It was bike-locked outside for the rest of term as I remember.

(Was she flirting?)

That's right.

Do you have a cigarette?

Sorry, I don't.

She got up, dispirited, and walked between the long tables toward the door. The hall that had once been so intimidating now seemed tiny. The people in it too seemed small, though in that previous life they had caused Anya to feel acute self-consciousness. Such shame and resentment toward her own family.

The man's name was Kieran, she remembered. Kieran what? Oh who cared, she was not there for him.

She was becoming warm and a little woozy from the wine. She could feel her cheeks flushing, a light sheen of sweat. If Christopher had been there, they would be outside smoking together, by now doing brutal caricatures of everyone in the hall. No one was in the smoking area to give her a cigarette. Someone from the kitchen staff was vaping. They smiled at each other politely. Then Anya was suddenly ashamed. She cringed, pretending to shiver so the young man would not be offended as she turned and left. She came back inside and sat down at the end of a table. Mimed a search for something on her phone. Scrolled through a property website. Aware all the time that *he* might at any moment catch sight of her and she would not want to look like she was waiting.

The woman opposite had brought her own food. Some kind of pale pink spread for slices of dark bread that she took out of Tupperware one by one as she ate them. The spread was applied with precise strokes. Anya now remembered the woman from her corridor. The first year. A Nat Sci? Christian society, that part she knew, a gaze she'd tried to avoid. Now she caught her eye and smiled awkwardly. The woman smiled back. Maybe she didn't recognise her. Clearly she didn't care what Anya thought of her as she sat there eating her plain, self-sufficient meal.

She finished her last slice and said hello, adding, as if she was well-rehearsed in how to have these conversations, that she'd studied Chemistry. Chosen due to her wish to be an art restorer, but she had failed at that. Now she was working as a French translator, for which she discovered she had a gift while living in Paris. She was just thinking she had misjudged the woman — refusing to eat hall food was really a mark of sophistication — when she trailed off. A presence had arrived at Anya's shoulder. Without turning to look at him, she knew.

Anya never called him Eddie until after he broke up with her, but Eddie was what everyone else in their college had called him. She'd expected to feel something when she saw him and had prepared for it. Hoped for it. Something very much in existence, set under permafrost, but when reviewed afterward, back on the outside of this, safely irrelevant.

He made amusing small talk with the translator, during which he described himself as *ostensibly single*. And what about you, he said, turning to Anya.

Only after he broke up with her had she found out he'd cheated. With their mutual friend. She'd lost both of them and the wider group she'd tangentially been a part of. He had tried to blame it on his parents – a divorce from years before which he'd once boasted hadn't affected him. That was a story he liked to tell. Instead of selling up and making him – sole child from that marriage – trek back and forth between two smaller homes that might end up being very far apart, his parents took out a second mortgage and built an extension, carrying on, essentially, in the same house. That way, as Eddie would explain it, no one's life had to be disrupted unnecessarily.

He was used to being the central fact of people's lives in this way, or he found a way to put himself there if he was not already. Every story revolved around his part in it, no matter how peripheral, so Anya knew, for example, that he'd been in Paris when the Bataclan attacks had taken place. She knew because he'd marked himself as *safe*. That was, she now remembered, the last time she'd spoken to him – online at least – and not when he'd been lost off Corsica. The status updates he had composed, apparently while lying for hours on the floor of a bar, managed to include a summary of his recent professional success. He was in Paris for the Airbnb conference, the company for whom he worked. Later he was posting again, offering strangers a bed using the hashtag #opendoors.

Soon the failed restorer had moved to another table. Anya silenced another unknown number and put her phone face down. At some point during their conversation, she found herself leaning in out of habit, resting her head on his shoulder. She realised quite how drunk she was when she kissed him lightly on the cheek. She kept her head there and he'd turned toward her, but as soon as her lips touched his she recoiled. It was Luke's skin she'd been expecting. Still, she wanted to forget about death. She wanted to stop feeling, just for a moment, that she had lost everything.

Eddie had requested, and paid extra for, his same room from first year. For old times' sake, he said. Anya went back with him *to see*. Luke did not want her so this was what he'd have to accept as the logical consequence. He was driving her to do this — the most self-destructive thing she could. The idea gave her a kind of nihilistic shiver. It was better to be complicit in the destruction.

Eddie placed his hand under her skirt as she climbed the narrow stairs in front. She didn't hesitate — that was her answer. She felt sick. Vicious. Aroused. In some kind of danger. She carried on walking at the same pace, down the familiar corridor toward his room. She recalled the feeling of being that young, which was the rush of feeling adult.

They'd used to talk about the experience after it was over, like they had both just emerged from a film. He was the first person to make her come, the body who'd revealed what hers could do if she climbed on top without self-consciousness. That was what he'd meant by *animal*. She could never quite access that place now, not in the way she once had. It was too bound up with shame, or worries about the future, which animals didn't have.

She would tell herself that because she knew what was possible, and that because sometimes she could still get close, even tantalisingly so, like the parallel curve on a hairpin bend, it was the same. But it wasn't, she thought with fresh clarity as Ed put his thumb to the back of her neck and held her throat, it was not at all the same. She felt sudden grief for all the wasted time, the sacrifice she'd made for Luke's empty promise of security.

He closed the door and began taking off his shirt. As it passed over his head she saw that he was perfectly preserved. It was as if he'd been frozen cryogenically in this room, which was also just as it had been. She remembered that she hadn't shaved or waxed in months. It hardly mattered now.

The first time she met him was at a party on Mill Road. He'd been set upon by several girls after arguing that females only liked guys who posed a sexual threat. She thought of this provocation again as he pushed her forward and put her hand between her legs to show her what she knew – that she was wet already. He nudged her legs apart with his knee and wound her long hair around his fist so that her neck yanked back and it was hard to breathe. Her body locked into position. She saw it just at the edge of her vision, eyeballs straining as her head bent back toward the ceiling, all reflected in the same mirror that, aged twenty-one, he'd screwed to the inside of the door.

Ed had once whispered he would like to fuck her pregnant. He found the taut bellies and breasts of pregnant women arousing. Now she told him, the only person she would tell, and he let her neck go slack for a moment so she made eye contact with her own reflection.

The lamp beside the bed fell and smashed, glass flying everywhere. He didn't stop. All she could do was hold her breath, his teeth pulling at her ear, the shadow of him on the ceiling.

At last he let her climb over him and a dark wall of heat came down.

She woke around dawn, tongue thick, the radiator on full blast, and tried to slip out of bed but he snorted and grabbed her wrist.

Where are you off to Annie?

The old name repelled her. She hadn't been planning to leave, only to get water, but now she decided
on leaving.

Don't.

He wrapped his arm around her back and pulled her
down against his chest. The smell in the cave of his arm
was overpowering. She looked down at their bodies —
his hairy and muscled, hers covered in smears of blood.
Tiny scratches. She'd forgotten the broken glass.

I really need to go.

But I *love* you! he whined in a girlish voice.

She wriggled free and started pulling on her clothes,
feet bleeding now too.

Will you tell your fiancé?

Who told you?

I can't remember. But you're getting married right?

Mm hm.

Next stop, death. That'll probably be the next thing I
hear about you.

Until he said that, her mother had not been dead.

It's pessimism that drives people to get married. To
lock something up so it can't run off.

I see.

She pulled her boots on but they were like hot irons
now. She took them off and held them in one hand.

Goodbye Ed.

Clasping the boots to her chest, she bent down, grabbed her bag and staggered through the door, down the stairs and out again into the cold. There was snow underfoot and she gasped.

For a moment she was disoriented – she knew this street, like the back of her hand, but was unable to place it on a map. The city was all made in the same stone, pretty much, seamless like a video game – no rough or discordant textures. At night it had always felt safe, if a little eerie. The homogenous unity meant walking along the empty street felt only marginally different to walking through the rooms of a house. She tipped her face to the sky and started walking, still barefoot. The street lamps seemed to be communicating with her, with each other. Communing even. She felt protected by their light and this oceanic feeling, like no harm could come to her. She walked the rest of the way as if she was being held.

On the train back to London the unknown caller became more insistent. I'd not wanted to answer because
then the hope that it was Luke would be extinguished
and I would instead have to have a conversation with
Daria about my mother, or maybe even one of Mira's
irate, book-burning Serbs who was probably hacking
into her messages. I wanted to put off that moment of
painful certainty, hoping it might somehow be averted.
That I would wake up as if from a nightmare, the way
my younger tutees ended all their stories.

When I finally answered, the caller was none of those.
My aunt said she'd heard about my mother and had
been trying to get hold of me. She was worried. She
was herself distressed by the news. As I submitted to her
gentle scolding, I found I could not contain myself any
longer. I turned my face toward the window to avoid the
other passengers.

She hadn't seen my mother for years but the people
she knew with Alzheimer's didn't have any sense of

danger, or were free of certain fears. One man near hers in Killin kept leaving his house and locking himself out, ending up in all sorts of places – the middle of the local stone circle or by a busy road. These people became a danger to themselves, yes, but they had to have their liberty. My father was right to leave her that. Even with what happened. Did I understand that? I stayed silent, not wanting to. We passed a whole field of cars tossed on top of each other like toys and it occurred to me how different things look depersonalised like that. The ball in my throat was back. Choking me. I could come and stay again, she said patiently, if I needed or wanted that. Her son Nikolaj, who went by Calum now, was working nearby and could drive me to and from the station.

The last time I stayed with her there, a house she had moved to an hour and a half north of Glasgow, was just after my first term at university. It was the first time I'd been back. Michaelmas term had ended. Drago was not yet dead. Life could now begin.

I get the train to Glasgow Central then walk from there to Queen Street. I have an hour until my next train and wander slowly to kill the time. The familiar hoppy smell makes me anxious and the pubs are full with jacked-up, warlike men. Celtic are playing Rangers. Whenever I feel intimidated by strangers on the street like that, I tell myself I'm more likely to be murdered by someone close to me. At Crianlarich, still fourteen miles from Killin, the line splits. I have to get off there and wait for Calum to get me. After Glasgow, the air is so pure and cold it hurts my lungs. There is snow on the ground and the sky throbs as if to promise more. Birds' nests sit exposed in the bare arms of trees. I pace beneath them, shivering in my charity-shop fur coat. After twenty minutes, I can't feel my hands or feet. I will learn to drive, I think, then I won't be dependent on men like him. I decide to ask Ed for lessons.

I try to picture Nikolaj. I try to remember to call him Calum. I've just spent eight weeks free of his tyranny, his face has blurred in my mind. He looks misshapen – a piece of overstuffed taxidermy. He's doing it on purpose, I know. Making me wait in this forbidding place, to establish who is powerful here. After three cars roar by I try calling him but get no answer. He has always hated me, but I'm expecting him to be merciless now I've started university. Finally his car swerves in beside me and he is grinning through the open window. Metallica, 'Fade to Black'. Happenin Oxford? He has called me this since the day I got in to Cambridge. He eyes my fur coat and sodden wheelie bag with amusement. His head's shaved and his teeth have dark rims as if he's swallowed ink. I notice, as he

drives, a new tattoo. The saltire, beside the existing kilted man dragging on a spliff.

As far as I know Calum's only political views
involve Scottish independence. To the extent that I
live in my head and cling to cities, my cousin exults
in his KGB carapace of muscle and bone, and hungers
for the wild. Before coming out here to work as a
ghillie he tried to be a participant on a reality show
that required people to survive on an uninhabited
island. He was not accepted, to my aunt's relief, but
while I was revising he would watch it and sneer at
the inexpert way the fud who had made the cut ahead
of him now tanned animal skins or whittled spoons
from logs.

He always resented his mother for leaving Yugoslavia when she did, before he was born, before he
got to have that opportunity. He used to get excited
at the sight of burning tanks and sparking wires, the
bodies sleeping in the sun, murmuring, as we watched
the news, that if he could he'd join the Tigers. The
paramilitaries all had names like that. Tigers, White
Eagles, Yellow Wasps. When he talked that way my
aunt slapped him.

On the back seat now, I can see his rifle. We pass
the falls – a white slalom against black rock – and he
tells me about the big estate he works for, which has

a haunted house. The wallpaper is laced with arsenic he says. But it's not the wallpaper he wants to show me. He will take me to the cottage he shares with his mother later, but first I'm to come with him. There is something immediately suspicious in the way he says this, but I know I can't refuse.

We get out by some sheds and he chucks me clothing from the boot. The dogs bark excitedly. I am strapped into Gore-tex, then he passes me a white lab coat. I ask if this is a joke. It's snowing up there, pure baltic he says, I'll need camouflage.

In the Argocat, we head up into the hills. He explains the general principles of managing the herd. Hunting deer is a matter of conservation. I have this as my frame of reference when Luke explains it to me, seven years later when we meet. I wonder if the move away from Glasgow has been good for him, a healthy outlet, or if he's just high on this new authority. He is doing real work while I'm a fandan at university.

Are you going to make me shoot a stag?

Pure gallus, Oxford. I'll shoot a hind.

Are they the women?

He rolls his eyes.

When we get to the top it is snowing heavily. In spite of the vast landscape, I feel trapped. I put the lab coat on and keep close behind, my head bowed against the wind as I follow his boots, which go quickly over the uneven terrain. Beneath the snow, the ground is either sharp rock or boggy, and every now and then I can hear the sound of water rushing away.

My eyes and nose stream. Each time we stop I look up in silence, confronted by a new scene, and wonder how I have ended up here, on the surface of another planet, with this man, in a lab coat. My lungs are in agony from running. I wonder if this is where I will die.

He points out a bird of prey and I collapse in the snow and then we are running again. My whole body is on fire except my hands and feet which are numb. Suddenly he drops down, behind a mossy verge, and I drop down beside him, relieved. He passes me a pair of binoculars – pointing out the group of hinds. They are in the distance, I know, but in the viewfinder they are right in front of me as if they have been cut out and placed there as Christmas decorations. As I'm looking, three stags dart across, only feet away, like dancers, antler arms aloft, then vanish into mist. We have to crawl up the burn, stopping every so often with the wind so they can't catch our scent.

Finally Calum holds up his hand and gives me some kind of signal, then disappears over the ridge. He is gone for a while. Inside my hood I can hear my heart beat inside my ears. I wonder if Calum counts as the kind of already-known person who might kill me, but otherwise it is peaceful, lying in the bright curve of the snow.

I return with the shot. Muffled as it was by my hood and the wind, I hear it, like a book falling flat from a shelf. I stand cautiously, stumbling toward the sound like there has been an accident. Calum is on his knees talking to it. Had a yearling, he says as I approach, we'll have to go after it in a bit. Too young to survive without a mother. Then he pulls out his knife and slits the soft belly open. The stomach must be cut out right now, he explains, and the animal bled, or the meat will spoil. The blood spills into the snow. I have never seen anything be taken apart like this. The stomach is a neat, translucent sack with a greenish tint. He slashes it open and soft, steaming grass swells from the incision, melting a patch of snow. He extracts the heart – the bullet is lodged inside. Wait here, he says. I sit beside the lifeless animal while he goes to find her young. The eyes are open but turning milky. Disembowelled, its skin looks like my coat. I stare at the entrails, splayed out on the snow, repulsed and in the same breath trans-fixed by them.

Beside their cottage on the estate, there is an outbuilding where he hangs the mother and then the child from hooks. He bifurcates and dismembers them in turn. I watch. He is surprisingly tender. Sliding into their flesh in a way that makes the swaying bodies open up for him like a folded-up toy – a puzzle all connected. He seems to delight in my expression, even more than the mutilation. He knows all the correct anatomical terms, and some I've never heard of. Knackery, stink pit. A stink pit, he laughs, is where dead animals are left as bait to trap more animals – foxes and other pests. He takes a cereal bar from his pocket with bloody gloves and I want to gag when he shows me pictures on his digital camera. Instead I dull my nausea with the thought of going back in a few weeks and handing in my essay on Shakespeare and the concept of authority. I will be cleansed and whole again, severing this person.

Anja? Are you still there?

She waited, listening to my breathing, then said, as she had once before, that my anger was a poison that would only end up hurting me. After she hung up I kept the phone to my ear. I clung to it first for its solidity, then as though I might break it.

When I get out at King's Cross the sky is huge. I am suspicious of the way winter is thawing, the bright blossom against pebble-dash houses. Things have come around too early.

The past keeps intruding. We are sick to death of it.

I find I am not welcome in my own home. My own country. Again and again this happens. I seem to be the common denominator. This realisation is, at first, the end of a cigarette in the dark, then a train sucking me toward it as it passes through my station. My brain is approaching the mode of concentration I know it is capable of. I focus my mind on this idea like a deeply rooted hair.

I am on the bus after my brother's suicide, not knowing I need to grieve until that moment, when I realise I can't, and I stumble off into the street where a group of men are playing saxophones. 'When the Saints Go Marching In'. It strikes me the song is not happy but apocalyptic. I am wild-eyed. I want to be in that number. Chain-smoking again. I put my hands out and watch them dance, throbbing like an electro-cuted cartoon character.

Ear-splitting sounds, the kind only children and animals can make, gasping for air in the intervals until my sister slaps me across the face. We are safe, she screams, shut the fuck up.

I walk from the bus stop, a woman is walking behind me in a pair of worn-down high heels, the rubber caps need replacing. Tack, tack, tack, tack. For a moment she is the target of all my rage. It hits me what a find my note-book will make for some other passenger sitting in that aircraft. Jenny Holzer's *Lustmord* is reproduced there. I google. Right under the text, at the end of the third section, the one voiced by an observer, is an ad featuring a red raw beef patty on a grill with an ice cube in the centre, melting like a puffy nipple on the meat.

After seeing why he places an ice cube on his burger when grilling, I'll never make one any other way.

The crowd parts as my mother, held up by my father and Mira's on either side, walks away from the grave like a too-thin carnival figure. Veering into people, her cardboard head jerking, eyes rolling, her hands shaking uncontrollably as she tries to drink from a small bottle. The one she didn't send away has left.

I reach the iron gate. I look up to see if Mira has the lights on. As I walk I imagine small creatures fleeing, moving out of my way. Shuffling and hopping and diving. Luke striding through the long grass with his scythe.

I no longer feel the need to hold myself together. I am just training my gaze.

13

Something had been unfrozen through fucking. It felt like a trick, the way parts of me were coming back to life. The raw, jellied pink, the uncooked meat at the centre of things. By the time I returned to the asylum, my arms imprinted with the strap of my bag, I suspected I'd got a UTI. Mira had just left a date and called to tell me about it while I tried to pee unsuccessfully.

He's an angry man. We went for dinner and he broke a plate. Stabbed his steak knife into it ranting about Eurocrats and must have hit a weak spot. It went all over the restaurant. But it was the end of the date, at least. The other one I'm on my way to now. He's an alcoholic, I think. When we had sex last time I could smell it, in his skin. How was your reunion thing?

I could see myself in the bathroom mirror as I laughed. My eyes were all pupil. I am saying I but it feels like *we*. That will sound like I have delusions of grandeur, yet there *is* someone else now, inside me. I has dissolved. It comes and goes. It's like I'm learning a new language.

The next morning Mira was still not back. Her phone went straight to voicemail. I could see she was not reading my messages. I tried to push paranoid thoughts from my mind but decided not to leave the flat until she returned to it. I could barricade myself in if necessary.

At a certain point I noticed it was dark again.

My first thought when Luke calls is that he's heard about Eddie. Then maybe that he has heard about my mother. It occurs to me I wasted my time translating for him when I could have been paying attention to the last words she was saying to me.

He asks questions about what I've been up to. He's nervous. He hates speaking on the phone. I prowl around the room to leach the adrenaline from my limbs, to settle. I feel canny and sharp-clawed. I use a formal, cold tone. I control the silences, letting them go on as long as he does. I put down slow, deliberate pauses. Brief answers between his questions.

Anyway, he says at last, the main reason I'm calling – I feel myself speed up again, slow slow – they found your book and stuff. I gave them your number when they called mine, but they said you never answered.

I'm silent for a long time.

The baggage people, he prompts. The company I found online.

Still I say nothing. I have stolen his silence.

Well, I thought you'd be pleased. When they called me again I just paid the fee and confirmed my address, so I've got it. The package arrived yesterday.

I move toward the sink, wanting background noise so it will sound as if I'm busy. I boil the kettle while he continues talking, unceasing now, about logistics – ways he could now get the package to me if I tell him where I am. My hands tremble slightly. Once the kettle has boiled I pour the water away down the drain, producing a cloud of steam.

A tiny screech and smudge of brown in the corner of my vision alerts me to my victim. The mouse has some-how found its way into the sink and is now making small cries. It seems to have lost a foot thanks to the action of my kettle, dragging itself in frenzied circles.

You need to put it out of its misery, he says when I tell him. Show no mercy. Do you have a hammer or anything? Something very heavy?

I go out into the garden to fetch a brick from by the chicken coop and Luke talks me through what I need to do. I say I'm worried I'll damage the sink and he says I will have to take the risk or it's inhumane. An amputated mouse will not survive in the wild. I don't tell him that she lived with us.

We are poised to do it, me trying to control the tremor in my hand, Luke coaxing me, but when I bring the brick down, his gentle encouragement in my ear, I feel faint. His tenderness makes me hesitate at the last moment, so that instead of dashing the mouse's brains out before it can feel more pain, I torture her with a slow, medieval death, slowly pressing into the softness of her body until there's a snap and then a crunch, like a plastic cup under a wheel.

I have tried to go back and explain who I was in those last moments, and what I return to is the mouse, the brick and that sound.

I try to explain that I felt my own power, godlike, and as I did, the way I saw things changed. I look at the head of a small dog now, and know that I could crush it. My chest felt cold but no longer tight as if something had unzipped it.

I gave Luke my new address and said that he could either post it or, if getting to the post office was too much trouble, drive it round to me that night.

Stay there, he said, as I knew he would, I'll come to you. Forty minutes. Forty-five.

Darkness presses in at the windows. Mira's still not back. I take my washbag to the bathroom and place it on the swirling linoleum before taking out a razor and tweezers. I stand before the mirror, serene and just visibly pregnant. I think of internal rupturing. The idea makes me giddy. I run the hot tap and hold the razor to my arm. Pause. If I start at my knuckles, why not drag the blade over every inch of me? I replace the razor and put my hand against my swollen stomach.

I notice a hangnail and as I pull, skin comes with it. At the sight of the pinkness, my mouth begins to water. I must be craving iron. The finger pulses and yes – I am craving meat.

Mira has a whole chorizo in the fridge. I take it, crouching on my haunches.

I can see the man at his window again, watching me eat, stark naked. I slide the mouse into the bin, still warm like a discarded teabag.

There is the swaying noise of a car alarm outside. Either it has just started or I have only just noticed it. Louder then quieter in waves but never ceasing. I try to decide whether it is really outside my head or only inside. It sounds almost like cicadas.

I start rifling for the box I know has souvenirs. All the mementos I kept from the early days. Venetian saints. I find the programme for the Olympics opening ceremony, *Isles of Wonder*, the intro by Danny Boyle.

I lie in wait with the brick beside the bed, imagining the scene, the road locked down, trembling cordons and blue lights glimmering. I take a picture, turning my phone's camera, staring directly into the eye of its black lens.

When Luke arrives at the front door I wait to buzz him in, then lope a few more times around the room to let off steam. I visualise smoothing fresh tarmac over everything, filling every crack, every flaw I have been picking at obsessively for years. The way is clear and new again.

I smell him in the hall before I see him.

The nowness of him in fisheye, the specificity, caught in my throat. This time I did not see a stranger. I saw exactly who he was. When he entered everything about him seemed enlarged. Certain. He gleamed and bulged. His pores, the shine of his teeth, the flakes inside his ears all magnified. He told me that I looked different though, his eyes sliding over my new frame as if afraid.

He is careful not to come too near. I'm a floating terror to him now. Shyly, he puts down the package and picks up the brick, inspects it with a frown, then wraps it in kitchen roll. Then, as if we haven't just spoken on the phone, he repeats most of what he's already said to me. I tell him I've started running. I've been learning how to drive.

It is inspired, what happens next.

Do you want to see me driving?

He is eyeing the bed in the centre of the room. When's Mira coming back?

Too soon. Let's go for a drive.

Anya wouldn't use that tone. He looks at me but I am deadly serious.

Aren't you going to open it? He nudges the package toward me.

I shake my head as if there's something I need more urgently and he takes my hand, kneading my fingers.

I guess you can drive me down your road, I'd like that. Then would you come back with me?

As the car slides forward, I feel everything go quiet. The past disappears and so does the future. I have only the present tense. My ears grow alert, my sense of smell so keen I can hold and separate every element inside the car. The leather seats, his sweat, his hair. The silence was like music. I keep my eyes on the road, moving very slowly in the direction of the station.

The car is automatic. Driving is easier than I expected.

I've had dreams in which I was put in charge of a car without knowing how to drive it, and those were horrifying and exhausting, but this! It feels like when I first broke into a run. I'll have to rethink what I'm capable of. What other things might come naturally to me.

I turn to him then again and, as when he'd come through the doorway, it is as if I am seeing him for the first time clearly, except that it feels final now, and when I turn back to the road what I see feels as good as an end.

The road stretches on and on. The buildings either side a blur like the edge of a black hole. No place to turn. Level and straight and stretching resolutely nowhere. I put my hand behind my passenger's head, warm, feeling the weight of his skull. I should have liked to have kept it.

I press my foot down on the accelerator. I do not see the curb. For a long time it is as if we have lifted off the road and are flying. My passenger, now my captive, holds on to the door. Shouting. Let me out, he repeats, let me out! As if I've lost control instead of taken it. Stop the car. Anya, fucking hell! Please, I beg you, stop. The longer I stay silent and the car careers on, the more it seems I can do this, just as he said. Faintly I hear him now. I press my foot down harder.

ACKNOWLEDGEMENTS

This book is dedicated to my grandparents and dispersed Balkan family past and present – from Montenegro to Mexico, Serbia to Scotland, Arizona to Acton. I made a tentative start on AR at the end of 2015, so it exists thanks to many people, conversations and acts of kindness over five years in which the world has changed significantly. It is a work of fiction, but one which draws on a sensitive history and painful reality for many. I'm indebted to the people I met in Bosnia, particularly Jasminko Halilović and the work of the War Childhood Museum. I'm also grateful for conversations with Vesna Petković, Ana Baric, Tamara Platiša, Svetlana Rakočević, Vesna Goldsworthy, Ana Russell-Omaljev, Maria Ratković Vidaković and Vladimir Unkovski-Korica, as well as the audiences at the Southeast European Future Festival and Serbian Literary Festival in London. I count my lucky stars for Emma Paterson and Angelique Tran Van Sang – thank you both for your transformative help. Thank you also to Saba Ahmed for her invaluable copyedit, Greg Heinimann for the cover, Lauren Whybrow for prising it out of my hands, and everyone at Bloomsbury and Aitken Alexander. In Brussels, thanks to Piet Joostens and Passa Porta who gave me the time, space and stipend to begin writing in earnest. Thanks to Thea Seger who read the first pages and alleviated second novel syndrome enough to keep going. Thanks to the supportive community of writers, readers and booksellers I've met online, I won't list you but I'm glad *Sympathy* did not deter you from making contact with an author via Instagram. Thank you to my friends and apologies for any fictionalised anecdotes you may find, also to my cousin who has the kilt/spliff tattoo. Thank you to my parents, uncle Branislav, and ONS, again.

A NOTE ON THE AUTHOR

Olivia Sudjic is a writer living in London. She is the author of *Sympathy*, her 2017 debut novel which was a finalist for the Salerno European Book Award and the Collyer Bristow Prize, and *Exposure*, a non-fiction work on anxiety named an *Irish Times*, *Evening Standard* and *White Review* Book of the Year for 2018. Her writing has appeared in publications including the *New York Times*, *Paris Review*, *Financial Times*, *Guardian*, *Vogue* and *Wired*.

A NOTE ON THE TYPE

The text of this book is set in Perpetua. This typeface is an adaptation of a style of letter that had been popularised for monumental work in stone by Eric Gill. Large scale drawings by Gill were given to Charles Malin, a Parisian punch-cutter, and his hand-cut punches were the basis for the font issued by Monotype. First used in a private translation called 'The Passion of Perpetua and Felicity', the italic was originally called Felicity.

SPECTRUMS

Our Mind-boggling Universe from Infinitesimal to Infinity

David Blatner

WALKER & COMPANY

New York

3 1571 00308 4400

Images on pages 36, 37, 43, 89, 119, and 147 courtesy of NASA and the NASA Earth Observatory; page 6, snowflake courtesy Kenneth G. Libbrecht, Caltech; page 13, coins by Proskurina Yuliya, Fotolia.com

Published by Walker Publishing Company, Inc., New York
A Division of Bloomsbury Publishing

LIBRARY OF CONGRESS CATALOGING-IN-PUBLICATION DATA

Blatner, David.
Spectrums: our mind-boggling universe from infinitesimal to infinity / David Blatner.
p. cm.
ISBN 978-0-8027-1770-2 (hardback)
1. Spectrum analysis. I. Title.
QC451.B53 2012
539.2—dc23
2012010727

Visit Walker & Company's website at www.walkerbooks.com

1 3 5 7 9 10 8 6 4 2

Designed by Scott Citron
www.scottcitrondesign.com

Printed in the U.S.A. by Quad/Graphics, Fairfield, Pennsylvania

SPECTRUMS

To Gabriel and Daniel,
who help me keep everything in perspective

Contents

Shades of Anger

Limpid
Quiescent
Tranquil
Phlegmatic
Composed
Mellow
Alert
Anxious
Fretful
Huffy
Grouchy
Cranky
Snappish
Stewed
Peevish
Chafed
Roiled
Mad
Indignant
Boiling
Irate
Enraged
Rabid
Possessed
Wrathful
Apoplectic
Nuclear

INTRODUCTION

**Science and art share a common mandate—
to find surprise in the ordinary by seeing it from
an unexpected point of view.**

—Howard Bloom

MY MOTHER MEANT WELL. "NEVER COMPARE YOURSELF TO others," she taught me. "It'll do nothing but bring you misery." I see her point, but comparing ourselves—whether to other people or to other things—is what we humans do. We compare; we contrast. We sift and segregate, then order, analyzing similarities and discovering differences. That's why we have eyes, ears, taste buds, nerve cells, brains: to compare ourselves with things larger or smaller, faster or slower, hotter or cooler. Through comparisons we create our understanding of the incredibly complex world around us, we realize aesthetic beauty, and we structure our societies.

When you compare two things, you create a duality: this or that, zero or one, black or white. But compare four, or eight, or sixteen things, and you begin to find spectrums—ranges, or continuums *from* this *to* that, a bit darker or lighter, a tad louder or more quiet. The more careful your observation, and the more sensitive your tools of measurement, the better you can gauge—and engage with— your environment.

I attempt, in this book, to provide a sense of scale across six spectrums with which we interact every day: numbers, size, light, sound, heat, and time. Certainly, there are many more spectrums we could explore—density, weight, chemical concentration (which we can sense through smell and taste), and so on—but these six are

> "My religion consists of a humble admiration of the illimitable superior spirit who reveals himself in the slight details we are able to perceive with our frail and feeble mind."
>
> —Albert Einstein, physicist

among the best understood in science and, themselves, represent a good spectrum of our everyday experience. True, in the process of discovery, we'll find that we must compare ourselves with others, but rather than misery, I believe we'll find awe, astonishment, and a sense of humility.

Human Scale In his classic novel *The Hitchhiker's Guide to the Galaxy*, Douglas Adams tells the tale of a massive fleet of alien spacecraft that attack Earth, only to discover that they have made a critical error in scale just before landing in a park and being eaten by a small dog. While none of us (I hope) is planning an interplanetary invasion, the lesson remains valid: It's crucial that we constantly evaluate our own perspectives and assumptions as we interact with the world.

Unfortunately, we tend to base our sense of reality on our own human scale and ignore the invisible and often surprisingly nonintuitive worlds beyond. As the biologist Richard Dawkins notes, "Our brains have evolved to help us survive within the orders of magnitude of size and speed which our bodies operate at." We're comfortable within these realms, which Dawkins calls the "middle world . . . the narrow range of reality which we judge to be normal, as opposed to the queerness of the very small, the very large and the very fast." The middle world encompasses distances easily walked, times and durations within our average life span, and temperatures more or less within the range we experience here on Earth, from ice to inferno.

No doubt it's crucial to consider these human scales in the fields of architecture, ergonomic design, retail, and entertainment. But for millennia, we've intuited that there is something more, beyond our senses, both greater and deeper. The idea that we live in a somewhat muted "middle world" inspired both shamanic traditions and many of our greatest myths. The ancient Greeks and Hindus described us as sandwiched by worlds above and below, which are populated by gods and demons. The Christian and Nordic theologies told of realms

I use the plural *spectrums* instead of *spectra* for a reason: While both are correct, the latter has unfortunately gained the supernatural connotation of ghosts and spirits. Although *spectrum*, *spectra*, *spectral*, and *specter* all derive from the Latin word for "vision," we often apply them to phenomena that have nothing to do with what we can see. This is similar to how, over the last century, a number of words with roots in science—such as *dimension*, *evolution*, and even *energy*—have expanded their meanings far beyond their original intention. Today, the word *spectrum* indicates virtually any broad range of characteristics or ideas.

to which we middle-worlders aspire (or fear), just beyond our mortal veil—worlds higher and lower, transcendent and immanent.

And true enough, as we look through microscopes, we find worlds within worlds, realms that explain our everyday rules of physics and biology, but in which, amazingly, those same rules don't always apply. As we peer through telescopes—not just at visible light, but also at the invisible wash of X-rays, gamma rays, and microwaves that we can detect—we discover a universe grander, and weirder, than anything we had imagined.

Science has led us to realize that there is far more outside our human scale than within it, and there is actually very little in this universe that we can feel, touch, see, hear, or possibly even comprehend. The vast range of phenomena around us boggles the mind. It's not an easy task to stretch our imagination to encompass both billions of years and billionths of seconds, or trillions of atoms and trillionths of a meter. And yet, we must explore all these spectrums to gain perspective on our place in the universe.

Spectrums, Everywhere Spectrums—not just the physical spectrums discussed in the chapters that follow but also the very concept of spectrums in general—are useful for far more than just analyzing the world in which we live. Spectrums allow us to communicate our insights and desires, no matter how mundane, with others.

If you're trying to describe a color to a graphic designer, for example, you might explain, "yellow, a bright sunshiny yellow like a pound of butter." In that one phrase you invoke two spectrums: hue and brightness (or, technically, frequency and amplitude). Each spectrum is like a model, or a map, that reflects a dimension of the world around us or within us. So if you hear a specific note played on a piano or violin, you can probably imagine another tone a little higher or lower. Sip your coffee and you viscerally know it would taste better if it were warmer. These daily comparisons may seem minor, but the fact that we can build internal maps like this, often

> "My task is to convince you not to turn away because it appears incomprehensible . . . You see, my physics students don't understand it . . . because the professor doesn't understand it. Nobody does. The thing that is exciting about this is that nature is as strange as can be! The rules of nature are so screwy you can't believe them . . . I don't understand it either! But the fun of it is that it's so mysterious!"
>
> —Richard Feynman, Nobel Prize–winning physicist

extrapolating beyond the ranges of our own personal experience, is an amazing example of what the human mind can do.

Of course, even tiny bacteria show their preferences, or fundamental tendencies, based on simple comparisons between more or less acidic environments. But as life becomes more complex, the more you can name spectrums, or categories, and the more you can name differences in those spectrums, the more you can comprehend, communicate, and thrive. After all, would you rather draw with a box of eight crayons or the jumbo 64-pack?

These spectrums can describe far more than physical measurement; we can use them to describe personal values and aesthetics, too. Any psychologist will tell you that if you're trying to explain how angry you are, it's more helpful to say "I'm about an eight on a scale of one to ten" than to insist on the binary "I'm angry" or "I'm not." The same rule applies, of course, to sports competitions such as Olympic ice dancing, where judges rate technical ability and style against an agreed-upon spectrum—everyone has an intuitive understanding of the difference between a 7.4 and a 7.8; one is just *that much* better.

Granted, not everything fits on a spectrum. In music, you can place rhythm on a spectrum, but not the timbre of individual instruments. Timbre—that extraordinary combination of overtones and harmonics that allows us to tell the difference between an oboe and a violin, even when they play the same note—is a quality, a texture, a shape in and of itself. A circle cannot be more or less circular; a Picasso cannot be more or less Picasso-ish. A sequence is similarly not a spectrum; sure, you can inscribe the life cycle of a butterfly along a line, and you can attempt to identify a caterpillar you've found against that ruler, but there isn't a single parameter, or dimension, you can look at, so there's no "spectrum of butterflyness."

Our richest experiences derive from the collisions of two or more spectrums. Music, for example, is an astonishingly complex

"We don't see things as they are, we see them as we are."

—Anaïs Nin

interaction among frequency (tone), amplitude (loudness), timing (rhythm), and more. But music itself is not a spectrum.

On the other hand, many ranges that certainly are spectrums are either completely subjective or extremely difficult to measure. Take humor. There's no doubt that one joke is funnier to you than another, but a joke that makes you snort milk out your nose is certain not to be funny to someone else; you might not even find it funny yourself in the presence of your children or a parent. Psychiatrists measure autism along a spectrum, and philosophers measure a spectrum of consciousness, but these are prone to debate (is a dolphin more conscious than a horse?) and require constant reevaluation.

Ultimately, although spectrums are important, they're no more "true" than any map or model, and it's easy to become fooled by looking at the map incorrectly, or through the lens of our own limited understanding. The sun and the moon appear about the same size in the sky, even though one has a diameter 400 times larger than the other. Similarly, it takes just a minuscule concentration of ammonia in the air for you to gasp in shock, while many other compounds hardly register to your nose, no matter how much you sniff. Clearly, when discussing spectrums, we must stand back and look at not just our experience but also how we measure and interpret what we sense.

Infinite Sensitivity We've come a long way in a short time. Just two centuries ago, we didn't realize that electricity had something to do with magnetism, and only a century ago we weren't sure if other galaxies existed beyond our own. But throughout the twentieth century, each decade saw breakthroughs beyond the previously assumed limit of one spectrum or another—radically expanding the age of the universe and the number of galaxies, measuring the size of an atom, smashing the sound barrier, or quantifying the unfathomable energy from an exploding star. Now, in the twenty-first century, we continue to make progress in leaps and bounds,

> **"Have you ever noticed that anybody driving slower than you is an idiot, and anyone going faster than you is a maniac?"**
> —George Carlin

but rather than pushing the outside limits of a spectrum, the breakthroughs tend to be increased sensitivity, finding exponentially smaller differences in measurements.

But how much is enough? Surely a millionth of a second makes no difference when playing soccer, nor an error of a billion years when discussing how much longer Earth will be habitable. It's obvious, but is worth stating anyway: There are optimal Goldilocks ranges when discussing any spectrum—both in range and sensitivity between values—based on who is talking, and about what.

Watch a professional musician fiddle with an instrument, and you'll be amazed at the small nuances in pitch or tone that she hears and that you simply don't. To you, such subtle distinctions don't matter, but the musician's more sensitive ear enables her to create a richer and more pleasing soundscape.

In fact, almost any expertise involves a deepening sensitivity to one or more spectrums. A typographer looks at a news headline and just feels that it would be more balanced if two letters were a tenth of a millimeter closer to each other. A photographer can see when

▲ Consider a single snowflake out of billions, just 3 mm from tip to tip.

a color print needs 1 percent more magenta. A perfumer knows when a fragrance should shift from citrus to dry woods, or toward greener notes.

As astonishing as this degree of awareness can seem, almost anyone can learn these skills. In fact, researchers have shown that people can even learn how to sniff out a scent trail almost as well as dogs. (Hint: Smelly molecules are heavier than air, so you need to get your nose to the ground to detect them.) The key to developing any of these abilities is simply feeling strong enough about it to try. The same is true in science: The intricate biological mechanisms that take place inside a cell's mitochondrion may be mind-blowing to one biologist and inconsequential to another who is focused on transcontinental ecosystems.

As the English anthropologist Gregory Bateson wrote, "Information is a difference that makes a difference." In order to increase our sensitivity, our abilities, we need first to wake up to the fact that there are differences. This is trickier than it seems; I met a man who told me that after ten years in the printing industry he had only recently noticed that there's a difference between the Times and Helvetica fonts—it had simply not been relevant to his work before. But when he was asked to create a flyer for a customer, what an incredible range of typeface design suddenly began to open to him!

You may even be married to someone who perceives differences that you don't, as she explains her discomfort over how a mutual friend is acting in a social situation, or how fast you're driving. It's tempting to grumble about being "too sensitive," but what if the truth is simply that you lack her awareness of differences in detail on that particular spectrum?

When the Hubble Space Telescope began sending images back to Earth, astronomers were stunned by not only the clarity but also the previously unknown range of the universe. What was a blurry blob in the dark sky suddenly became a crisp set of multiple galaxies, and both our understanding and our expectations grew. We believe that there is even more now—more out there, and more inside,

> **"When you are put into the Vortex you are given just one momentary glimpse of the entire unimaginable infinity of creation, and somewhere in it a tiny little marker, a microscopic dot on a microscopic dot, which says, 'You are here.' . . . In an infinite universe, the one thing sentient life cannot afford to have is a sense of proportion."**
>
> —Douglas Adams,
> *The Hitchhiker's Guide to the Galaxy*

too, in the realms of the subatomic, the superfast, or even the most mysterious dimension of all: the mind. What if we could develop a telescope in space with a thousand times the sensitivity of Hubble? Or an instrument a trillion times more sensitive than our most advanced microscope? The interfaith campaigner Wayne Teasdale describes God as "infinite sensitivity." Surely, whatever your sense of faith or science, it's a dream to aim for.

Paths to Wonderment Before we launch into our exploration, I have to warn you: Each of these spectrums ranges from interesting to awe-inspiring to truly vertigo-inducing. It's hard to imagine how amazingly small and seemingly insignificant we are in the universe. It's also hard to imagine how amazingly huge and overwhelmingly significant we are in the universe.

Clearly, you need your feet on the ground if you're going to reach for the stars. But where do we find a firm foundation on which to stand? It's a tricky question because—and I know it's not a particularly polite thing for an author to say at the beginning of a book—you really have no idea what's going on. I don't intend any disrespect to you, the reader; it's simply that none of us does. Here's the problem: In our hubris, we humans want to know, we think we *can* know, the whole of the universe. But we can't.

For example, it's obvious that objects have mass, heft, weight, but we don't really know why. Yes, gravity of course, but we don't know why gravity works! It's a mystery. Why does time appear to move forward rather than backward? Is it true that a hundred billion billion times smaller than the proton inside an atom there are just wiggly little strings of energy? We don't know, and it's increasingly clear that we may never know.

We may be like the old story of the blind men and the elephant, where each blind man describes a different aspect of the elephant— the tail, the trunk, the feet—but none of them can understand the whole. As thoroughly as we search the universe for answers, as finely

> "Now my own suspicion is that the Universe is not only queerer than we suppose, but queerer than we *can* suppose."
>
> —J. B. S. Haldane, 20th-century evolutionary biologist

as we tune our instruments, we may be equipped to see only a few parts of the "whole beast."

The result is that as we stretch toward the extremes searching for answers, we find little but more questions, and our most advanced science begins to read like a tract on philosophy or a science-fiction novel. Is there really such a thing as three-dimensional space, as we've all been brought up to believe, or are time and distance a façade, like a hologram that cleverly disguises a far stranger set of realities? It's possible that the Hindus and Buddhists have been right all along, and our universe is all *maya*, or illusion; or that Plato's allegory of the cave in which we see only shadows cast on a wall truly reflects the limits of our senses, and perhaps even our ability to comprehend what we sense.

Nevertheless, just because we can't know it all doesn't mean we can't keep trying and—along the way—enjoy the sense of wonder, awe, delight, and recognition that we are each an integral part of this spectrum of mystery. If we retain a sense of curiosity, and "become like little children" without fear of exploration or shame that we don't yet have the answers, we are bound to learn more, discover more, and slowly develop our abilities over time—exploring the range and depth of our spectrums, opening to their possibilities.

> **"Man is equally incapable of seeing the nothingness from which he emerges and the infinity in which he is engulfed."**
>
> Blaise Pascal, 17th-century mathematician

NUMBERS

None of us really understands what's going on with all these numbers.

—David Stockman, budget director in the Reagan administration

WE ALL LIKE TO THINK WE HAVE SOME SENSE FOR NUMBERS.
You may not have enjoyed math in school, but chances are you can peruse your bank statement, squint at a thermometer reading, or count the weeks until Christmas.

We humans are good at these kinds of small numbers. But as keen and insightful as we consider ourselves, as able at digit juggling and mathematical maneuvers as we may be, we are still constrained by our own human limitations: Big numbers (and very tiny ones) are our weakness.

Nevertheless, we are subjected daily to these outliers, especially when exploring the sorts of spectrums discussed in the rest of this book. Even if we can't truly understand the biggest and smallest values, we can at least gain a better intuitive grasp of them.

However, it's no use starting up in the stratosphere, with billions or trillions. We must, instead, start small.

Imagine one: one button, or one person, or one of anything that comes to mind. It's easy to imagine one, or three, or even as many as seven. When imagining a small number of objects, you're likely to see or experience the group as a pattern—perhaps a triangle, a pentagon, or a cross. The technical term is *subitize*: You know the number, you feel it, even without counting.

Beyond six or seven, however, you need to count, or to group small, basic patterns into collections. For example, to conceive "ten,"

you might see two groups of five; to think about "fifty," you might lay out five of those groups of ten.

But unfortunately, it doesn't take a number much larger than that before our human minds get blurry and imprecise. We begin to approximate values, or compare them to a known quantity. For example, asked to consider one thousand, you might picture the seats in a midsized auditorium.

But that's very different from the way you grasped "three." Three is concrete, innate, elemental. Three is an easy pattern, and if there is one thing humans are good at, it's recognizing patterns. Studies show that even human babies on their first day of life are capable of understanding small abstract numbers, correctly matching a pattern of repetitive audio signals to visual stimuli. Australian Aboriginal children who speak Warlpiri (which contains the number words for only *one*, *two*, *few*, and *many*) can similarly distinctly identify groups of five or six—they intuitively understand the patterns even without language for them.

The Meaning Behind the Symbols This method of grouping objects into patterns extends to the sometimes odd symbols and conventions that mathematicians have come up with over the years. For example, multiplication is, at its heart, a way to define a pattern. So 5×3 means *add* three groups of five ($5 + 5 + 5$). That is, multiplication is a way of defining a pattern of adding.

Now, how do you define a pattern of multiplying? The answer is the notion of an exponent—a fancy way of saying, "multiply it *this* many times." For example, 5^3 (which you may see as 5^3) means multiply 5 by itself three times: $5 \times 5 \times 5$.

It sounds complex, but you work with exponents every day without thinking about it. Everyone knows that ten pennies are a dime, ten dimes are a dollar, ten dollars are . . . well, ten dollars. You get the idea. That's exponents—take the whole group and multiply it by the same number. So 10^1 is just 10, 10^2 equals 100, 10^3 is 1,000, and so on. Our basic systems of math and finances are all based on

There are more insects in a single square mile of good, fertile soil than there are human beings on Earth.

Using exponents makes math with huge numbers easy, because you can add and subtract instead of multiply and divide. For example, a million (10^6) times a trillion (10^9) equals 10^{15} (because 6 + 9 = 15). Conversely, a trillion divided by a million equals a thousand (10^3, because 9 − 6 = 3).

exponents—in this case, exponents of the number 10. These are easy to handle because the exponent simply describes the number of zeros after the 1: Ten (10^1) has a 1 followed by one zero, a hundred (10^2) has two zeros, a thousand (10^3) has three zeros, and so on.

We can do this with pictures, too: Imagine five pennies in a row, then repeat that row five times. That's 5^2, or 5×5, or 25 pennies. Now repeat *that* grid 5 times—for example, you might stack four more pennies on top of each one on the first layer, making a "cube" 5 long, 5 wide, and 5 tall—a total of 5^3 or 125 pennies.

This method of writing numbers is key to understanding what's called scientific notation, such as 4.5×10^9. Once you understand that 10^9 is a billion—a 1 with nine zeros, or 1,000,000,000—then you understand the notation to mean "4.5 billion."

> **"Learning to compare is learning to count."**
> —Edward Kasner and James Newman, *Mathematics and the Imagination*

Even in math there are controversies and disagreements. One such is over the naming of numbers such as 10^9. In North America, we use the "short scale" nomenclature, in which 9 zeros equal a "billion." Residents of many other countries rely on the "long scale," referring to this as a "milliard" or "a thousand million." What Americans call a trillion they then refer to as a billion. Fortunately, after several hundred years of confusion, the long scale has been dwindling in usage worldwide since the 1970s. This is for the best, as otherwise scientific papers on pathologies in duck populations might have to discuss "a milliard mallard maladies." In this book, we'll use only the short scale.

▲ 5^2 pennies (top) versus 5^3 pennies (5 x 5 x 5)

How Big Is Big? The tricky (and powerful) thing about exponential numbers is that very small changes in exponents can reflect really huge changes in the value. For example, the difference between 10^2 (100) and 10^3 (1,000) is 900, but the difference between 10^3 and 10^4 is 9,000! Increasing the exponent by just 1 reflects the difference between the length of the state of California (about 770 miles) and the diameter of Earth (about 7,900 miles). Add 1 more to the exponent (10^5) and you're a third of the way (about 79,000 miles) to the moon.

The difference is even greater when you talk about things like volume. For example, let's say you have a "cube" 100 pennies wide by 100 pennies deep by 100 pennies tall, in other words, 10^2 on each side. That's a total of one *million* pennies, or $10,000. Increase the value of the exponent to just 10^3 pennies per side, and the total number of pennies goes up by 999 million, to a *billion* pennies, or $10 million.

This kind of overwhelming "exponential growth" can lead to startling outcomes. There's an old story of a craftsman who presents a king with an exquisite chessboard and asks, in return, for a single grain of rice on the first square, two grains on the second, four on the third, eight on the fourth, and so on, for all 64 squares. It seems like a reasonable request, so the king quickly agrees.

Unfortunately, the king does not understand the power of exponents. Doubling is a way of saying "2 to the n" or 2^n. So the second square requires 2^1 grains of rice, the third has 2^2 (just 4) grains, and the eighth square at the end of the first row requires only 2^7 grains of rice—a meager 128 grains. But keep going . . . the twenty-first square would need to hold over a million grains, and the forty-first square would hold over a trillion. When you finish the math, you find a total of $2^{64} - 1$ grains of rice. (You have to subtract 1 because you're starting with only one grain, technically 2^0, on the first square.) That's 18,446,744,073,709,551,615 (1.84×10^{19}) grains—enough to fill a box 4 miles long, 4 miles wide, and 6 miles high—taller than Mt. Everest.

Of course, the story goes on to explain that the king, while not wise in numbers, is the perfect politician: He proclaims that in order for the craftsman to receive his payment, he needs to count each and every grain given to him. If the man counted one each second, it would take over half a trillion years—about 42 times the age of our universe—to count the grains!

The story explains beautifully the idea of just how huge numbers can become when working with exponents, and why the phrase "the second half of the chessboard" is sometimes used to describe a situation that has grown far out of control.

Number Numbness Unfortunately, somewhere in the first third of the chessboard the human brain develops what the cognitive scientist Douglas R. Hofstadter calls "number numbness." After all, we can see a thousand objects, so we have a sense—albeit an imprecise

Computer scientists often refer to the speed of a computer in "flops"—floating point operations per second. While most computers today can process megaflops or gigaflops (millions or billions of operations), the fastest computers are just this year breaking the petaflop barrier (quadrillions of operations per second—10^{15}).

one—of what that number means. We can even see ten thousand or a hundred thousand things at the same time—visualize a sold-out football game or political rally where you can see nothing but acres of tiny heads.

The upper boundary of our visual perception, however, is between one and ten million—you could print out a large poster with a million dots on it and stand close enough both to see them all and to resolve each one more or less distinctly. The phrase "I'll believe it when I see it," is applicable: As soon as it's no longer possible for us to see these numbers, we tend to lose any sense of meaning for them. So to many people, any *-illion* word is functionally the same, whether it's *million*, *billion*, *trillion*, or *megazillion* (no, that's not actually a number).

The basic incomprehensibility of large numbers wouldn't be such a problem if it weren't for the fact that modern politics and economics (not to mention science and mathematics) require their comprehension. But how can we grasp a billion when it's a thousand times larger than a million, and a trillion is a million million (10^{12})?

Once again, we do better when we use images to grapple with numbers of this magnitude. So imagine a stack of 100 hundred-dollar bills—just $10,000, small enough to fit easily in a jacket pocket. A hundred of those packets—a pile small enough to fit into a small box or a grocery bag—equals $1 million. Add 99 more of these piles and you've got $100 million sitting just over six feet tall on a shipping pallet.

Now to jump to $1 billion, you need ten of those pallets. Is $1 trillion just a little more? No, you'd need a *thousand* more groups of these 10 pallets to reach $1 trillion.

This unbelievable, mind-stretching number is big. Really big. As one blogger put it, "Your brain can't handle its biggitude." Now double it—match each and every one of the trillion pieces of paper with another—and you get only 2 trillion. You don't add a zero to the number—increasing from 10^{12} to 10^{13}—until you reach 10 trillion. This seems eye-rollingly obvious, but the implications are huge: Each

"Not everything that counts can be counted, and not everything that can be counted counts."
—Albert Einstein

Each cell in the human body contains more atoms than there are stars in the Milky Way galaxy.

$100

$10,000

$1,000,000 ($1 million)

$1,000,000,000 ($1 billion)

$1,000,000,000,000 ($1 trillion)

additional zero means duplicate the previous already-inconceivable group 10 times; each additional "illion" means multiply 1,000 times.

There are myriad examples of how much surprisingly larger these numbers are than each other. For example, take the subject of length: You could stroll a million millimeters in less than an hour, but it takes 10 hours to drive a billion millimeters. A trillion millimeters? That's 25 times around Earth.

Or time: A million seconds is about a week and a half. A billion seconds is 30 years, which is a long time until you notice that Neanderthals were walking around a trillion seconds ago (30,000 years).

Or let's look at dollars again (it always seems to come back to money, doesn't it?). A well-paid professional with $100,000 in the bank can feel confident but may aspire to $1 million. Okay, now create a bar graph where 1 inch = $1 million, and the professional can see that her tenth-of-an-inch bar is paltry against the millionaire's. But now compare the millionaire to Warren Buffett's $65 billion: At this scale, Warren's lot would require a graph more than 1 mile (1.6 km) tall!

Looking at these numbers, you can start to get a sense of how minuscule is a million.

Heading farther into the unfathomable, consider that our own Milky Way galaxy holds about 200 billion (2×10^{11}) stars, and according to observations from the Hubble Space Telescope, we know there are almost 150 billion galaxies in the entire universe. That's an extraordinarily large number, but compare it with something ordinary sitting on your own desk: You can store a trillion bits of information on a common computer hard drive—so if each galaxy were represented by a zero or a one, you could store six universes. And even that number pales compared with the approximately 100 trillion (10^{14}) cells you have in your body.

From time immemorial, humans have been asking which is greater, the biblical "grains of sands of the earth" or the number of stars in the sky. Obviously, neither number is countable, but

Prefix	Abbreviation for Meters	Size	Name
yotta-	Ym	10^{24}	septillions, from the Greek *okto* ("eight," as this is the eighth group of thousands—that is, $1,000^8$)
zetta-	Zm	10^{21}	sextillions, from the French *sept* ("seven")
exa-	Em	10^{18}	quintillions, from the Greek *hex* ("six")
peta-	Pm	10^{15}	quadrillions, from the Greek *pente* ("five")
tera-	Tm	10^{12}	trillions, from the Greek *teras* ("monster")
giga-	Gm	10^{9}	billions, from the Greek *giga* ("giant")
mega-	Mm	10^{6}	millions, from the Greek word for "great" (Alexander the Great was *Megas Alexandros*)
kilo-	km	10^{3}	thousands, from the Greek *khiloi* ("thousand"); 1 mile equals 1.6 km
hecto-	hm	10^{2}	hundreds, from the Greek *hekaton* ("hundred")
deca-	dam	10^{1}	tens, from the Greek *deka* ("ten")
deci-	dm	10^{-1}	tenths, from the Latin *decimus* ("tenth")
centi-	cm	10^{-2}	hundredths, from the Latin *centum* ("hundred")
milli-	mm	10^{-3}	thousandths, from the Latin *mille* ("thousand"); 1 inch is about 25½ mm
micro-	µm	10^{-6}	millionths, from the Greek *mikros* ("small"); sometimes called microns
nano-	nm	10^{-9}	billionths, from the Latin *nanus* ("dwarf")
pico-	pm	10^{-12}	trillionths, from the Celtic *beccus* ("beak" or "sharp point")
femto-	fm	10^{-15}	quadrillionths, from the Danish *femten* ("fifteen")
atto-	am	10^{-18}	quintillionths, from the Danish *atten* ("eighteen"); note that an attometer is 1,000 zeptometers and a thousandth of a femtometer
zepto-	zm	10^{-21}	sextillionths, from the Latin *septem* ("seven," as this is the seventh group of thousandths—that is, $1,000^{-7}$)
yocto-	ym	10^{-24}	septillionths, from the Greek *octo* ("eight")

University of Hawaii researchers (who should know) estimate Earth has about 7.5 billion billion (7.5 × 10^{18}) grains of sand. And even though we can see no more than a few thousand stars with the unaided eye, astronomers currently think there are about 16 sextillion stars throughout the known universe (give or take a few)—that's 16 × 10^{21}. That's an unbelievably large number, but it turns out to be about how many molecules you'd find in just ten drops of water.

Yes, molecules really are that small, and of course atoms are even smaller. In only 12 grams (just under half an ounce) of pure carbon 12 there are 6.02 × 10^{23} atoms. That seemingly arbitrary number happens to be so central to the study of chemistry that it has its own name: Avogadro's constant. This value defines the size of a "mole"—that is, 1 mole of any substance contains exactly that many molecules. Armed with this knowledge, you can glance at a table of chemical weights and find that a single grain of sugar contains a trillion (10^{12}) molecules of sucrose. That's insignificant compared with a grain of salt, which contains just over a quintillion (1.03 × 10^{18}) molecules of the very compact sodium chloride.

Chunking The idea that you can take a number like 602,214,179,300,000,000,000,000 and give it a simple name like Avogadro is called chunking, and it's what keeps us sane when dealing with extreme values. We chunk numbers all the time: It's far easier to think in terms of dollars than in hundreds of pennies. Even numbers like "a million" are chunks, but no one wants to think about "two million pennies" when you could say "20,000 dollars"—or, even better, chunk it down to the easier "20 grand." Because we have an intuitive understanding of both "20" and "a grand," we don't have to convert it to smaller units. The chunk is a kind of psychological reality; we know what it is, so we can work with it, mulling the number over and deciding whether the car in the ad is worth that much.

Similarly, we use the term "one hertz" instead of "times per second." Then we add prefixes to make ever-bigger chunks, so

You have about 25 trillion (2.5 x 10^{13}) red blood cells in your body right now.

Three moles of water would fill about a quarter cup. Three moles of M&M candies would fill all the oceans of the world.

kilohertz (kHz) means thousands of times each second, and megahertz (MHz) means millions. (In the example above, it would make far more sense to say "the car costs 2 megacents," but people would look at you funny.)

Astronomers chunk the average distance between Earth and the sun, calling it 1 astronomical unit (1 AU)—easier than writing 150 million kilometers—and they chunk 63,000 AU into a single light-year. You may have no intuitive sense of what a light-year is (the distance light travels through space in one Earth year), but you can certainly understand that an astrophysicist discussing the distance from here to Vega is far happier scribbling 25 ly rather than 147,962,000,000,000 miles or even 2.37×10^{17} meters. Of course, it seems that no matter how large the chunk, the numbers still get out of hand, growing cosmically—one might even say comically—huge. The farthest object ever detected—a gamma ray blast from an exploding star—sits at such a length: some 13,140,000,000 light-years (1.2×10^{26} meters) away.

Beyond the Possible In 1938, the mathematician Edward Kasner asked his nine-year-old nephew Milton to name a number so huge, so out of this world, that it would boggle the mind. The reply was "a googol,"* which he precociously defined as 1 followed by a hundred zeros (10^{100}). Urged toward greater heights, Milton then followed up with the googolplex, which he originally determined would be contrived by writing zeros until your hand got tired but was later standardized as a 1 followed by a googol zeros.

> Googol + 267 is the first prime number over a googol.

These numbers are bigger than anything we've encountered so far. In fact, not only can we not imagine a googol of anything, there isn't even a googol of anything to imagine! A googol is bigger than the number of molecules in every substance on our planet; it's more than all the hydrogen atoms in our sun. Astonishingly, when you

*Note that this number is spelled differently from the trademarked name of a certain Internet search company.

count up *every atom in the known universe*, it still comes to only about 10^{81} particles, a quintillion times less than a googol.

So if numbers like a googol (not to mention the even more insanely enormous googolplex) are beyond any correspondence with physical matter, why even bother with them? Because mathematics demands it. While most students' experience of mathematics stops not far beyond arithmetic, professional mathematicians drive farther and delve far deeper, past the shallow solving of equations, in an attempt to understand the underlying nature of numbers and, indeed, the universe itself. To describe the universe—or one of the many potential multiverses—you must go beyond its boundaries, just as the paper you draw on must be larger than the picture you're drawing.

You can't really avoid "very large numbers" (as they're quaintly described in textbooks) when doing higher math or studying code breaking or cosmology. For example, we earlier looked at the meaning of the simple number 4^4, which equals 256. But what about 4^{4^4}? That seems innocuous enough at first, but the answer is actually more than 154 digits long (it's 1.34×10^{154})! Mathematicians call this tetration—as in "4 tetrated to 3"—or sometimes call it superpower, superdegree, or a term nine-year-old Milton would be proud of: hyper4.

Hyper4 numbers take mathematics to a whole different playing field, one beyond the simple number crunching of electronic computers. Sure, a computer can brute-force analyze all the possible moves in a game of chess (the total number of moves in an entire game is probably on the order of 10^{50}), but in the ancient game of Go—played with simple black and white stones on a 19-by-19 grid—there are more than 10^{150} possible positions.

The patterns of logic and number spiral out ever higher. In 1933, the South African mathematician Stanley Skewes was studying how prime numbers* are distributed across the spectrum of numbers

In Darren Aronofsky's movie π, the protagonist, Max, tells a group of Jewish kabbalists that he knows they have written down every possible 216-digit number. Of course, as a mathematician, Max must know this is impossible. Even a million supercomputers working steadily from the big bang until today couldn't achieve that goal.

---

*A prime number is any number greater than 1 that is evenly divisible by only 1 and itself.

when he published 1.397×10^{316} in his research—a number so large that it was given a name (Skewes' number) and dubbed by the famous mathematician G. H. Hardy as "the largest number which has ever served any definite purpose in mathematics." But the record was not to last, and Skewes' number looks positively quaint compared with today's most advanced math functions, which regularly include numbers such as $10^{10^{600}}$. Very large indeed.

Going Negative It appears to be a universal adage that "as above so below," and this is seen nowhere as clearly as in the world of the number. The inverse of the number 2 is ½—one half of 1. The inverse of 3 is ⅓, smaller than a half. As you raise the number to 4, 5, 10, 100, and greater, its inverse decreases (¹⁄₁₀, ¹⁄₁₀₀, and so on), approaching, yet never reaching, zero. What's smaller than 1/googol? Of course the answer is 1/googolplex!

By the way, you can describe extremely small numbers using much the same notation as very large ones. Where 1×10^3 means "move the decimal point 3 places to the right" (1,000), the notation 1×10^{-3} means move the decimal point 3 places to the left (0.001, or one thousandth, ¹⁄₁,₀₀₀). A millionth is 10^{-6}, a billionth is 10^{-9}, and so on.

But at some point you're bound to hit zero . . . and then what? Just as you cannot count a googol objects, you can't count fewer than zero. The ancient Greeks, who even twenty-five hundred years ago could do far more precise math than you might expect, had a serious weakness: They rejected any numbers that wouldn't fit into their geometries. Can't draw a picture of a number less than zero? Then, in their world, it didn't exist. Granted, it's not an entirely unreasonable assumption: Ask a six-year-old to solve "2 take away 2," and she can tell you; ask her "2 take away 3" and you'll see her little eyebrows screw up in an innocent imitation of Mr. Spock: That does not compute!

However, the Chinese and the Hindus of the pre-Christian era didn't need to represent numbers with pictures or countable objects,

> **"Every time you drink a glass of water, you are probably imbibing at least one atom that passed through the bladder of Aristotle. A tantalisingly surprising result, but it follows [from the] observation that there are many more molecules in a glass of water than there are glasses of water in the sea."**
> —Richard Dawkins

and both came up with a fairly radical idea at the time: the negative number. You can't count it, but you know it's there because it makes sense that it should be. As the great mathematician Carl Friedrich Gauss wrote, "Just as in general arithmetic no one would hesitate to admit fractions, although there are so many countable things where a fraction has no meaning, so we would not deny to negative numbers the rights accorded to positives."

So once again we find pairs of numbers: 15 is matched with –15, 10^{261} (sexoctogintillion) is mirrored by -10^{261}, and so on.

And so on? If you stop and think about it, the phrase "and so on" is just as radical a concept as negative numbers: It connotes forever, eternally, the infinite. Here, once again, we are asked to extrapolate beyond the comfortable countable universe. It is a basic premise of our mathematics that there is such a thing as the infinitely large and the infinitely small. But dealing with infinity—known by many terms, including "aleph null" and "the set of N"—is a slippery business not to be undertaken by the faint of heart.

Remember, infinity is not a destination but rather an idea. There is no point where the very large numbers begin to merge subtly into infinity. The astronomer Carl Sagan wrote, "A googolplex is precisely as far from infinity as is the number 1 . . . No matter what number you have in mind, infinity is larger."

Even doing math with infinity takes on a bizarre fun-house-mirror quality. Infinity plus 1 is infinity. Infinity plus infinity equals infinity. While it appears that the list of odd numbers would be half the size of the list of all the numbers, it is not so—rather, both are (you guessed it) infinite. As Philip Davis and Reuben Hersh wrote in *The Mathematical Experience*:

> The set of N is an inexhaustible jar, a miraculous jar recalling the miracle of the loaves and the fishes in Matthew 15:34.
> This miraculous jar with all its magical properties, properties which appear to go against all the experiences of our finite lives, is an absolutely basic object in mathematics, and thought to be well within

the grasp of children in the elementary schools. Mathematics asks us to believe in this miraculous jar and we shan't get far if we don't . . .

The infinite is that which is without end. It is the eternal, the immortal, the self-renewable, the *apeiron* of the Greeks, the *ein-sof* of the Kabbalah.

You could say that plus and minus infinity define the endpoints of the spectrum of numbers, except that, by their very definition, they cannot be endpoints at all.

Thinking Outside the Box With a number line stretching out toward negative and positive infinity, like a railway traversing eternity, we should be able to pinpoint the answer to any mathematical problem we encounter, right? Amazingly, you don't have to search long before you find an equation for which there is no train station on that line, no place at which you can definitively say, "This is the solution."

Instead, we have to deal with numbers like the irrational—those that can be written as an infinitely long decimal sequence but cannot be described simply by dividing two integers. For example, find a number that you can multiply by itself to result in 2—the square root of 2 (or $\sqrt{2}$). We can estimate it by dividing 90 by 63, or we can write it as 1.4142135 . . . But that "dot dot dot" at the end means we can never isolate its value exactly—the digits simply rattle off, without pattern, forever.

Then there are the transcendental numbers. Originally named when mathematicians thought these values were exceedingly rare, we now know they are as common as dust scattered throughout mathematics. A transcendental number is not only irrational but also nonalgebraic. That is, it cannot be described by a simple, finite algebraic equation. Many irrational numbers are also transcendental, such as the famous constants π and *e.*

However, both irrational and transcendental numbers do live somewhere on the number line, even if we can't put our finger on them precisely. There's another class of number so weird that we have to step off the tracks entirely to grasp it. Let's look at a simple π =

3.141592653589793238462643383279502884197169399375105820974944592307816406286208998628034
8253421170679821480865132823066470938446095505822317253594081284811174502841027019385211
0555964462294895493038196442881097566593344612847564823378678316527120190914564856692346
0348610454326648213393607260249141273724587006606315588174881520920962829254091715364367892590360011330
530548820466521384146951941511609433057270365759591953092186117381932611793105118548074462379962749567
35188575272489122793818301194912983367336244065664308602139494639522473719070217986094370277053921717
6293176752384674818467669405132000568127145263560827785771342757789609173637178721468440901224953430146
5495853710507922796892589235420199561121290219608640344181598136297747713099605187072113499999983729784
049951059731732816096318595024459455346908302642522308253344685035261931188171010003137838752886587533320
8381420617177669147303598253490428755468731159562863882353787593751957781857780532171226806613001927
8766111959092164201989380952572010654858632788659361533818279682303019520353018529689957736225994138912
497217752834791315155748572424541506959508295331168617278558890750983817546374649393192550604009277016
711390098488240128583616035637076601047101819429555961989467678374494482553797747268471040475346462008
04668425906949129331367702898915210475216205696602405803815019351125338243003558764024749647326391419
927260426992279678235478163600934172164121992458631503028618297455570674983850549458858692699569092721
0797509302955321165344987202755960236480665499119881834797753566369807426542527862551818417574672890977
7727938000816470600161452491921732172147723501414419735685481613611573525521334757418494684385233239073
9941433345477624168625189835694855620992192221842725502542568876717904946016534668049886272327917860857
84383827967976681454100953883786360950680064225125205117392984896084128488626945604241965285022210661
1863067442786220391949450471237137869609563643719172874677646575739624138908658326459958133904780279...

e =

2.7182818284590452353602874713526624977572470936999595749669676277240766303535475945713821
7852516642742746639193200305992181741359662904357290033429526059563073813232862794349076323
3829880753195251019011573834187930702154089149934884167509244761460668082264800168477411
18537423454424371075390777449920696551702761838606261331384583000752044933826560297606737113200709328709
1274437470472306969772093101416928368190255151086574637721112523897844250569536967707854499699679468644545
90598793163688923009879312773618152499922957635148220826989519366803318252886939849646510582093
9239829488793320362509443117301238197068416140397019837679320683282376464804295311802328782509819455815301756717361332
0698112509961818815930416903515988885193458072738667385894228792284998920868058257492796104841984443634632449684875602336
24827041978623209002160990235304369941849146314093431781436405462531520961836908887070167683964243781405927145635490613
0310720851038375050101157477041718986106873969655212671546889570350535402123407849819334321068170121005627880235193033224745015
8539047304199577770935036604169973297250886876966403555707162268447162560798826517871341951246652010305921236677194325278675398558944896970
96409754591856956380236370162112047742722836489613422516445078182442352948636372141740238893441247963574370263755294448337998016125492278509257782562092
62264832627793338656648162772516401910590049164499828931505660472580277863186415519565324425869829469593080191529872117255634
754639644791014590409058629849679128740687050489585867174798546675757320568128845920541334053922000113786300945560688167400169842055804033637953764520304024322566135278369511778838638744396
6253224985065499588623428189970773327617178392803494650143455889707194258639877275471096295374152111516835062752602326484728703920764310059584116612054529703023647254929666938115137322575
36450988890136020572481765851180630364428123149655070475102544650117272115551948668508003685322818315219600373562527944951582841882947876108526398 13...

algebraic equation: $x^2 - 1 = 0$. To solve this, we add 1 to both sides and find $x^2 = 1$. In other words: What number multiplied by itself equals 1? The answer is obviously 1. (Technically, the answer could also be −1, because a negative value multiplied by itself always results in a positive.)

Okay, so now let's make a tiny change to the equation, changing the minus to a plus: $x^2 + 1 = 0$. What number when multiplied by itself equals −1? Up go the Spock eyebrows, and clank goes the brain. You could take the easy way out, like the Greeks on negative numbers, and say, "That does not exist." Or instead, you could look into the fog, step off the number line, and use your imagination. As the great mathematician Leonhard Euler wrote, the answers to these sorts of questions "are neither nothing, nor greater than nothing, nor less than nothing; which necessarily constitutes them imaginary."

He wasn't saying they didn't exist; he was literally naming them: imaginary numbers, typically described by the letter i, those living on an alternate spectrum of numbers than the one we're used to. While imaginary numbers and their "complex number" friends (such as "2 + 3i") don't show up on household electronic calculators, they are a standard—indeed, an essential—element in the mathematician's toolbox. Without imaginary and complex numbers, scientists could not figure rocket trajectories or work out quantum dynamics. They exist because they should exist, they must exist in a logical system of math—just like negative numbers exist—not because we can see them or count them. As the brilliant seventeenth-century inventor of calculus, Gottfried Leibniz, wrote, "Imaginary numbers are a fine and wonderful refuge of the Holy Spirit, a sort of amphibian between being and not being."

From a foundation of patterns we have built cathedrals of numbers, from the highest spires to the darkest catacombs. The numbers shimmer in our architecture, expressing both the countable and the ineffable, the real and the imaginary. Imagine one. Then imagine it all.

SIZE

Distance lends enchantment to the view.

—Mark Twain

WHAT IF A SINGLE E. COLI BACTERIUM—ONE OF THE MICROSCOPIC creatures that are currently massed in your digestive tract—suddenly, improbably gained self-awareness and intelligence? It would not, could not, comprehend its place in its world—a human body tens of millions of times larger than itself and yet a world of which it is intimately a part. How then are we to understand our place in a universe that is absurdly large and complex in comparison with our nearly insignificant size?

On the other hand, as we consider that tiny bacterium, we realize that from our human perspective we ourselves are incredibly huge, each of us truly containing multitudes. For there are more than 10 trillion cells in the human body, and ten times that many bacteria living inside it (yes, we are more "they" than "us," at least in number). If each cell were a star, your body would contain hundreds of galaxies.

And upon even closer exploration, we find inside each cell billions and billions of atoms, bound together into molecules of water, DNA, and other structures. Your body contains more atoms than there are stars in the universe.

So perhaps our rank depends entirely on our perspective—we are either teeny or enormous, irrelevant or gods, based on how we look at it.

Of course, part of the trouble with gaining perspective is that from our viewpoint we see only a tiny slice of the whole. Just as our

> "You shall not pervert justice in measurement of length, weight, or quantity. You shall have true scales, true weights, true measurements of dry and liquid."
> —Leviticus 19:35–37

eyes can see only a portion of electromagnetic radiation (visible light), or hear a segment of a sound spectrum that extends beyond our reach, we experience size and distance only at our human scale. It is only through our scientific instruments that we start to recognize the worlds within and the heavens around us.

Common Measurements To comprehend size—and, more important here, to discuss it—we must take a detour to explore standards of measurement. The standards have changed over time, of course, in both name and precision. The ancient Hebrews and Egyptians used the cubit (the distance from fingertip to elbow), divided into seven palms of four digits each. Unfortunately, there were a number of different cubits: The Egyptian cubit was around 52 centimeters (20.5 in); the Hebrew cubit was shorter, only about 45 cm (17.7 in).

The Romans, interested in larger scales, developed the *mille passuum*, from which our concept of a "mile" originated. Their "thousand paces" was about 5,000 feet (1,500 m) long, which seems to indicate either really that Romans were really tall or that one pace equaled two steps.

Unfortunately, both of these examples reinforce the common misconception that the ancients were sloppy or ignorant with their math and physics. Not so. Take the case of Eratosthenes of Alexandria, Egypt, who in 240 BCE not only proved that the world was round but also calculated Earth's circumference using stadia (the common length of sports stadiums at the time). His result was within 2 percent (a couple hundred miles) of what we know today to be correct.

The stadium may seem like an odd value, but measurements have always been somewhat arbitrary and usually based on a very human scale. The 12-inch foot appears to have originated by the length of some long-forgotten royal foot (though that, too, likely stretched the royal truth). The post-Roman mile was defined as eight furlongs, each of which described a conveniently sized "furrow long" when plowing.

The only countries that haven't standardized on the metric system are the United States, Myanmar, and Liberia.

There are at least 18 different measurements called the "barrel" (including for beer, oil, cranberries, cornmeal, cement, and brandy).

The acre, from the Latin *ager* ("field"), reflected the land that could be plowed by a yoke of oxen in one day.

And, of course, for most of the first two millennia C.E., every town, province, and industry seemed to boast its own measurement system, often with similar names but very different values. Even today we have to be careful when comparing gallons (the British "imperial" gallon is a fifth larger than the American gallon); pounds (a pound may equal the 16 "avoirdupois" ounces that most Americans use or the 12 "troy" ounces used when weighing precious metals); or miles (the nautical mile is 15 percent longer than one on land).

So in the eighteenth century, France, in the heat of the revolution, set out to standardize a metric that everyone could use: The meter (or metre, if you're feeling continental) would be land based, not human based, calculated at one 10-millionth the distance from pole to equator—or, one 40-millionth of Earth's circumference. Unfortunately, as Earth is neither smooth nor truly spherical, even this ideal fell to an arbitrary human compromise. The meter ended up defined as the distance between two lines someone etched on a bar of platinum-iridium alloy—just under 40 inches (3.25 ft).

Desperate to find a true meter in nature, scientists at the 1960 General Conference on Weights and Measures decided to base the meter on the wavelength of a particular orange-red spectrum-emission line of the krypton 86 atom. Still too arbitrary? In 1983, the meter was finally redefined as the "length of the path travelled by light in vacuum during a time interval of 1/299,792,458 of a second." A more self-justified argument for a value would be hard to find, but at least it is a firm standard one can hold on to in these changing times.

The greatest benefit of the meter, of course, is not its definition but rather our ability to use the unit at any scale. The simple, though sometimes obscure, prefixes you can attach to the word make it easy to describe exponential differences in size. For example, add *kilo-* to describe a thousand (10^3) meters. Change it to *mega-* to describe something a thousand times longer (10^6, or a million meters). Or

> "Metric is definitely communist. One monetary system, one language, one weight and measurement system, one world—all communist! We know the West was won by the inch, foot, yard, and mile."
> —Dean Krakel, director of the National Cowboy Hall of Fame

Few Americans know that America has been debating the adoption of metric measurements for more than 200 years. To argue the use of meters vs. miles is as American as apple pie and George Washington, who brought the discussion to the public's attention in his first inaugural address. Even fewer Americans know that even the foot and yard are legally based on the value of the meter. One yard equals exactly 0.9144 meter.

switch it to *micro-* to describe 10^{-6} meters—that is, millionths of a meter.

Getting Big, on Earth We have an innate comprehension of the world that we can see and easily measure. That is, we "get" things that are larger than a mote of dust and smaller than, say, our neighborhood. These boundaries define what's known as "human scale," easily measured from thousandths to hundreds of meters.

You're probably shorter than two meters in height, though some people are taller—the American Robert Wadlow (who died in 1940 at the age of twenty-two) broke the record at 2.72 meters (8 ft 11 in). The tallest animal, the giraffe, can grow as high as 5.5 m (18 ft). The tallest living tree is about 115 m (378 ft). The longest baseball throw on record was about 136 m (446 ft), which also happens to be about the height of the Great Pyramid at Giza—the tallest structure in the world for almost four thousand years.

The world record for the shortest human is held by the 72-year-old Nepalese Chandra Bahadur Dangi at 21.5 inches (54.6 cm) tall.

There are no human-made objects that reach as high as 1 kilometer (1,000 m); the Empire State Building is only 381 meters (1,250 ft) tall; and the tallest structure in the world at the time of this writing, the Burj Khalifa skyscraper in Dubai, is only 828 m (2,717 ft). Seeing it rise majestically into the haze evokes the dream of the Tower of Babel, which was to reach to the heavens themselves.

Of course, a kilometer is impressively high, but the same measurement doesn't pack the same punch when describing a length—the Golden Gate Bridge spans 1.28 km from one tower to the next, and the biggest bridges are far longer.

The Washington Monument in D.C. was built in 1884 to be 555 ft 5 in. (170 m) tall.

And yet, these human-scale measurements are all easy for us to comprehend, largely because we have personal experiences with things this size. The phrase "seeing is believing" has a kernel of truth, as we tend to deeply understand—to *grok*, using a word coined by the science-fiction author Robert Heinlein—that which we can see. We can see a tree, walk around it, or even climb it, and thereby get an internal understanding of its size in relation to our own.

However, as we look at objects longer than a kilometer or two, we tend to lose track of scale. We may be able to see it, to believe it, but we don't know it in the same way we can know that tree, because we can no longer correlate it to our own human scale.

That's not to say we don't know it in a different way. After all, it's possible to know a forest better than you know an individual tree, just as you know the tree better than its trillions of constituent cells. What we understand—what we see—is always just a portion of the whole picture, as each object is both itself a complex system and part of an even more complex system. We know the shape of our continent from satellite photography, but that does not imply we comprehend how truly large that landmass is. Our understanding, too, exists on a spectrum.

If we're standing on level ground, Earth's natural curvature prevents us from seeing farther than the horizon, about 5 kilometers (3 mi) away, though from a small mountaintop you can see 190 km (120 mi) or more. Mount Everest reaches only about 9 km above sea level. Few people realize that the Hawaiian island mountain of Mauna Kea is actually almost a mile taller than Everest, but the base of the mountain rests 19,684 feet (6 km) below the waves. The deepest ocean trenches extend far lower, at about 10 or 11 km below sea level.

Most weather occurs within the troposphere, up to 11 km (36,000 ft) from the surface of Earth, though the highest clouds may extend about 24 km (80,000 ft) into the stratosphere. We have a sense that our atmosphere is a huge cushion around us, protecting us from the harsh vacuum and radiation of space. However, think of it this way: If Earth were shrunk to the size of a wet tennis ball, our atmosphere would be no thicker than the water clinging to the surface.

Returning to sea level, it's slightly easier to wrap our heads around these sizes when considering geographic landmarks. Manhattan island is about 22 km (22,000 m, or 72,000 ft) long. You can measure the distance from San Francisco to Honolulu as 3,860 km, but at this

The largest living thing on Earth: the 2,400-year-old, 2,200-acre (8.9 km^2) giant fungus living underground in Oregon.

length it starts to become easier to measure in the millions of meters, so we write 3.86 Mm. Flying from Chicago to Tokyo covers 10.16 Mm, almost the diameter of Earth itself (12.75 Mm). The circumference of that big blue ball we call home is a convenient-to-remember 40 Mm (40 million meters . . . well, technically 40,075,160 m around the equator, but who's counting?).

It's impossible for us to simply grasp Earth's size as an absolute; instead, we must rely on comparing its size with objects around us. It would take 14,615 Golden Gate bridges to circumscribe the globe. And you could stack 15,400 Burj Khalifas to span from Beijing through the center of Earth to its antipode, Buenos Aires.

Of course, if we have trouble grokking our own planet, what's to become of us as we leave the comfort of our terrestrial home and begin to explore the size of the cosmos?

The Great Beyond It seems as though space—that ultimate frontier—is unimaginably far away. But jetliners traverse the sky only about 10 kilometers high (about 6 mi), and you need travel only 100 km (62 mi) up before you are no longer considered an aeronaut and are now an astronaut. In fact, the distance from the surface of Earth to

> **The diameter of the Earth** from pole to pole is is just over 500,500,000 inches.

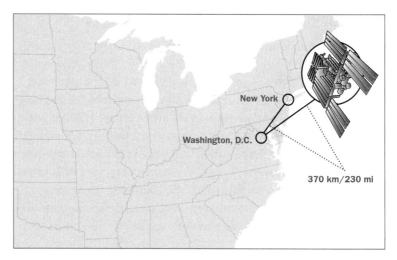

New York

Washington, D.C.

370 km/230 mi

the International Space Station is shorter than the train ride from New York to Washington, D.C., about 370 km (230 mi).

Of course, the hardest part about making "one small step for man" isn't the distance it takes to get into space but rather the force it takes to break free from the bonds of gravity. And ironically, gravity may be the weakest force in the universe! After all, in a battle between the entire mass of Earth and a tiny magnet, the tiny magnet easily wins, picking up a paper clip with ease. Electromagnetism is billions of times stronger than gravity. Nevertheless, it requires tremendous force and speed for a huge rocket to escape the gravitational pull of the planet to reach 250 km (160 mi) from the surface, where it can begin to orbit, or continue on past Earth's exosphere and toward the moon.

It is at this point in our journey outward, however, that the sizes begin to get mind-numbingly large. The exact distance between any two celestial bodies varies, of course, as orbits tend to be elliptical rather than spherical. But the moon is generally around 378 Mm from Earth—that's 378,000 km, about a quarter million miles, or ten times the circumference of our own planet.

The closest planet to us, and the brightest object in the night sky after the moon, is Venus, about 38 billion meters (41 Gm) at its closest—that's more than 100 times the distance between the moon and us. The sun is about 1.4 Gm in diameter, and is, on average, 150 Gm away.

Think about these numbers this way: If Earth were the size of the period at the end of this sentence, the moon would be about 15 millimeters away (about the thickness of your finger), and the sun would be about the size of a child's fist and 6 meters (20 ft) away. In fact, the sun is so large that if Earth were placed at the center of the sun (ignoring the fact that we'd all vaporize), our moon's orbit would reach a bit more than halfway to the solar surface.

When you're discussing planetary distances, it's awkward to count in meters—even gigameters. Instead, a more handy measure is the average distance from Earth to the sun; scientists call this value 1

Voyager 1 set out in 1977, and is currently traveling at about 3.6 AU (538 Gm) per year, or 61,400 km/h. At this rate, it won't reach the Oort cloud for more than 1,000 years, and it will take more than 73,000 years before reaching the nearest star.

▲ Earth as a tiny dot of light, seen through the rings of Saturn from the Cassini spacecraft in 2006.

astronomical unit (1 AU). So Jupiter, for example, orbits about 5 AU from the sun.

Jupiter, by the way, is an astonishingly large gaseous planet, with more than twice the mass of all the other planets put together. It's so big that its easily identifiable red dot—thought to be a huge storm that has raged for almost two centuries—is larger than the diameter of Earth. Here's a helpful comparison: If the sun's diameter were equal to the height of a man, Jupiter would be about the size of his head and Earth would be slightly bigger than the iris of his eye.

Heading farther out into our solar system, we find the planets Saturn at just under 10 AU, Uranus at almost 20 AU, and then Neptune at about 30 AU (around 4.5 trillion meters, or terameters) from the sun. Beyond Neptune, stretched across a massive 25 AU of space, is an enormous ring of more than 100,000 rocky icy objects collectively called the Kuiper belt. These chunks of space debris orbiting far from the sun include Pluto and several other frozen dwarf planets, such as Haumea and Makemake. (All large Kuiper belt objects besides Pluto are named after creator deities; Haumea is the

Hawaiian goddess of fertility, and Makemake is the fertility goddess of the Rapanui people of Easter Island.)

The farthest known object in our solar system is Sedna, a rock about two thirds the size of Pluto, which has an extremely elongated orbit. At its closest (the perihelion of its orbit), Sedna is about 76 AU away; after fifty-five hundred years, when Sedna reaches the other end of its orbit (its aphelion), it reaches 937 AU, more than 140 trillion meters into space from the sun. No wonder it was named after an Inuit goddess who is said to live in the darkest, coldest part of the Atlantic Ocean.

Most of us were taught that Pluto marks the outer edge of the solar system, but there is likely far more out there, endlessly orbiting the sun, bound by the same gravitational force that holds our planet in place. Unfortunately, we don't know what else is out beyond the Kuiper belt—it's simply too dark for us to see. Astronomers believe that there is likely nothing at all for an expanse of several thousand AU, spare an occasional comet, followed by a huge swarm of trillions of comets that surround our solar system between 5,000 and 100,000 AU away. This is the theoretical Oort cloud, the outer edge of which is considered the boundary of our solar system.

Light It's all very well and good to bandy about distances like 100,000 AU, but what do they really mean? Once again, the numbers are just too big. So imagine that the solar system (out past the Oort cloud, to the boundary between the solar wind and interstellar space) is the size of a typical elementary school classroom. The sun—by far the largest object in the room—would float in the middle of the classroom, smaller than a grain of salt. Earth, about the size of a microscopic bacterium, would be orbiting about 10 centimeters away.

Or let's flip it around: If Earth were the size of a grain of salt, our solar system (only out to Neptune!) would be 352 meters wide—that's a grain of salt sitting inside about three and a half football fields of space. If you include the whole solar system (out to the Oort cloud), it's more than 2,000 times more space: a grain of salt in a region

▲ The "Blue Marble" photo of Earth was taken by Apollo 17 in 1972, 45 Mm (28,000 mi) from the surface.

If our solar system (out to the Oort cloud) were the size of a grain of salt, the Milky Way galaxy would be about the length of a football field. If the Milky Way galaxy were the size of a grain of salt, the visible universe would be about as large as the 110-story Sears Tower in Chicago.

If the universe were shrunk so that Earth were the size of a period on this page, our nearest star would be 1,500 km (930 mi) away. The center of the Milky Way would be about 8 Gm or 5 million miles away.

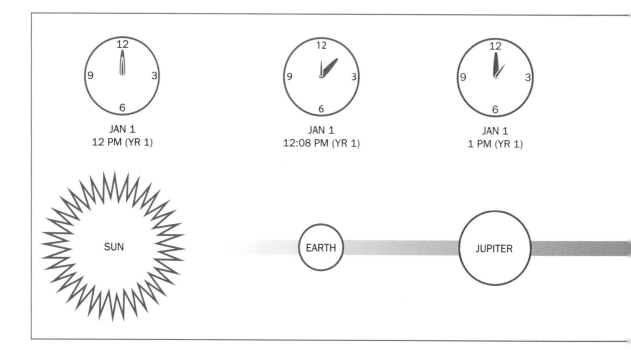

JAN 1
12 PM (YR 1)

JAN 1
12:08 PM (YR 1)

JAN 1
1 PM (YR 1)

SUN

EARTH

JUPITER

about 450 miles wide. (That's like flying from San Francisco to Seattle—a two-hour flight—and encountering virtually nothing but a few specks along the way.)

Of course, no one wants to deal with numbers like 100,000 AU or trillions of meters. There are too many zeros for comfort! Instead, astronomers tend to simplify these enormous values by using parsecs. A parsec is defined in a way that only a mathematician could love, but it's based on the tiny discrepancy we can see when we view distant stars from different positions along Earth's orbit. You're already familiar with this effect, called parallax: Hold your finger up at arm's length and close one eye, then open it and close the other, and you'll see the finger appear to change position against the background scene. Astronomers use parallax to measure distances in parsecs.

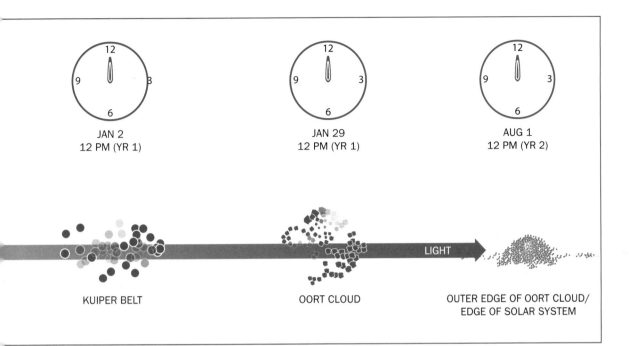

KUIPER BELT

OORT CLOUD

OUTER EDGE OF OORT CLOUD/
EDGE OF SOLAR SYSTEM

The rest of us rely on a much simpler measurement: the light-year. Light always travels at the same speed; in a vacuum, that's almost exactly 299,792,458 meters a second—though it's easier to round up to 300 Mm/sec (which you can write 3×10^8 m/sec). Imagine traveling seven and a half times around the equator in a single light-second.

You can visualize a package of light leaving the surface of the sun at the stroke of 12:00 a.m., January 1. At just after 12:08, it would reach Earth (1 AU away). By 1:00 a.m. (a light-hour), the light would have traveled past Jupiter. By midnight (a light-day), it has traveled 26 Tm, far past the Kuiper belt. But that light would not reach the inner edge of the Oort cloud for another 27 days. It then travels through the cloud for a long, long time. At midnight on December 31, after one light-year, it is still making its way past the icy debris. That same parcel of light wouldn't reach the outer edge of our solar system until the following August, 20 months after it left the sun.

The "year" in "light-year" is the Julian year, which is always exactly 365.25 days of 86,400 seconds each.

Clearly, a light-year is a very long way indeed. In case you're prepping for a game show: a light-year is 9.46 Pm (petameters, that's 10^{15} m); about 6 trillion miles; 63,200 AU; or 31,557,600 light-seconds. For reference, the moon is a bit over 1 light-second from Earth.

But the size of a light-year is truly a matter of perspective, and we'll quickly see that a mere light-year is a measly measurement. After all, to explore the galaxy in which our own solar system belongs, we must rely on kilolight-years (abbreviated kly); traveling between galaxies requires megalight-years (Mly); and supergalactic structures in our universe span gigalight-years (Gly)—literally billions and billions of light-years.

To Infinity . . . and Beyond! On a clear night, in the countryside or from a mountaintop, you can't help but be awed at the sight of kerjillions of stars sparkling overhead. As it turns out, you can actually see only about two thousand stars with the unaided eye from any one spot on Earth, and mostly likely every single one you see is a star in our own galaxy. Until a century ago, astronomers thought that our galaxy was the extent of the universe; as we'll soon see, there's a bit more to the universe than that.

The closest stars to us, deep in the southern sky, are the small cluster of Alpha Centauri A, Alpha Centauri B, and Proxima Centauri, only about 4.2 light-years (about 1.3 parsecs, or 40 petameters) away. To get a sense of the distance, if our sun were the size of a grapefruit in Los Angeles, then Alpha Centauri A would be another, slightly larger, grapefruit in Chicago. If we could send a rocket toward these stars at 80,000 km/h (50,000 mph), it would take 57,000 years to arrive.

This distance between the stars is pretty typical throughout the galaxy, though there are many instances of clusters of two or three stars that are much closer together, like those in Centauri. There is far greater variation in the size of the stars themselves: Some, such as red dwarfs, are much smaller than our own sun, and some are far greater. For comparison, take the red supergiant Betelgeuse—about

> "The cells of our body are as small relative to our own size as a mountain is large."
>
> —Christopher Potter,
> *You Are Here*

640 light-years away and one of the brightest stars in the night sky—in the constellation Orion. With a radius almost 1,200 times larger than our own sun, if you placed Betelgeuse in the center of our solar system, Earth, Mars, and even Jupiter would be inside it.

That's nothing compared with the largest star currently known, VY Canis Majoris, 5,000 ly away from us and twice the size of Betelgeuse. If this star were the size of Mount Everest, our sun would be only 15 feet (4.5 m) wide.

About 27,000 ly from us, in the constellation Sagittarius, there appears to be a supermassive black hole (called Sagittarius A), with a gravitational pull so great that it acts as the centerpoint around which our entire galaxy revolves. We call our galaxy the Milky Way, reflecting the greater density of stars along a cloudy band that streams across the night sky. That river of light is our view of billions of stars spiraling around in a relatively flat plane, about 1,000 ly thick and as much as 100,000 ly (30 kiloparsecs, or 9.5×10^{20} meters) wide. Imagine: If our solar system (out to Pluto) were shrunk to the size of a quarter, our galaxy would be as big as the western half of the United States.

The fact that we can see a similar number of stars on either side of this plane indicates that we are somewhat centered between the "top" and "bottom" of the spiral, with many stars on every side of us. However, if we can see only 2,000 stars unaided, how many stars are really there? Look through the telescope, do the math, and you'll find there are somewhere between 200 and 400 billion stars in the Milky Way, each rotating around Sagittarius A about once every 250 million years.

Residents of the southern hemisphere looking into the nighttime sky may notice two tiny clouds that appear to have broken away from the Milky Way. These are the Magellanic Clouds, first identified by the crew of Ferdinand Magellan's sixteenth-century expedition past South America. More specifically, they are galaxies—the Large Magellanic Cloud (LMC) and the Small Magellanic Cloud (SMC)—and the only objects outside of the Milky Way that we can see without a

"Space is big. Really big. You just won't believe how vastly hugely mind-bogglingly big it is. I mean, you may think it's a long way down the road to the chemist, but that's just peanuts to space."

—Douglas Adams,
The Hitchhiker's Guide to the Galaxy

telescope. Both are dwarf galaxies, less than a seventh the size of our own, with only perhaps 350 million stars between them, and both are more than 160,000 light-years away from us.

Of course, the greater the mass, the larger the gravitational pull—and just as planets are held to stars by gravity, and stars are drawn to black holes in galaxies, whole galaxies are pulled together, too. Those little Magellanic Clouds will likely someday be consumed by the greater collective mass of the Milky Way. But lest we fall pray to braggadocio, we need only look to the Andromeda galaxy, a mere 2.5 million light-years away and containing perhaps as many as a trillion stars. Andromeda appears to be approaching us at 500,000 km/h, and the collision—about two billion years from now—promises to be spectacular.

It might seem that we're starting to get a grasp on the size of the universe, but the Milky Way, Magellanic, and Andromeda galaxies make up only a small part of what's called the Local Group—a small cluster that includes about 30 separate galaxies. The American Museum of Natural History in New York City offers a beautiful reference to the size of the Local Group: In the museum sits the Hayden Sphere, 87 feet (26.5 m) in diameter, and a sign explaining that if the Local Group were shrunk to the size of the sphere, the Milky Way would be about 2.5 feet (80 cm) large. Between those handful of galaxies in the cluster is . . . we don't know, but it's likely pretty much *bubkes.* As the saying goes, "They don't call it *space* for nothing."

The Local Group is, in turn, a tiny piece of the Virgo supercluster, which is about 100 billion times larger than the Milky Way and contains hundreds or even thousands of galaxies. If you don't have vertigo yet, consider this: There are likely around 10 million superclusters in the universe, containing billions (possibly trillions) of galaxies, and likely about 3×10^{22} stars. Astronomers now believe that a large number of these harbor planets, but if even only a tiny percentage have habitable planets, the odds are almost certain that there is sentient life out there, waiting to be found.

The Canis Major dwarf galaxy is just outside our own. In fact, it's actually closer to Earth than is the center of the Milky Way, at only 25,000 ly away.

"There is no smallest among the small and no largest among the large, but always something still smaller and something still larger."

—Anaxagoras, fifth-century Greek philosopher

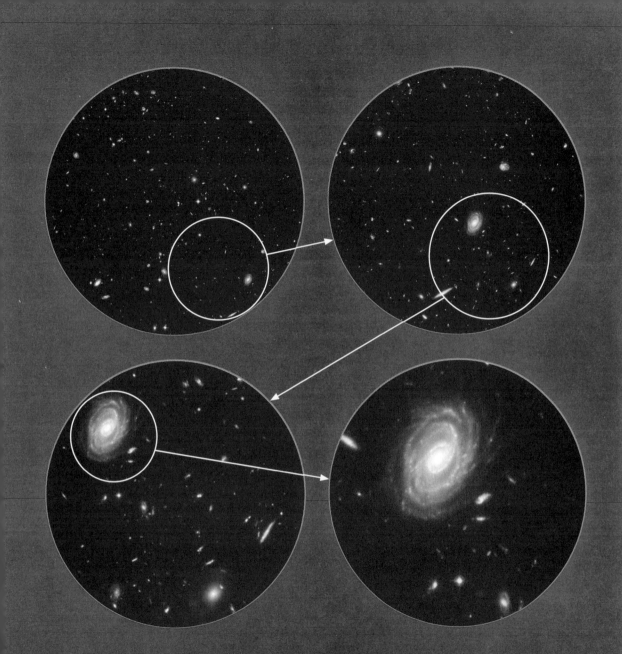

▲ The top-left image, called the Hubble Space Telescope Ultra-Deep Field, represents a span the size of a pen point against the night sky.

When you look up tonight, make a mental note that there are millions of galaxies (that's *galaxies*, not stars) in the "bowl" of the Big Dipper alone.

We cannot see each star in each galaxy, no matter how powerful our telescope. Rather, the lights of whole galaxies blend together to form pinpoints, like the thousands of individual street and house lights of a city coalesce into a single fuzzy spot in a satellite photo. And similar to the patterns of these city lights you can see from space, clusters of galaxies form intricate, cotton-candy-like webs of filaments across the cosmos.

The largest of these filaments is the Sloan Great Wall, discovered in 2003. About 1 billion light-years away, constructed from countless galaxies, and stretching almost 1.5 billion light-years long, the wall is sandwiched between two enormous voids in space. And yet, as unfathomably large as it is, the wall spans only about 1/60 the diameter of the known universe—when you see it against the computer-generated map of all we know about the cosmos,

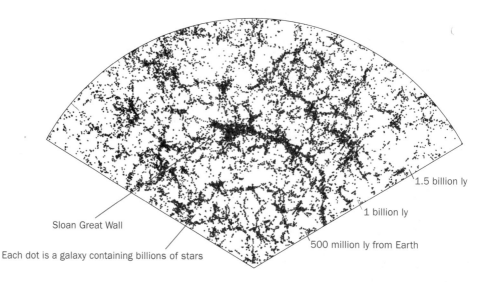

1.5 billion ly

1 billion ly

500 million ly from Earth

Sloan Great Wall

Each dot is a galaxy containing billions of stars

M. Blanton and SDSS Collaboration, www.sdss.org

it's hardly more than a smudge, like something spattered on a windshield.

Looking out into the universe is like looking through a smoky room on a sunny afternoon, seeing motes of dust and ash caught in beams of light. But imagine: Each speck is itself a cluster of galaxies, separated by unimaginably vast amounts of space. And each galaxy in that particle is itself a dusty room containing uncountable number of stars, like ours, the sun.

As far as astronomers can tell, our universe likely has a radius of about 46 billion light-years (435 yottameters, or 4.35×10^{26} m). This is far, far larger than it should be if the universe is—as astrophysicists also believe—"only" 13.7 billion years old. So is the size a fiction? No; space itself is far stranger than fiction.

Getting Small In contrast to the breathtaking size of the universe is the world of the very, very small. It's easy to overlook that world; the very small goes largely unnoticed even though it is every bit as awe-inspiring. Even the largest superclusters in the cosmos are built from the same things we are: atoms, subatomic particles, and perhaps things even tinier than that.

Most of the objects we can hold in our hand fall into the range of a few centimeters, and the smallest can be measured in millimeters. This is a level of the human scale we are intimately aware of—we can see it, even play with it. The smallest mammals, the Etruscan pygmy shrew and the bumblebee bat, are just over 3 cm long. A penny is about 1.9 cm wide. The head of a pin is about 1.5 millimeters, and a grain of salt is about 0.5 mm. You can also write that measurement as 500 micrometers—labeled μm, which is a thousandth of a millimeter, or a millionth of a meter, and is sometimes still called by its old name: a micron.

The spectrum of our human vision extends down as far as about 100 to 200 μm (1or 2 *tenths* of a millimeter). Here we find the diameter of dust mites and the human ovum (the largest cell in the human body), or the thickness of a thin human hair or a dollar bill.

However, even though we can see a single grain of sand or a minuscule gnat, it's hard for us to understand that the microworld works differently from our macro expectations. To a tiny insect, the air we breathe and walk through so effortlessly is actually rather thick with molecules—what we would call flying, it would consider swimming. As we then step beyond the seeable, into a world until recently hidden from us, we must begin to learn new sets of rules, ones that become increasingly bizarre from our human perspective.

A glimpse through almost any microscope shows a world where even the smoothest surfaces suddenly become jagged, with unexpected crevices and outcroppings. Like psychedelic fractal artwork, a tiny rock takes on the form of a craggy mountain, and bread mold becomes a field of flowering plants.

Optical microscopes bend light like a set of fun-house mirrors, allowing us to extend our sight below 100 μm, where we find individual animal and plant cells. A paramecium swimming in lake water is as small as 60 μm. Red blood corpuscles are disks about

▼ This moth's eye is 800 μm wide, a hundred times larger than a single red blood cell (bottom right); the large spiked pollen from the Hibiscus flower is about 110 μm wide.

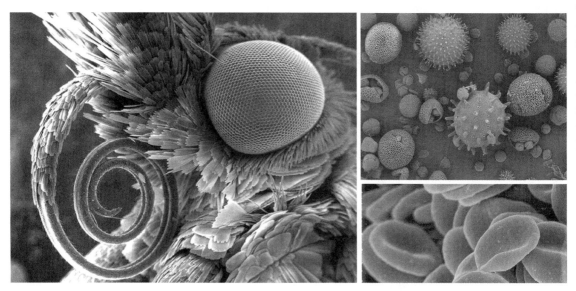

Moth and pollen courtesy Dartmouth University; blood cell courtesy Tina Carvalho

7.7 µm wide and 3.7 µm thick. To get a sense for how tiny this is: If a red blood cell were expanded to the size of an apple, an apple enlarged the same amount would be twice as tall as the Empire State Building.

There are far smaller cells, too: The head of a sperm cell is only about 5 µm long, more than twice the size of that hot-dog-shaped *E. coli* bacterium that thrives in our large intestine. In their world, even pure water is as thick as honey, and astonishingly, about 200,000 of these little creatures could live in the period at the end of this sentence.

With the most powerful optical microscopes, we can magnify objects more than 1,000 times, letting us see organelles inside cells even smaller than a micrometer—things measured in the hundreds of nanometers, or *billionths* of meters. To visualize one billionth of anything, consider half the width of your little fingernail compared with the distance from New York to Los Angeles.

We could make more powerful magnifying lenses, but at this size visible light itself fails us. After all, a single light wave is as small as 400 nm. In order for us to see something, a light wave must be affected by it—either reflected back, refracted away, or absorbed by it. An influenza virus is about 115 nm long, too small to have much effect on a wave of light; a rhinovirus (the predominant cause of the common cold) is even tinier: a small sphere only 20 nm wide.

At this size, we're dealing with tightly packed groups of molecules. And the difference in size between a light wave and a small molecule of atoms is like a 40 m (130 ft) ocean wave encountering a pebble on the beach—the wave may be affected by the entire beach but certainly not by a single rock, or even a pile of them.

Instead, to get a sense of what's going on in the realm of the nanometer, scientists use X-rays, or electrons with wavelengths about 100,000 times shorter than visible light, and watch how their minute electrical charges fluctuate as they interact with molecules. Or, in atomic force microscopy, scientists probe the surface of a material

One billionth: A nanometer is a billionth of a meter; a dime (or 1-yen coin) is about a billionth of the diameter of Earth.

"A cloud is made of billows upon billows upon billows that look like clouds. As you come closer to a cloud you don't get something smooth, but irregularities at a smaller scale."

—Benoit Mandelbrot, mathematician

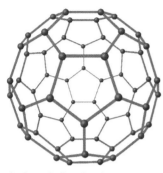

▲ Buckyball molecule

The ink that forms a single letter *A* on this page contains enough atoms so that not only could every person on Earth have one but also every person on every planet in the Milky Way, assuming every star had a planet like ours.

with a sliver of a sliver of a needle, "feeling" the hills and valleys to build a picture of a world beyond seeing.

DNA, that tightly wound double helix of molecular instructions, is only about 2 nm wide—though if you unfurled the coils, the strands of DNA in a single cell would stretch over 2 m (6 ft) long. A single molecule of table sugar (sucrose) is about 1 nm across, as is the soccer-ball-shaped molecule called the buckminsterfullerene or buckyball. Named after the inventor of the geodesic dome and found in tiny quantities in ordinary soot, this molecule is made of 60 carbon atoms fused together, and when compressed it is twice as hard as diamond.

Clap your hands in the "real world," and you can feel the collision generating sound and heat. But in the world of the nanometer—and even smaller, the picometer, which counts out trillionths of a meter—we find that something completely different is happening. Atoms and molecules rarely actually collide (outside of a sun or a supercollider). Instead, they constantly attract or repulse each other, like tiny magnets. As one hand approaches the other, the molecules in your skin strain to hold together and push back against the opposing hand, harder and harder, until no further passage is possible. This whole process is so fast and occurs at such a microscopic level that we are fooled into believing that our hands are solid. Similarly, you may feel your behind against your chair, or your car bumper hitting a concrete wall—the illusion of firm boundaries all around us is compelling, but you're experiencing nothing more than electromagnetism in action.

Atoms are generally a few tenths of a nanometer across, around 100–500 picometers. The smallest atoms (hydrogen, carbon, oxygen, and so on) are all roughly 100 pm in diameter, a measurement that is sometimes called an angstrom (labeled with the Scandinavian Å). They may be magnetically locked together to form solid structures, like crystals; or loosely affiliated in a liquid; or floating free form in a gas, where molecules tend to be well spaced, about 5 to 10 diameters apart.

Once again, it is virtually impossible to truly understand the near-infinitesimal size of atoms, but here's an attempt, using the previously mentioned Hayden Sphere, 87 feet (27 m) in diameter: If a red blood cell were expanded to the size of the sphere—bigger than a six-story building—then a rhinovirus would be about 3 inches (7 cm) in diameter. And if that rhinovirus were expanded to the size of the sphere, then a water molecule would be the size of an inflatable exercise ball, and a single atom would be the size of a basketball.

Or consider this: If you magnified everything so that an apple appeared as large as our Earth, a flea would be as large as a small country, and an amoeba or a human body cell would be the size of a midsized city. A human chromosome would be the size of a baseball field, a virus would fit inside the infield, and a single molecule would fit on home plate.

Dividing the Indivisible Materialists insist that each and every thing is inevitably made of even smaller things. So although the word *atom* by definition (from the Latin *atomus* and the Greek *atomos*, meaning "invisible") implies that there can be nothing smaller, every high school student knows that there's more to be found below the angstrom. On the one hand, you can discover a great deal about the universe inside a single atom; on the other hand, you'll find virtually nothing there.

If you've never been inside the enormous Houston Astrodome, imagine a huge, round sports building, able to seat sixty-five thousand people for a football game. Now imagine a single watermelon seed sitting at the 50-yard line. That tiny pit is like the nucleus of an atom, surrounded by a huge spherical cloud of electrons, far, far away, separated from the nucleus by nothing but space. The size of a hydrogen atom, for example, is about 50,000 times larger than the nucleus itself. Given that the atom (defined by the diameter of that electron cloud) is about 100 pm or 1Å, the nucleus containing a single proton is only a couple of femtometers wide.

OBJECT SIZES

Infinitesimal
String scale
Nano scale
Sub-atomic scale
Atomic
Molecular
Mitochondriatic
Cellular
Microscopic
Minuscule
Tiny
Lilliputian
Small
Medium
Bulky
Large
Immense
Massive
Giant
Mammoth
Colossal
Leviathan
Vast
Galactic
Cosmic
Universal

from *Hatch's Order of Magnitude*

A femtometer (fm) is really, really small: a millionth of a nanometer—that is, a millionth of a billionth of a meter (10^{-15} m). And it's important to note that words often have different meanings at this subatomic level than in our daily lives. For instance, electrons aren't *things* with size and mass that revolve around the nucleus in the way they're often drawn in diagrams. Rather, each electron is in a constant probability cloud ("it could be here, or here, or here . . ."). Most of the time, in most places, there's no *there* there. No matter how strong our microscopes, we'll never capture more than a blurry photo of an atom, because reality itself at this level is impossible to focus—it's all about probability, not certainty.

▲ Olympicene—named after the Olympic logo—is a single molecule only 1.2 nm wide, made of five interconnected rings of carbon atoms.

What's more, an electron, like a photon of light, is considered an elementary particle—something that truly cannot be broken down into smaller pieces because it does not actually have any size at all. Or, perhaps more accurately, elementary particles do have size, but only sometimes. At other times, they are more like waves of energy, potentialities constantly crossing the threshold between what is and what could be.

The femtometer-sized nucleus—which accounts for 99.9 percent of the mass of the entire atom—is made of one or more protons and neutrons (except for hydrogen, which contains only a proton), and these particles do have mass and can be smashed apart. The result is a menagerie of elementary particles that have individual characteristics and names, but they share a common oddity: Like electrons, they affect space but do not necessarily extend into space as structures with size. Again, at this lowest level, it becomes difficult to discern between energy and matter, so these are sometimes described as being *at most* an attometer (10^{-18}, or a billionth of a billionth of a meter).

Scientists have given these elementary particles the most wonderful names, such as quarks, muons, and leptons, each bonded together with "force carriers" such as gluons and bosons. We know these exist, though several others are only currently hypothesized, such as the tachyon, graviton, and Higgs boson—also called the "God particle" because scientists think it confers mass on other particles, basically turning light to matter.

And just as the American inventor and statesman Benjamin Franklin arbitrarily applied the terms *positive* and *negative* to describe two different types of electric charge, scientists today apply adjectives to the "particle zoo," including *up*, *down*, *top*, *bottom*, *spin*, and *flavor*. For example, a proton is made of two up quarks and one down quark; a neutron is made of one up quark and two down quarks—though try hard enough and you may find a red charm quark, or perhaps even an antiblue antidown quark! The adjectives themselves don't describe the particles—there is no "up" or "down"

If Earth were the size of a baseball sitting at home plate in a baseball park, the moon would be the size of a cherry, about 7.5 feet away. Mars is only about a third of a mile away. The sun would be 27 feet across, three quarters of a mile away. The next planet out, Jupiter, would be about 3 miles away. At this scale, the nearest star outside our solar system would be located far off any map of the world.

If Earth were the size of a grain of sand in San Francisco, the nearest star (apart from our own sun) would be the size of a peppercorn, hundreds of miles away, near the Grand Canyon. Sirius, the brightest star in the night sky, is as big as a baseball, halfway across the United States.

or visible color at this level—but they're helpful in distinguishing one category from another.

So if it stops making sense to apply size at this subatomic level, why continue? Isn't delving deeper like bringing a footstool to the peak of Everest to stand on, just to say you went a little higher? For better or worse, scientists are, if nothing else, driven by insatiable curiosity—the word *science* itself derives from the Latin word meaning to know, or to separate one thing from another. So might quarks and other astonishingly small particles such as the elusive neutrino be made of something finer?

Here it all just becomes theory, though theory based on extraordinary research and consideration. The leading idea is that underneath it all, everything is made of "vibrating strings" in an 11-dimensional universe. These strings are about 1.6×10^{-35} meters long, a size called the Planck length. In other words, compare the size of a single atom to the length of your arm; that's about how much smaller a string would be compared to an entire atom. Or imagine: If you magnified a single atom to the size of our entire solar system, one Planck length would be the width of a strand of DNA.

The Planck length also marks the smallest measurement that makes any sense. That is, given the speed of light, the force of gravity, and other universal constants, physicists have calculated that nothing *can* be smaller. If you think of our reality as being created out of tiny squares, like pixels on a computer screen, then each pixel is 1 Planck length tall and wide. We simply cannot venture smaller.

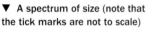
▼ A spectrum of size (note that the tick marks are not to scale)

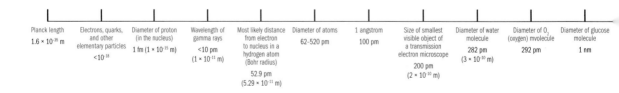

| Planck length 1.6×10^{-35} m | Electrons, quarks, and other elementary particles $<10^{-18}$ | Diameter of proton (in the nucleus) 1 fm $(1 \times 10^{-15}$ m) | Wavelength of gamma rays <10 pm $(1 \times 10^{-11}$ m) | Most likely distance from electron to nucleus in a hydrogen atom (Bohr radius) 52.9 pm $(5.29 \times 10^{-11}$ m) | Diameter of atoms 62–520 pm | 1 angstrom 100 pm | Size of smallest visible object of a transmission electron microscope 200 pm $(2 \times 10^{-10}$ m) | Diameter of water molecule 282 pm $(3 \times 10^{-10}$ m) | Diameter of O_2 (oxygen) molecule 292 pm | Diameter of glucose molecule 1 nm |

Size Depends on Space Unfortunately, there is a fundamental problem with any discussion of the spectrum of size and dimension: Size depends on space; that is, every measurement is based on how much space (length, width, and height) something takes up. And—as weird as this may sound—scientists still don't understand what space is or how it works.

Everyone knows that science and math go hand in hand, but few people understand the extent to which scientists and mathematicians rely on philosophy to get the job done. As much as we want to believe that science teaches absolute truth, the absolute truth is that science is based on assumptions and hypotheses, and in some cases we may simply not be able to prove that some of those assumptions are valid. This is perhaps never more true than when discussing space.

The brilliant physicist Isaac Newton made his opinions clear in his late-seventeenth-century opus, the *Principia Mathematica*: Space and time are absolutes, a standard in which all things have their place and order. Newton's firm grip on reality—with its rigid, invisible scaffolding that gives the cosmos its shape—is comforting. In Newton's world, a ruler is a ruler is a ruler—the very essence of modernism. But of course, we're also talking about a guy who, in the name of science, stuck a blunt needle between his own eye and ocular bone just to see what was back there.

While Newton was probing his absolute universe, the mathematician Gottfried Leibniz was arguing that everything in our

▲ Sir Isaac Newton

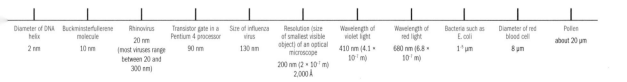

Diameter of DNA helix	Buckminsterfullerene molecule	Rhinovirus	Transistor gate in a Pentium 4 processor	Size of influenza virus	Resolution (size of smallest visible object) of an optical microscope	Wavelength of violet light	Wavelength of red light	Bacteria such as E. coli	Diameter of red blood cell	Pollen
2 nm	10 nm	20 nm (most viruses range between 20 and 300 nm)	90 nm	130 nm	200 nm (2×10^{-7} m) 2,000 Å	410 nm (4.1×10^{-7} m)	680 nm (6.8×10^{-7} m)	1^{-5} μm	8 μm	about 20 μm

universe is positioned and moves relative to everything else. That is, objects don't exist inside a fixed space; space itself is defined as the relation between the objects.

▲ **Gottfried Leibniz**

This may seem like nitpicking, but these underlying assumptions about what space is turn out to have radical implications on science and how we measure things. For example, the data that astronomers collect from distant stars would have to be interpreted completely differently with each model, leading to very different understandings of the cosmos.

However, in the early twentieth century, Einstein's theory of relativity prompted a complete rethinking of the matter. Space, it turns out, *is* based on your frame of reference, and, what's more, it's far from absolute; rather, it is warped by mass and motion. For example, an object traveling faster becomes shorter and heavier, but only compared to one moving more slowly—that is, it's relative. Here's another oddity: The more massive an object, the more it can literally warp space and time, like a block of spongy foam twisted and stretched. From any one point inside space it doesn't appear warped, but careful measurements of light moving through space expose the truth. Einstein's theories have since been repeatedly validated with experimental data: The fabric of space is elastic, not concrete.

Based on Einstein's descriptions, the physicist Hans Reichenbach wrote *The Philosophy of Space and Time* (1928), in which he pointed out that you cannot know the inherent, absolute size of an object; you can know it only relative to another object. Of course, if everything is relative, including time and space, we end up in a vicious circle: How

Length of sperm cell (head to tail)
50 μm (5×10^{-5} m)

Size of smallest dust particles
0.1 mm
100 μm (1×10^{-4} m)

Thickness of a dollar bill or average human hair
110 μm
(1.1×10^{-4} m);
0.0043 in., 0.11 mm

Largest cell in human body; ovum
140 μm

Dust mite
200 μm

Dot at end of a sentence
300–500 μm

Grain of salt
0.5 mm
(500 microns)

Length of jump of common flea, 1.5 mm (0.06 in) long
330 mm (13 in.)

Diameter of the head of an average pin
1.7 mm
(1.7×10^{-3} m)

Height of a line of text in 12-point type
4.234 mm
(4.234×10^{-3} m)

Length of smallest vertebrate
Paedophryne amauensis frogs of Papua New Guinea
7.5 mm

can we understand the underlying forces of nature if we can't get a grip on the geometry of space-time? And how can we understand the geometry of space-time if we don't understand the underlying forces? "It appears," wrote Reichenbach, "that the solution of the problem of time and space is reserved to philosophers who, like Leibniz, are mathematicians, or to mathematicians who, like Einstein, are philosophers."

Ultimately, we humans experience our universe like the proverbial blind men and the elephant, where different perspectives result in very different "truths." We start by understanding things within our reach—on our human scale—and at this level Newton's laws generally work. Then, as we extend our reach by using instruments, we gather data that makes no sense from our original perspective; it's as though the rules change in the worlds of the very large and the very small.

▲ Albert Einstein

For example, a traditional model says that stars and galaxies are all flying farther away, like the detritus of some massive explosion. But current theories actually point to something else: that space itself—the "nothingness" between these massive bodies—is stretching, like the surface of a balloon being blown up, or expanding, like bread rising in an oven, largely with the help of what cosmologists call dark energy. (This should not be confused with dark matter, which is, no pun intended, a different matter entirely.)

As far as we can tell, space is expanding at about 70 kilometers per second per megaparsec (3.2 light-years). In other words, let's say you could stretch a tape measure out to Proxima Centauri. You could look down at the number on the tape to see just how far away

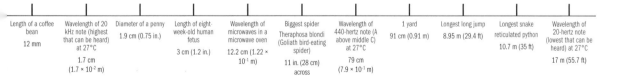

Length of a coffee bean	Wavelength of 20 kHz note (highest that can be heard) at 27°C	Diameter of a penny	Length of eight-week-old human fetus	Wavelength of microwaves in a microwave oven	Biggest spider Theraphosa blondi (Goliath bird-eating spider)	Wavelength of 440-hertz note (A above middle C) at 27°C	1 yard	Longest long jump	Longest snake reticulated python	Wavelength of 20-hertz note (lowest that can be heard) at 27°C
12 mm	1.7 cm $(1.7 \times 10^{-2}$ m$)$	1.9 cm (0.75 in.)	3 cm (1.2 in.)	12.2 cm $(1.22 \times 10^{-1}$ m$)$	11 in. (28 cm) across	79 cm $(7.9 \times 10^{-1}$ m$)$	91 cm (0.91 m)	8.95 m (29.4 ft)	10.7 m (35 ft)	17 m (55.7 ft)

it was—but when you brought the tape measure back in, you'd see that the distances between the marks had literally changed; the tape measure had actually stretched, invalidating the measurement you had just taken.

Astronomers see the effects from space-time expansion every day, as light emitted from far-off superclusters of galaxies travels through unimaginable amounts of space to reach us. As space stretches, the light waves themselves also become elongated, causing the color to shift toward the red end of the spectrum (called "redshift").

The fact that space is stretching leads us to another astonishing possibility: Extremely distant objects may be moving away from us at a speed greater than the speed of light. The objects themselves aren't breaking any speed laws, but the cumulative effect of the expansion of space adds up. If this is so, then there may be far more to our universe than we can observe—it would be impossible for light from beyond that far horizon to ever reach us.

Innerspace When we take our eyes off the stars for a moment, and turn toward the atomic and subatomic worlds, similarly bizarre effects await us. Remember that all material is made of molecules, which are made of atoms; that the atoms don't even touch each other but are held together by electromagnetic forces; and that the atoms themselves are virtually all just space.

If you closely inspect a color photograph printed in a newspaper or magazine, you'll find that, at its heart, the vibrant and compelling images are all constructed from tiny dots arrayed on a grid. Even the rich spectrum of color is a trick, as the spots are printed using

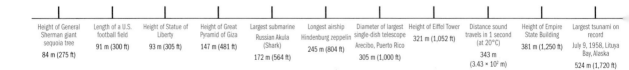

Height of General Sherman giant sequoia tree
84 m (275 ft)

Length of a U.S. football field
91 m (300 ft)

Height of Statue of Liberty
93 m (305 ft)

Height of Great Pyramid of Giza
147 m (481 ft)

Largest submarine Russian Akula (Shark)
172 m (564 ft)

Longest airship Hindenburg zeppelin
245 m (804 ft)

Diameter of largest single-dish telescope Arecibo, Puerto Rico
305 m (1,000 ft)

Height of Eiffel Tower
321 m (1,052 ft)

Distance sound travels in 1 second (at 20°C)
343 m
(3.43×10^2 m)

Height of Empire State Building
381 m (1,250 ft)

Largest tsunami on record
July 9, 1958, Lituya Bay, Alaska
524 m (1,720 ft)

only four pigments. From a distance, it all blurs together to convey a picture. But is what we call reality any different? Is it not just a series of dots—matter loosely held together—that we interpret as Truth?

And just as the ink can't perform its magic without paper, atoms cannot manifest without space. Space itself—which we ignore, like the black-clad puppeteers in a Japanese Bunraku play—turns out to be a medium. The spaces between are not empty, after all. Rather, space is woven tightly with a tempest of electrons, gluons, photons, bosons, neutrinos, waves of probability, fields of potential. And these elements play by rules we don't yet understand. For example, in certain circumstances particles can become entangled in such a way that they behave as a single entity, no matter how far apart they are. This has been repeatedly demonstrated, even though it completely violates the rules of classical physics, leading Einstein to famously call it *spukhafte Fernwirkung*, or "spooky action at a distance."

Then, as we peer closer, far down below the attometer, the fabric of space-time loses its smooth peculiar-but-reliable uniformity and becomes unruly. Like driving out of range of an analog radio station, the signal is slowly replaced by static. Get small enough and probability gives way entirely to randomness, so that physicists now believe that, at the Planck scale, space is a foamy, frothy sea of possibility. At this quantum level, virtual particles form out of energy and dissolve almost instantly, black holes may suddenly pop in and out of existence, and wormholes leading from one part of the universe to another (or possibly even into other universes) may appear then disappear in an instant.

Height of Burj Khalifa	Tallest waterfall Angel Falls in Venezuela	1 mile	Depth of Lake Baikal, deepest freshwater lake	Average depth of world's oceans	Height of Mt. Everest	Depth of Marianas Trench in the Pacific Ocean	Height of the troposphere at equator	Average altitude of International Space Station above sea level	Length of Grand Canyon	Diameter of moon
829.84 m (2,723 ft)	979 m (3,212 ft)	1.61 km (5,280 ft)	1,620 m (5315 ft)	3,790 m (12,434 ft)	8,848 m (29,028 ft)	10,918 m (35,820 ft)	17 km (56,000 ft)	370 km (230 mi)	446 km (277 mi)	3.47×10^6 m

Of course, once again, nobody knows if any of this is really How It Is. We've built myriad mathematical constructs that attempt to describe our universe—some that are completely at odds with each other—and discovered that there may be more than one correct answer, depending upon your perspective. While most people imagine the universe to be roughly spherical, it turns out that space-time may actually be the shape of a hyperbolic saddle, or perhaps (the current forerunner idea) based on a buckyball-shaped Poincaré dodecahedron. Superstring theory, a sweet mix of philosophy and mathematics, tells us that space may contain five or six additional, infinitesimally small dimensions that are twisted in intricately folded shapes called Calabi–Yau manifolds.

The math clearly tells us that the universe should contain gravitational waves that literally stretch and compress space, but in reality the effects are so minute that no one has yet detected them. One difficulty is that noise creeps into the experimental data—a meaningless static that obscures our view, like poor reception on an old rabbit-eared television. A reasonable (though controversial) explanation is that we are actually seeing evidence of Planck-length froth at much larger sizes, and that we're seeing it because—sit down for this one—the universe as we know it may actually be a hologram based on some far more complex reality played out on an insanely large membrane, like the way we see a three-dimensional image on a flat credit card. Could it be that, once again, our fundamental assumptions are based on illusions?

> **You know about measuring in** three dimensions: length, width, and breadth (or height). But many scientists envision a fourth spatial dimension—sometimes called ana/kata. A 4-D cube is called a tesseract.

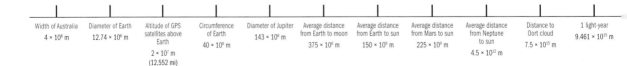

Width of Australia	Diameter of Earth	Altitude of GPS satellites above Earth	Circumference of Earth	Diameter of Jupiter	Average distance from Earth to moon	Average distance from Earth to sun	Average distance from Mars to sun	Average distance from Neptune to sun	Distance to Oort cloud	1 light-year
4×10^6 m	12.74×10^6 m	2×10^7 m (12,552 mi)	40×10^6 m	143×10^6 m	375×10^6 m	150×10^9 m	225×10^9 m	4.5×10^{12} m	7.5×10^{15} m	9.461×10^{15} m

As we go looking for answers, we should keep in mind the words of the twentieth-century British mathematician and philosopher Alfred North Whitehead: "There are no whole truths; all truths are half-truths. It is trying to treat them as whole truths that plays the devil."

Stretching Beyond *Homo sapiens* have been around for 100,000 years or so, but only in the past few hundred years have we had even a vague sense of the universe—big and small. Recognizing the orbiting planets led to theories of the stars; other explorers looked in the other direction, guessing that there was such a thing as microscopic life. But it wasn't until a century ago that we found the multitude of galaxies and uncovered the truth of subatomic particles.

Each discovery has led us to new mysteries; each mystery has led to new ideas. And at every step, there have been some who declare that now, finally, we understand, and others who understand that only now, finally, we can learn more. As the science writer Isaac Asimov wrote, "We have been misled before, and it may be that in time to come, additional vastness and intricacy will unfold and we will come to realize that what we now know, or think we know, is but a tiny part of a still greater whole."

Distance to Alpha Centauri A	Width of Milky Way galaxy	Distance to Andromeda galaxy	Diameter of Local Group (few dozen galaxies)	Diameter of Virgo Supercluster (1,000+ galaxies)	Length of Sloan Great Wall	Distance to edge of the observable universe	. . .
4.3 ly	100,000 ly	2.5 million ly	10 million ly	110 million ly	1.37 billion ly	46 billion ly	
$(4 \times 10^{16}$ m)	$(9.5 \times 10^{20}$ m)	$(2.4 \times 10^{22}$ m)	$(9.5 \times 10^{22}$ m)	$(1 \times 10^{24}$ m)	$(1.30 \times 10^{25}$ m)	$(4.35 \times 10^{26}$ m)	

LIGHT

What is to give light must endure burning.

—Viktor Frankl

WHAT IF YOU COULD WATCH MUSIC AS IT STREAMED OUT FROM A
radio tower, like an enormous lightbulb shining in the sky? What
if turning on your television made your eyes blink from the bright
flash—not from the screen but from the tip of your remote control?
What if your microwave heated your food with light, like one of
those old toy ovens from your childhood? In fact, all these things—
radio, cell phones, microwave ovens, and remote controls—are
based on light. They use light that, even though we cannot see it, is
nevertheless the same in every way as the light that we can see.

We are constantly awash in an astonishing spectrum of light,
everflowing and everlasting. Even in the darkest room we cannot
escape light, if only because our own bodies radiate it through the
very act of living.

Of course, humans are mercifully sensitive to only a small
portion—less than a thousandth of 1 percent—of the full spectrum
of light. Our eyes see the edges of a rainbow fade gradually away to
what seems like nothingness. But electronic instruments uncover for
us a world far beyond the red (on one side) and violet (on the other).
The universe truly is far stranger (and brighter!) than we can imagine.

Such Stuff as Light Is Made On Light—that is, the light that the
physiology of our eyes is tuned to see—is part of a phenomenon
called electromagnetic radiation (or EMR) that describes how
electricity and magnetism radiate, or travel, from one place to

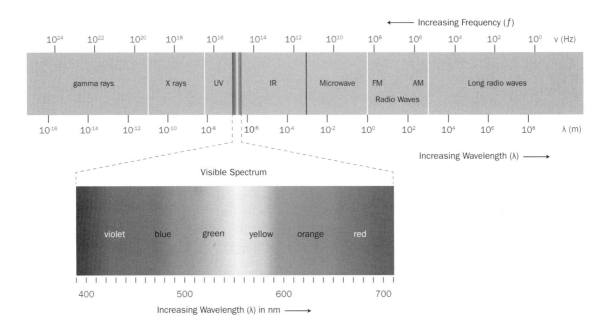

Increasing Frequency (*f*)

| 10^{24} | 10^{22} | 10^{20} | 10^{18} | 10^{16} | 10^{14} | 10^{12} | 10^{10} | 10^{8} | 10^{6} | 10^{4} | 10^{2} | 10^{0} | v (Hz) |

| gamma rays | X rays | UV | IR | Microwave | FM AM Radio Waves | Long radio waves |

| 10^{-16} | 10^{-14} | 10^{-12} | 10^{-10} | 10^{-8} | 10^{-6} | 10^{-4} | 10^{-2} | 10^{0} | 10^{2} | 10^{4} | 10^{6} | 10^{8} | λ (m) |

Increasing Wavelength (λ) ⟶

Visible Spectrum

violet   blue   green   yellow   orange   red

400   500   600   700

Increasing Wavelength (λ) in nm ⟶

▲ Visible light spectrum

another. Understanding EMR is necessarily technical, but the more you understand about light, the more amazing it is.

When an electrical current flows from one place to another, such as through a wire or the nerve system in your body, it generates a magnetic field. That's why an electrical current flowing near a compass moves the needle. It's why your favorite tune can be converted from an electrical pulse in a wire, to a magnet in a speaker, to the sound you hear. Control the current, and you control the magnet, which controls the speaker vibrations we hear as sound.

Conversely, when you move a magnet near a coil of wire, it creates electricity in that wire. This intimate bond between electricity and magnetism is what makes it possible for us to create motors, or, in fact, to create electricity itself in a generator.

So a changing electrical current creates a magnetic field, and a changing magnetic field creates an electrical field. And an amazing thing happens if you oscillate them by varying these fields back and forth: You create a wave effect, where the changing electric field actually generates the magnetic field, which creates the next electric field, and so on, potentially forever.

This self-propagating "electromagnetic" wave is what we call "light," and it can travel through the vacuum of space without slowing, without fading. This explains why the burning plasma of a distant star, aglow with the dance of free-floating electrons, can throw its radiation waves out across trillions of kilometers to be captured by our eyes and instruments.

Electromagnetic radiation—where energy is moved through space as light enables us not only to see our own sun but also to feel its warmth and, indeed, be burned by it, even on a cloudy day. And it allows us to send and receive seemingly invisible messages with satellites in orbit or with a cell phone tower on a hill.

Making Light Technically, there are two ways to create light: incandescence and luminescence. The former comes from heating a material, such as the nuclear reactions in the sun, or from electricity being passed through a tiny wire filament inside an incandescent lightbulb until it glows white-hot at over 2,000°F.

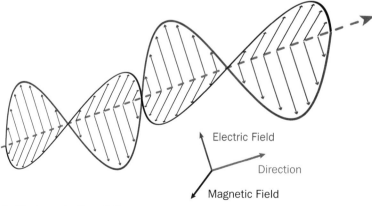

Electric Field

Direction

Magnetic Field

▲ **Electromagnetic radiation**

Luminescence is light without heat. For example, a watch dial painted with a phosphorescent substance will absorb energy in a lit room and then gently continue to glow in the dark. A firefly generates bioluminescence with a chemical reaction inside its abdomen. The phosphor in some laundry detergents is called a "brightener"—making white clothes "whiter"—because it literally glows with cool, visible light when energy from the sun hits it.

You can see this effect most clearly in a disco or an amusement park fun house that has black lights—special lightbulbs that emit ultraviolet radiation and make the phosphorescent materials in the room glow. Laundered white shirts and socks, natural phosphors in your teeth, and fluorescent paint all pop out brightly because they respond to the energy by giving off light we can see.

If you paint the inside of one of these lights with a phosphorescent coating, the surface itself glows white instead of your T-shirt. The result is the most common form of luminescence we see around us: a plain fluorescent lightbulb.

Both incandescence and luminescence derive from the same underlying mechanism: Electrons in an atom absorb energy of some sort and then emit it in the form of a bit of electromagnetic radiation. In incandescence, atoms are heated until their electrons get so excited that they break free and travel from one atom to another before settling down, releasing their energy as light. In luminescence, electrons are energized but remain within their atoms, quickly emitting the absorbed energy and dropping back to their original level. In both cases, the process continues until you stop adding energy, flicking off the switch.

How Fast, How Red Of course, there are many kinds of light: blue, infrared, ultraviolet . . . and the difference? It's the result of wavelength. Like ripples on a pond, or waves in an ocean, light waves radiate with energy, created by the constant rise and fall of electric and magnetic fields. If the waves gently undulate back and forth, we say they have a long wavelength and a low frequency. That is, it takes

▼ High frequency, small wavelength, more power

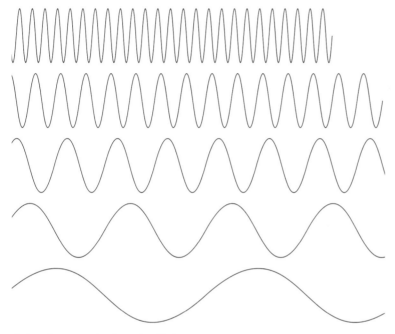

▲ Low frequency, long wavelength, less power

more time for each long wave to crest, so the frequency of those waves is slower.

On the other hand, a fast wave—one that goes from electric to magnetic, crest to trough, quickly—has a very short wavelength and a fast frequency.

Frequency and wavelength are always inextricably tied because of a crucial universal constant: the speed of light. This law tells us that there is one speed at which all light—indeed all electromagnetic radiation—travels in a vacuum. It's important to add the vacuum caveat because light does travel slightly slower in a gas, liquid, or clear solid. Place the tip of a stick in a clear brook and you'll see it "bend" underwater because the speed of light is literally slower beneath the surface than it is in air.

Pass light through a diamond and it slows to about 40 percent its normal speed. In fact, through some exceedingly clever tricks involving shooting lasers into extremely cold clouds of rubidium and helium gas, scientists have even been able to slow a beam of light until it is virtually standing still, apparently extinguished, but actually just on pause.

But in the vacuum of space, light travels at about 300,000 kilometers per second (just over 186,200 miles per second). Nothing travels faster.

So if light is radiating out at, well, the speed of light, then the number of waves that pass by a given point in space each second (frequency) is always tied to how long those waves are. Longer wave, fewer of them can go by each second; short little wave, you can cram a bunch of them in each second.

Note that because the speed of light is so (unbelievably, shockingly) fast, when you look at wavelength and frequency, you have to deal with some really huge (and small) numbers.

Red light—that is, light that our human eyes perceive as red—has a frequency of about 420 THz (teraherz). That means those electric fields and magnetic fields are flipping back and forth about 420 trillion times each second. If your car wheels revolved that quickly, you could drive from one end of our solar system to the other in the time it takes to blink an eye.

At that rate, each of those red-colored light waves is about 700 nm (700 billionths of a meter) long, about a tenth the size of a red blood cell, even smaller than a typical microscopic bacterium.

As you shorten the wavelength—that is, increase the frequency, so you get more waves per second—red becomes yellow, then green, then blue, and then, at about twice the frequency of red, purple. Speed up the frequency even more and the light changes, moving beyond what we can see into the ultraviolet (UV) range, then X-rays, then gamma rays. More about those bad boys in a minute.

"Come forth into the light of things, Let Nature be your teacher."

—William Wordsworth, "An Evening Scene on the Same Subject"

"Colours seen by candle-light Will not look the same by day."

—Elizabeth Barrett Browning, "The Lady's 'Yes'"

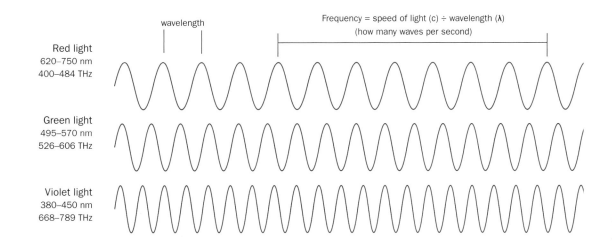

wavelength

Frequency = speed of light (c) ÷ wavelength (λ)
(how many waves per second)

Red light
620–750 nm
400–484 THz

Green light
495–570 nm
526–606 THz

Violet light
380–450 nm
668–789 THz

On the other side of the spectrum, if you slow the frequency (stretching out the wavelength), your red light becomes invisible infrared ("below red"), then microwaves, and then radio waves. The electromagnetic waves of your favorite FM radio station are radiating only at somewhere between 88 and 107 MHz (megahertz, or million cycles per second). Do the math and you'll find that each of those musical waves is about 3 meters (9.8 ft) long. That's longer than you might expect, but remember that each of those light waves speeds by unbelievably quickly—if radio signals could bend, they could travel around the globe 7 times each second.

We know of no longest wavelength in the universe. On Earth, telluric currents—extraordinarily subtle shifts in electromagnetic waves within Earth's crust or oceans, often due to weather or even the silent interaction between the solar wind and Earth's magnetosphere—may be as slow as a few hundred cycles per second. Waves at that rate are called extremely low frequency (ELF). Even longer, in the field of ultra low frequency, are the intricate but slow-flipping waves of our own brains. Each message that fires through

"It is sometimes said that scientists are unromantic, that their passion to figure out robs the world of beauty and mystery. But . . . it does no harm to the romance of the sunset to know a little bit about it."

—Carl Sagan

the brain's electrochemical connections has an electromagnetic result—we are each walking transmitters, though fortunately our signals are weak.

As the frequency drops even lower, to a single cycle each second (1 Hz), such as can be found deep in the movements of Earth itself, the wavelength becomes stretched out across 300 million meters—about 80 percent of the way from Earth to the moon.

It's All Energy As light radiates, it carries energy. You might even say that light is energy in motion. And the amount of energy transmitted through light is based entirely on the light's frequency or wavelength. The higher the frequency, the more energy. In other words, visible light contains more energy than infrared or radio waves. However, more energy doesn't necessarily result in effects you might expect.

> "To gaze is to think."
> —Salvador Dalí

While the light we can see will illuminate us, it doesn't warm us much. Most visible light bounces off our skin or is absorbed in ways that don't translate into heat. On the other hand, we are warmed by infrared light; it's invisible and transmits less energy, but it penetrates deeper, and is quickly absorbed by many materials, causing them to warm up.

Lower the frequency even more and you get microwaves, which can melt butter in seconds! Turn on a microwave oven and you send invisible electromagnetic radiation through the air to your food. This light energy has a frequency of 2.45 GHz (gigahertz, or billions of cycles per second)—lower than infrared but still far higher than radio waves. The choice of frequency results in some interesting effects: Microwaves at these frequencies are absorbed by particular kinds of molecules, such as those in water, fats, and sugars, causing them to vibrate, bang into each other, and heat up. The waves just pass by other molecules, such as the dry exterior of a kernel of popcorn or a potato, leading people to exclaim, erroneously, that microwaves cook from the inside out.

	Radio	Microwave	Infrared	Visible light	Ultraviolet	X-ray	Gamma ray
Frequency	30 kHz–300 MHz	300 MHz–3,000 GHz	3–400 THz	400–790 THz	790 THz–30 PHz	30 PHz–3 EHz	3 EHz–3 ZHz (and beyond)
Wavelength	1 Mm–1 m	1 mm–100 µm	750 nm–100 µm	750–400 nm	400–10 nm	10 nm–100 pm	<100 pm
Energy	128 peV–1.25 µeV	1.25 µeV–12 meV	12 meV–3 eV	1.6–3 eV	1.6–3 eV	120 eV–12 keV	12 keV+

▲ Electromagnetic radiation (EMR or "light"). Note: There are no strict boundaries between one type of radiation and another, so these numbers are all approximations.

If you worry about those microwaves escaping the oven, fret not: Waves at this frequency are about 122 millimeters (4.8 in) long—far larger than those of visible light. So the visible light waves can escape through those tiny holes in the glass door, letting us see our food being cooked, while the long microwaves remain inside, bouncing around the chamber.

When you hear that microwaves are electromagnetic radiation, you might get nervous about that word: *radiation*. After all, it's touching stuff you're going to put in your mouth. Fortunately, EMR at the energy of visible light and lower is safe because it's *non-ionizing*. Ionizing radiation in high-frequency, tiny-wavelength light (from ultraviolet light to X-rays and gamma rays) packs such an energy wallop that it can knock electrons right out of their atoms, making for an unstable chemical situation. These reactive atoms are called free radicals and are infamous for their destructive effects.

It's the infrared that makes you sweat on a hot day, but it's the ultraviolet that can give you a sunburn or worse. In the upper atmosphere, seemingly innocuous chlorofluorocarbons, escapees from old refrigerators and air conditioners, are bombarded with ionizing ultraviolet light from the sun. As electrons are blasted off, the newly radicalized molecules do their best to destroy our planet's ozone layer.

It's the ozone layer, of course, that has traditionally helped block much of that same dangerous light from getting down to us. But inevitably some high-powered ultraviolet light pushes through anyway, striking our skin hard enough to break down the fundamental building blocks that keep us alive. When atoms in our DNA are radicalized, the result can be mutant or cancerous cells,

"A 60 W tungsten bulb, a normal household bulb, consumes more than six times the electrical power of a 9 W compact fluorescent lamp but they are both perceived as producing approximately equal amounts of light . . . This is because a lot of the power used by a tungsten bulb is given out in the infrared part of the spectrum where the eye has no response. The light given out by the fluorescent lamp corresponds more closely to the peak sensitivity of the eye."

—UK National Physical Laboratory

so damaged that our internal defense mechanisms can no longer repair them.

You can run inside, but you can't hide. Glass reflects, absorbs, or scatters about 37 percent of low-powered ultraviolet light (called UVA)—that's about as good as putting on sunscreen, but you can still get a sunburn inside your car on a long drive. Small doses of the more powerful (higher-frequency) UVB rays are good for us—they get our body to produce essential vitamin D, but too much exposure is a major cause of melanoma.

Scientists measure the energy in light by electron volts (eV). For example, the light we can see contains only 1 or 2 eV. At 3 or 4 eV, light becomes ionizing. When the light waves speed up to about 30 PHz (petahertz, or 3×10^{16} cycles per second), they carry charges in the hundreds of electron volts. This kind of light has such peculiar properties that the researchers who first discovered them labeled them "X" rays. So powerful, with wavelengths so small, X-rays can slip between molecules of soft material like our skin and organs, stopping only when they encounter dense material such as metal or bone.

Sure, X-rays leave a path of destruction in their wake, but with short, infrequent doses the risk is low and your body generally repairs minor damage. Most of the X-rays we encounter in our lives are natural: exposure to tiny bits of radioactive rocks in the earth, radiation from the sun, and so on. Again, score one for our upper atmosphere, protecting us from the worst of it.

But as the energy in light increases, so does the danger. When you boost the energy into the tens of thousands of electron volts, the light wavelengths are reduced to picometers—trillionths of a meter, even smaller than atoms. This is the realm of gamma rays.

Gamma rays are just another form of light, but with electromagnetic frequencies measured in exahertz, over a thousand times greater than some X-rays and a million times greater than visible light. Doctors can shine gamma rays emitted from radioactive materials on our body to create incredibly detailed pictures of what's

> "Light is not so much something that reveals, as it is itself the revelation."
>
> —James Turrell, artist

going on inside tissue or bone, or concentrate these rays on an area of cancerous cells to destroy them. Customs officials can bombard shipping containers with gamma rays to "look" through 18 cm (7 in.) of steel and find stowaways or contraband inside.

Like X-rays, gamma rays naturally occur all around us in tiny amounts. When government officials attempt to locate nuclear material with gamma ray detectors, they're often stymied by a wide variety of food. Bananas and Brazil nuts, for example, tend to have higher than average quantities of naturally occurring radioactive material, causing false positives for investigators. It gives new meaning to getting high energy from eating fruits and nuts.

Of course, while these ubiquitous gamma rays are powerful, they're paltry compared to the far end of the electromagnetic spectrum, where gamma rays carrying 20 million electron volts flash from the tops of thunderclouds during lightning storms here on Earth. Traveling outside our terrestrial bubble, the most energetic phenomena in the universe—black holes and supernova—blast out gamma rays that radiate at 10^{27} Hz and more than 5 trillion electron volts.

If these numbers seem extraordinary, it's worth putting them in perspective. It takes 1 joule* of energy to lift an apple off a table, and 1 joule is about 6 exa-electron volts—6 *billion* billion (6×10^{18}) eV. In other words, light is extremely powerful . . . to extremely small things. Light can shatter the infinitesimal world of subatomic particles, but it exerts hardly any pressure on our everyday "macro" world.

That said, with enough light you can achieve the seemingly impossible. Proof came in 2010 with the launch of the Japanese spacecraft IKAROS (Interplanetary Kite-craft Accelerated by Radiation Of the Sun). Outfitted with a microthin solar sail 14 m (45 ft) wide filled with pressure from gentle waves of light, this lightweight unmanned vessel slowly, methodically gained momentum outside

> "Every man takes the limits of his own field of vision for the limits of the world."
> —Arthur Schopenhauer

The sun is like a 4×10^{26} watt lightbulb. That's brighter than the average star, but there are far brighter ones out there. Epsilon Orionis (the middle star of Orion's belt) is 1,300 light-years away and 400,000 times as bright as the sun. There's a star in the Large Magellanic Cloud called R136a1 that is as bright as almost 9 million suns. Of course exploding stars, called supernovae, are even brighter; the brightest on record peaked at about 100 billion suns.

*A joule is a measurement that describes energy or work.

the drag of Earth's gravity, like Aesop's tortoise. Once considered the stuff of science fiction, IKAROS has already sailed past Venus on the force of light, and solar sailing is thought by many to be the future of interplanetary travel.

A Discrete, Not a Continuous Spectrum So far we've been discussing light as though it were simply "wave energy," but the bigger picture is far more weird.

If you reduce the energy of light, you would expect a smooth continuum, smaller and smaller, like turning down the volume on a stereo until you finally hit zero. But light doesn't work like that. It turns out that light can exist only at particular energy levels—as though the volume knob had notches in it at 3, 2, 1, and 0, nothing between.

The only reasonable explanation for this is that light, at its core, is made of particles. A single particle of light, called a photon, is like a little packet with a discrete amount of energy.

The intensity of light involves the number of photons, but the energy of the photons is something completely different. Imagine a photon as a Ping-Pong ball. If the ball is moving slowly when it hits you, you barely feel it. Now let's increase the intensity by throwing 100 slow-moving Ping-Pong balls at you. More pressure, but because each ball is low powered, it isn't much more than annoying. Now let's shoot just one of these little balls out of a cannon at you. Ouch.

Photons are all moving at the same speed (the speed of light), but they contain different energies—what we've expressed before as frequencies or wavelengths. So a low-frequency photon doesn't deliver much kick, but a high-frequency photon can pack a wallop.

Unfortunately, there's a problem with this argument: It's relatively easy to prove that light absolutely, positively behaves like a wave, not a particle. The fact that light refracts (bends) when moving from one medium to another; the fact that it diffracts (like ripples in a pond interacting with a stick poking through the surface) . . . waves do these things, not particles, which travel in straight lines. But if

> "In the beginning there was nothing. God said, 'Let there be light!' And there was light. There was still nothing, but you could see it a whole lot better."
>
> —Ellen DeGeneres

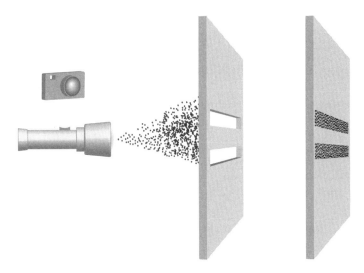

▲ Sending one photon toward a board with two slits and observing to see which slit it passes through, you can prove that it acts like a particle, traveling through one slit or the other.

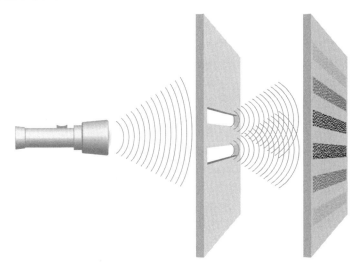

▲ If you don't watch, or if you send many through at the same time, the light acts like a wave, diffracting and creating interference patterns.

you fire light through two slits in a piece of cardboard, and use very careful measurements, you can determine that each photon is going through only one or the other slit, so there's also no doubt that it behaves like a particle.

You could dismiss this paradox, called the wave-particle duality, as just another wacky this-and-that fact of nature, like the old *Saturday Night Live* joke "It's a floor wax *and* a dessert topping." But actually, this is one of the greatest and most troubling mysteries in science today. It calls into question everything we think we know about the universe. We like to think that "stuff" is here or it's not, that it's matter or it's energy, but in fact everything is likely both: here and not, matter and energy. And if that doesn't confuse you, you don't understand it.

Fortunately, while the scientists and philosophers are arguing over the nature of reality, we needn't fully understand light in order to see it, measure it, and even use it to our advantage.

What We See The majority of what we humans understand is due to light, whether the reflections of the physical world around us or the glimmer of far-off stars. We gather information from what we see with our eyes and—perhaps even more important—our photosensitive instruments that can detect the invisible light around us.

Of course, color doesn't actually exist in the universe. We see color only because our eyes can register light at certain wavelengths and our brain attempts to make sense of those wavelengths by assigning them a visual meaning.

As we've seen, our ability to sense electromagnetic radiation is limited to a tiny range of wavelengths starting at about 380 nm (which we see as violet) and extending to about 750 nm (red). In musical notation, an octave is a doubling of a sound wave's frequency, and if you do the math, our spectrum of visible light equates to only about a single octave. Compare that to our 10-octave

> "Yet mystery and reality emerge from the same source. This source is called darkness. Darkness born from darkness. The beginning of all understanding."
>
> —Lao-tzu, *Tao Te Ching*

range of hearing, or the 45 octaves between AM radio waves and gamma rays.

Nevertheless, we can sense that little segment called visible light because of four particular types of nerve cells that we've developed in the tissue along the rear wall of our eyes: three types of cone cells and one rod cell—each named for its general physical appearance under a microscope. All are sensitive to light—that is, they can absorb electromagnetic energy and transmit it as a signal to the brain—but each is tuned to different wavelengths.

The three kinds of cones are most sensitive to light waves in the red, green, and blue frequencies, though each cone can also pick up a wide range of light. So, for example, the "green" cone can pick up some blue, yellow, and red, but it's most sensitive to the wavelengths we see as lime green. When light enters the eye, the cones quickly react, sending signals to the brain, which combines them—first finding edges (areas of widely different color contrast), then filling in the rest with color details until we determine what we're looking at.

Rods are far more sensitive, but they work best in very low light. Able to respond to even a single photon entering the eye, rods excel at night vision and for sensing very quick, small motions. They also tend to "wake up" more slowly than cones. For example, when you walk into a dark room, like a cinema, it can take several minutes for your eyes to adjust: Your cones aren't receiving enough light to function well, and your rods need time to get activated. After five minutes, your rods are working great, but you can barely make out any colors—just areas of light and dark.

Even more telling is the placement of rods and cones on the retina: Your eye contains about 6 million cone cells densely packed into the center, directly behind your pupil and lens. Surrounding the cones are about 100 million rod cells, like a ring around a bull's-eye target. This explains why, when walking outside on a dark night, you might see a star shimmer in your peripheral vision: The very dim

The only animal that can see both infrared and ultraviolet light is the goldfish.

"**The principal person in a picture is light.**"
—Edouard Manet

light hitting the outside edges of that target excites the rods but is often nowhere near bright enough to see when you try to focus your less-sensitive cones on it. Conversely, when you're in good light and you want to discern color or detail (such as these words), you need to look directly at it, focusing the image on your cones.

Granted, when we talk about humans, there are always exceptions. Some people lack one type of cone, resulting in what we call color blindness. They can still see color but must make do with only two signals instead of three. Conversely, some people—primarily women—have developed a mutant fourth cone. Where most of us are trichromats, these people are tetrachromats, able to see more colors—or, more accurately, more distinctions among colors, especially in the red to yellow tones. A tetrachromatic mother might be better suited to seeing tiny changes in a child's complexion or perhaps even notice subtle infrared heat radiating from a fever in a way that most of the rest of us could not.

It's unclear how many bands of color a tetrachromat sees looking at a rainbow. When Isaac Newton first used a prism to split white light into a rainbow in 1672, he named the five colors that most of us identify: red, yellow, green, blue, and violet. Later, however, in an effort to synchronize the spectrum with the seven notes of a Western musical scale, he somewhat arbitrarily inserted two additional bands of color: orange and indigo. Thus the primary-school mnemonic was born: ROY G. BIV.

Today, few people identify indigo as a hue separate from blue or violet. That doesn't mean we no longer see that color, but most of us probably don't call it out as notably different from the colors around it.

Curiously, we can identify colors that are not in the spectrum at all. Most notable is magenta—that hot pink color found on fuchsia flowers and in nearly every color printer in the world. You can easily create magenta on a computer screen by mixing red and blue light. Our eyes pick up the red and blue wavelengths and our brains mix them together. The result should be halfway between red and

"The French philosopher Auguste Comte demonstrated that it would always be impossible for the human mind to discover the chemical constitution of the stars. Yet, not long after this statement was made the spectroscope was applied to the light of the stars, and we now know more about their chemical constitution, including those of the distant nebulae, than we know about the contents of our medicine chest."

—Edward Kasner and James Newman, *Mathematics and the Imagination* blue, but on the light spectrum that color is green! We can tell that the color we're seeing isn't green, so, in a that-does-not-compute moment, the brain makes up a color to see: magenta.

Messages in the Light If light is energy in motion, then it is information in motion, too. At its simplest, someone might light a bonfire on a hill fifty miles away in order to warn his tribe of danger—the information from the light is able to travel far faster than a messenger or even sound. If the tribe had particularly clever gadgetry, such as telescopes and prisms, they might even be able to learn what the folks on the hill were burning. This is due to a curious (but incredibly helpful) phenomenon: Different elements, when heated, give off specific wavelengths of light. Sodium gives off a different pattern of frequencies than carbon or hydrogen.

Armed with this knowledge, we can point our telescopes toward the sun and stars, carefully analyzing the light we capture and learning things we would not otherwise know: what the sun is made of, where black holes are hiding, how light follows the warped fabric of space-time as gravity bends reality. Our ability to tease apart light, to reveal its makeup, is called spectroscopy.

Of course, the sun and stars (and everything else in the universe) exhibit more than visible light. Radio waves and microwaves reach out across the cosmos, helping us map the solar system and the constellations. X-rays and gamma rays help us determine massive centers of otherwise invisible energy in the universe, such as pulsars and quasars. Everywhere we turn our instruments, we gather information, looking for understanding, searching for meaning.

And if we can find answers in the spectrums of natural light, then we can also encode our own messages in light that we create. The trick to doing this is called modulation: taking a known wave and adjusting it over time.

For example, let's say you tune in to an AM station at 700 on your radio dial—that's 700 kHz, or an electromagnetic wave oscillating back and forth at 700,000 cycles each second. AM stands

> **"What is essential is invisible to the eye."**
> Antoine de Saint-Exupéry,
> *The Little Prince*

Extremely low frequency (ELF) transmissions for naval communication frequency

3 Hz–3 MHz

Power lines

50–60 Hz

AM radio

520–1,620 kHz (1.62 MHz)

Shortwave radio

5.9–26.1 MHz

Garage door opener

40 MHz

Baby monitor

49 MHz

Radio-controlled airplane

72 MHz

Television stations

54–88 and 174–220 MHz

FM radio

88–108 MHz

Wildlife tracking collar

220 MHz

Cell phone

824–849 MHz

Cordless telephone

900 MHz

Global Positioning System (GPS)

1.2–1.6 GHz

Microwave oven

2.45 GHz

Short-range ("X band") radar tracking

8–12 GHz

Red light

400–484 THz (620–750 nm)

Yellow light

508–526 THz (570–590 nm)

Green light

526–606 THz (495–570 nm)

Blue light

606–668 THz (450–495 nm)

Violet light

668–789 THz (380–450 nm)

▲ Examples of light energy